PRAISE FOR THE GUIDE TO

"This original chick lit novel is fun, entertaining, and a wonderfully eye-opening take on older women who don't expect much from men, even though they'd like to. Cathy, Betsy and Linda are well introduced on the first page but the reader will find many more aspects of their personalities and certainly their lives to be discovered. I was engaged and delighted page after page."

—Next Generation Indie Book Awards - (Grand Prize Winner 3rd Place Fiction-2023)

"Jannette's 'showing not telling' approach to establish the characters made them quite endearing. …Loved the mutual affection Cathy, Linda, and Betsy shared, each ready to do their best for the others. At the same time, they gave each other space and respected their decisions. Throughout the story, Jannette showed how our non-human friends bring us unconditional love. Jannette's portrayals of various age-related issues and the associated uncertainties tugged at my heart. Yet, the novel also showed how age could be less of a constraint if we have supportive friends to see us through life's ordeals.…Reading this wholesome, comforting book was like sipping a warm cup of tea at the end of an exhausting day."

—Readers' Favorite - (Bronze Medal Winner Readers' Favorite International Book Award Competition-2023)

"Jannette has written a comforting story of healing…This is a story of strength, of finding the spark and passion inside of oneself to face challenges and overcome obstacles. Life is full of the unexpected, and this novel teaches readers that even those moments, while they might look bad at the start, can lead to beautiful discoveries. The Tea Drinker's Guide to Adventure is a beautifully written women's adventure novel. The bonds of friendship between the characters and the sparks of romance they feel will keep readers engaged and following the trio through this unexpected journey they end up on together."

—Literary Titan - (Silver Medal Winner)

"The Tea Drinker's Guide to Adventure by Andrée Jannette is a thoroughly enjoyable later-in-life romance, and a peek into how friendship can carry you through the ups and downs of life. This is a really beautiful tale. Andrée Jannette has captured the essence of life and friendship perfectly, in this easy-to-read, light-hearted escapade. Her writing style brought the people and places to life. Sweetly romantic, uplifting, and a real page-turner, The Tea Drinker's Guide to Adventure by Andrée Jannette comes very highly recommended."

—Chick Lit Café - (Winner CLC Book Excellence Award)

"This is a sweet tale that shows how bonds between friends can become more meaningful with age. Will appeal most to sentimentalists and dog lovers."

—Kirkus Reviews

"Andree Jannette's The Tea Drinker's Guide to Adventure is a warm wholesome story that makes it clear that new friends and new adventures aren't limited to the young, with a touch of romance and a couple of adorable dogs to sweeten the pot. The story doesn't make light of, or smooth over, the difficulties, pains, and stresses of old age and chronic illness, but neither does it treat old age and chronic illness as life-ending tragedies that reduce people to helpless victims. All in all, it's a lovely book that offers a gentle dose of hope, the warmth of friendship, sisterhood, and community."

—IndieReader

"Jannette does a good job of bringing together three different women through a shared connection, and showing how a lifetime of experience can bring both a willingness and reluctance for change. Just as in real life, the change Cathy, Betsy, and Linda encounter may not necessarily be the change they were prepared for. But Jannette's storytelling makes the heartening case that it's while facing hurdles that the women open their hearts, learn to share their fears, and form new friendships... The novel is consistently entertaining, boasting memorable dialogue and characters, plus loads of heart, wonderfully described dogs, and a reminder that life is to be lived."

—BookLife

"Refreshing older heroines and their strong friendship carry the day. This cozy tale offers much to enjoy."

—Publisher's Weekly

THE TEA DRINKER'S GUIDE TO ADVENTURE

3 WOMEN, 2 DOGS, 1 RV: ON THE ROAD TRIP OF A LIFETIME

a novel by
ANDRÉE JANNETTE

This is a work of fiction. Names, characters, and incidents are the product of the author's imagination or are used fictitiously. Any resemblance to actual persons living or dead, events, or incidents is purely coincidental.

All rights reserved. No part of this publication may be reproduced or transmitted in any form or by any means, electronic or mechanical, including photocopy, recording, or any information storage and retrieval system, without permission in writing from the publisher.

Printed in the United States.

Copyright © 2022 by Andrée Jannette

ISBN 979-8-9863742-1-5 (paperback)
ISBN 979-8-9863742-0-8 (Ebook)

*To Jeanne, my partner in everything.
To my extended family: Cathy, Mike, Sharon, Mary,
and all my nieces and nephews, thank you
for welcoming me so warmly into your lives.*

*Many thanks to those stalwart individuals who agreed to
read this book in its various iterations, especially Jeanne
Cook and Catherine Roseman Smith.*

*Thanks to my editor, Rosanna Aponte, for her
valuable suggestions, and my designer, Asya Blue,
for her wonderful cover design.*

CHAPTER 1

Cathy's eyes were gritty and dry, and her eyelids impossibly heavy. She could feel how desperately she wanted to close them for just a moment or two. But she knew it was dangerous to give in to that urge. She glanced up briefly into the rearview mirror, seeing her blue eyes and red glasses reflected there. It had been a long day of driving. Opening the driver's side window, she took a deep breath of the crisp New Mexico night air as the elderly RV buzzed and hummed down the dark road. Its headlights carving out a brilliant tunnel of light surrounded by the pitch-black landscape.

Cathy glanced in the rearview mirror again at the two women sitting behind her at the dining table. It was a peaceful scene; Betsy was sipping a cup of green tea with mint and doing a crossword puzzle while Linda was playing a game of solitaire.

Like Cathy, Betsy was 63 years old, a comfortable and curvy 5'4," give or take a pint or two of Häagen-Dazs. Her gentle hazel eyes belied her wicked sense of humor. For this trip, while Cathy had gotten her silver curls cut short for convenience, Betsy had dyed a long strand of her silver hair blue. She said it was to remind her of blue skies ahead. Linda was the third and oldest member of the group at 65. Long and lean, at 5'7," with a super-short silver hairstyle á la Jamie Lee Curtis, Linda was a devotee of all things yoga. Even now, she was doing gentle stretches as she played solitaire.

Six months ago, the women had met at a book club in their hometown of West Chester, a college town forty minutes outside of Philadelphia. The three of them quickly discovered that though they came from different backgrounds—Cathy, a guidance counselor; Betsy, a teacher; Linda, an ER nurse—they had similar tastes in literature. They often found themselves at odds with the club leader's choices, which seemed to begin and end with novels about sex-crazed vampires. As Betsy noted, "It was almost enough to put me off garlic for life."

So, the women decided to form their own book club. As the group became known for freewheeling and fun discussions, women of all ages started signing up. While the three of them enjoyed being involved with the book-loving community, the administrative aspect of the book club, given its popularity, was wearing thin. They hoped to make a decision about the club's future on this trip.

More importantly, it was also a time to grieve for Alice, the fourth founding member of the club, who recently died of cancer. Near the end of her life, she had made the three women promise to go together to Georgia O'Keefe's Ghost

Ranch in Abiquiu, New Mexico, a place especially important to her and spread her ashes there. To fulfill that promise, they elected to rent an RV and drive out, camping along the way. The women were a little uneasy about spending that much time cooped up in a camper, especially since they knew nothing about RVing. But they decided to view it as an adventure.

Stifling a yawn, Cathy glanced at the dashboard clock. "It's getting close to midnight. We need to figure out where we want to camp and...shit!" she suddenly yelled, stomping on the brake as the RV veered almost out of control. "Hold on!" For a long, anxious moment, it felt like it was going to tip. It swung back and forth across the road, with Cathy frantically pumping the brake pedal. Finally, the brakes caught hold, and she was able to bring the vehicle to a shuddering, tension-filled stop. Her heart pounding, she climbed out of the driver's seat and back into the cabin.

Linda was already up and about. "Is everyone okay?"

"Fine," said Betsy, her voice a bit shaky, as she began clearing up the mess of playing cards and tea that had been catapulted onto the floor. "What the hell happened?"

"Something ran across the road right in front of me. I think it was a dog." Cathy grabbed a flashlight from the utility drawer and started for the door. "I don't know whether I hit it or not."

Linda asked, "Where do you think you're going? You don't know what's out there."

"I'm fairly sure it was a dog. I want to check and see if it's okay."

Helping Betsy wipe up the last of the tea, Linda said, "Hold on, I'll go with you."

Cathy cautiously opened the door. Linda followed her out. As they stood there, getting their bearings, the engine startled them, making crackling and popping noises as it cooled. Inside the vehicle, Betsy switched on lights to make it more visible to other drivers.

Cathy strode down the road, playing the flashlight back and forth over nearby bushes. Linda followed slowly, looking carefully at the ground for tracks. They walked a little distance from the camper. So far, there was no sign of a dog anywhere.

Cathy shrugged. "Either I imagined it because I'm so tired, or it was here, got scared, and ran away." Without any further discussion, they turned back and started to return to the vehicle. Suddenly there was a low whimper. They both froze, not even sure they had heard anything. They glanced at each other. Out of a tangle of shrubs and trash came another quiet whimper.

Linda whispered, "I'm going to get some food to try to coax whatever that is out into the light."

"Let Betsy know what's happening," murmured Cathy. She was trying to look, without being obvious, at the area where she thought the whimper was coming from.

Linda walked quickly back to the vehicle. She rifled through the fridge and found a leftover hamburger from the previous night. While she was doing that, she explained the situation to Betsy. She returned to Cathy's side, and Betsy quietly joined them, leaning heavily on her cane.

Crumbling the hamburger in her hands, Linda started tossing small pieces in the general direction where they had heard the sound. She paused and stood still. Suddenly a small black dog pushed through the shrubbery and approached the food. The women watched and waited. Cathy caught Linda's eye, nodding at the dog. Linda looked closer and caught her breath. Her face tightened in anger. An arrow, heavily chewed at one end, protruded between its ribs. Someone had been using the little dog for target practice.

With their focus on the animal, the women didn't pay much attention to the headlights coming up the road. The vehicle pulled in behind them, and an overhead array of lights switched on. The dog immediately disappeared back into the shrubs. When they turned around, they saw that it was a police cruiser. They looked at each other in dismay.

The police officer had his interior lights on and was talking on his radio. After a few minutes, he opened his car door. He tugged on his hat, adjusted his gun belt, and walked over to the women.

"Having car troubles?" he asked.

"No, sir," answered Cathy.

"Registration and license."

Cathy said, "This is a rental vehicle; the papers are all inside. Are you OK with me going into the RV?"

The police officer nodded. As Cathy walked back to the camper, Betsy and Linda started explaining to him what had happened.

Cathy returned and handed him the paperwork.

"So let me get this straight. You almost crash when an animal, most likely a dog, runs in front of your RV. You stop to check if it was injured, and you see it has an arrow in its side. Is that accurate?"

Cathy answered, "Yes, that's right."

The officer looked at the three of them before saying, "I need to run these, and then I'll get back to you. Just wait here a moment." He walked back to his vehicle.

"I hate it when they do that. It makes me feel like I've done something wrong, and I don't even know what," said Linda.

Cathy chimed in. "I feel the same way. Kind of a knee-jerk, guilty reaction to God knows what."

"Original sin?" murmured Betsy.

Cathy snorted with laughter. "He's probably finishing up today's Wordle."

Giggling, she tried to imagine how they must appear to the officer. Betsy and Linda eyed each other, suddenly cracking up. All three were looking like it was way past their bedtime. While Cathy was dressed in sneakers, a sweatshirt, and jeans, Linda was in flannel pajamas and a bathrobe covered with images of sheep jumping over fences. Betsy was also wearing pajamas and a flannel bathrobe. A fan of Harry Potter, hers had little wizards all over them. Linda had grabbed some Wellington boots before they headed outside, but Betsy was still wearing her fluffy bunny slippers. As such, they were the most unlikely candidates to be arch criminals.

The officer got out of his squad car and walked back

to the women. "Everything checks out. Are you trying to catch the dog?"

"Yes," said Cathy.

"I have a dog crate in my vehicle you can use and a pair of heavy-duty gloves so you won't risk getting bitten."

Cathy looked at him. "Thanks. You're very helpful."

The officer smiled slightly. "Well, I do generally try to be of assistance."

Cathy wasn't sure how to respond. "We need to get him to a veterinarian. Do you know of any nearby?"

"Let me get the crate out for you, and then I'll check on the nearest vet." As he started to head to his cruiser, he turned back. "The reason I stopped is that your camper is sticking out on the road. It is a hazard for other vehicles, especially at night."

Cathy stammered, "S-s-sorry about that. I'll move it now." The officer returned to his cruiser. Cathy quickly got into the RV, maneuvered it off the road, and parked it.

When she walked back to Linda and Betsy, she found the police officer had brought the dog crate out and placed it near the bushes where they had first heard the sound. Linda and Betsy were carefully arranging a blanket at the bottom of the crate so that it would be a cozy bed for the dog. Transporting an animal with an arrow sticking out of it was not going to be a cakewalk no matter what they did to make it a smooth ride. They scattered pieces of hamburger on the blanket, hoping to entice the dog into the crate.

The three women moved away from the crate and closer

to the police car to give the dog some space. The police officer returned to his vehicle. About ten minutes ticked by. It was quiet except for the murmur of the police officer talking on his car radio. They heard some rustling, and suddenly the dog popped out of the bushes onto the roadway, close by the crate. The women remained still. A slight movement caught Cathy's eye, and she saw that the police officer was about to get out of his car. He had not spied the dog yet. Cathy shifted slightly and raised her hand to indicate he should stay in place. He caught her gesture and relaxed back into his seat.

The little dog crept slowly out of the brush and approached a piece of hamburger on the ground. He glanced around and quickly gulped it down. The dog spotted another piece. Even though it was aware of the people watching it, the animal's hunger drove it forward to grab more food. The dog approached the crate where the smell of meat was strongest. It hesitantly crept inside and quickly started gobbling the food down. Linda sprang forward, shut the crate door, and latched it.

"Good job, Linda," murmured Betsy.

Realizing it had been trapped, the dog freaked out. It spun around in circles barking and growling. Then, oddly enough, it just stopped in its tracks. It was like the terrified animal suddenly realized that it wouldn't be going anywhere soon. Panting from stress and fear, it stared out at the people gathered around the crate. The dog looked intently at each one, seemingly determined to meet their eyes. Finally, it turned to the hamburger bits left on the blanket and finished eating them. Then it lay down, struggling a bit to get comfortable.

"Cute dog," said the police officer who had joined them once the dog was in the crate. He peered at the animal. "It's a male; it looks like a Shih Tzu mix of some sort." He added, "His eyes are nice and bright. That's a good sign. Some of the dogs I've seen rescued along this highway look like they have totally given up."

Betsy asked, "Do you get many dogs abandoned here?"

"Unfortunately, yes. They might have a chance if we get them early enough after they've been dumped. But there are a lot of predators in this area—coyotes and mountain lions, not to mention poisonous snakes. The odds for long-term survival are just not in their favor. Especially for a little guy like this."

Linda said, "Well, we hope we can give this one a second chance."

The officer knelt next to the crate and looked more closely at the dog, who gazed steadily back at him. The police officer grinned at him, and the dog cautiously wagged its tail. The officer stood up, brushing the dust off his pants before leaning against his cruiser. "I think I may have found a vet for you," he said. "About twenty miles south of here, there's a ranch that the owner has turned into an RV community. It is an older crowd, mostly professionals. A retired veterinarian, her name is Alfreda, often camps there. I just talked with Ben, the ranch owner, and he says she's there now.

"Follow this road to the Golden Dawn Truck Stop. Take

a right onto Arden Way; go until you cross a bridge over a river, and you will see huge gates to the Arden Ranch. Just head right up to the main ranch house. If the lights are on, he's awake. It doesn't matter what time it is. Feel free to knock or use the buzzer if there are lights on anywhere in the house."

Linda said, "You've been a tremendous help. Thank you so much." Cathy murmured in agreement.

"What's your name?" asked Betsy.

"Peter Jones. I am the police chief for Candor County."

"I'm Betsy Flynn. These are my friends Linda Smith and Cathy Rosen."

He tipped his hat, started walking back to his cruiser, and then stopped. "Do you need help loading the crate?"

"No, we're fine, thank you," answered Cathy.

Suddenly Betsy said, "I need to sit down for a bit."

Linda turned to her, concerned. "Are you all right?"

"Yes, just a bit shaky."

Although she didn't talk about it a lot or make much of it, Betsy had Parkinson's. The other women knew when Betsy said she needed to sit or lie down; she must not be feeling too great. She headed for the door of the camper. Linda followed slowly behind, keeping an eye on her.

The police chief sized up the situation. "Here, let me just take the crate and put it in the RV."

Cathy hesitated. But then a thought occurred to her. 'Why am I so quick to turn down an offer of help, especially from a man?' She determined to change that habitual reaction here and now. "Thanks, that would be great," she said.

Inside the camper he settled the crate under the dining room table so it wouldn't slide around. "You can leave the crate and gloves with the vet, and I'll pick them up later." He said goodbye and left.

Cathy, Betsy, and Linda looked at each other.

"Wow," murmured Betsy in a throaty growl. The women started laughing.

"God, was he gorgeous," said Linda. "He reminded me of the actor Sam Neill."

"Beautiful blue eyes, thick salt-and-pepper hair, lots of lovely laugh lines," Betsy grinned. "What's not to like?"

Cathy looked at her. "Really?"

"Just because I have Parkinson's and am in my sixties doesn't mean I can't appreciate a good-looking man."

"Well, we certainly just got a surprise boost of testosterone," Linda added.

Cathy stood up. "OK, enough already; let's get this show on the road."

CHAPTER 2

"Unless you need me for something, I'm heading to bed," Betsy said to the two women.

"I think we're fine. Have a good night's sleep." Cathy turned to Linda. "Are you okay with driving the rest of the way?"

Linda answered, "I'll be fine with a cup of coffee. However, I'm not sure about the directions. I tend to listen to the first few, like turn right or left, and then I zone out. Everything beyond that is gone with the wind."

Cathy laughed. "I do the same thing. I am always hopeful that someone with me can catch the last part."

"Well," said Linda, "once we get closer to the RV park, there might be signs or indications of where it is. Or maybe between us, we will remember the landmarks Peter, the police chief, mentioned."

Linda swung into the driver's chair. As she secured her seatbelt, she asked, "How's the dog?"

"Hold off driving away for a moment so I can put more food and water in the crate. He looks somewhat calmer but still anxious." Cathy kept a close eye on him to make sure there were no signs of aggression. Carefully she put a bowl of water in the crate. Although he looked at her steadily and maintained eye contact, he didn't show any signs of hostility. In fact, as she put crumbled up hamburger in the crate, he wagged his tail slightly.

She said to Linda, "I think this is a nice dog. I mean, he's been through the wars, yet here I'm putting food in the crate, and he wags his tail at me."

Linda turned to look at Cathy, "You know it always amazes me how forgiving dogs can be, no matter how badly they have been abused and mistreated by humans."

Cathy nodded and then yawned so wide she could hear her jaw creak.

"I'm fine driving," said Linda, "why don't you get some rest?"

"Okay then, I'll probably just read a bit and keep an eye on the dog."

Linda put the turn signals on and checked to see if the police chief had moved yet. "He is still sitting there," she muttered. "Well, I am going to go." She carefully steered the RV onto the road and blinked her lights as a 'thank you.' The cruiser responded with a few blinks of its own and then pulled out onto the road, turned in the opposite direction, and sped off.

They continued down the road. Occasionally a car would pass them in the night. But generally, there was nobody else out there. As Linda looked through the windshield, she was awed by the dazzling display of stars in the night sky overhead. She said to Cathy, "Put this on the list; we've got to buy a telescope."

Cathy moved forward and peered up through the windshield. "Wow! How beautiful is that? We definitely need a good telescope. One of those with computer tracking."

She decided to put a little more food into the crate. The dog sniffed the food and looked at her. Then he lay down and closed his eyes. Cathy carefully poked her finger through the mesh and softly stroked the dog's head between the ears. She could feel the animal tremble. Cathy wondered if the little dog had ever known a gentle touch.

"What a good boy," she said, sitting back in her seat and closing her eyes.

She dozed fitfully as the camper rumbled into the night. After about twenty miles, they came across the twenty-four-hour truck stop the police chief had mentioned. They decided to stop and get gas and stretch their legs. Cathy walked inside to pay for the gas. Immediately she didn't like the vibe of the place. A couple of customers turned around to watch her as she wandered the aisles looking for snacks. It gave her the creeps. She paid for the gas and left quickly.

She climbed into the RV and strongly advised Linda to forgo the delights of this particular truck stop. A few of the customers came outside and wandered toward the RV. Linda started the vehicle and gunned it out of the parking lot, spewing gravel in her wake.

"Okay, I'll need some help here," she said.

Cathy climbed into the passenger side chair and looked

out the windshield. "This is where we turn onto Arden Way for a few miles until we come to a bridge."

"Glad you remember the directions," said Linda. The paved road gave way to a dirt one. She slowed down as the RV shimmied over the deeply rutted surface. Five miles felt like fifty as they bumped along at a snail-like pace. "There it is. There's the entrance to the ranch." The seven-foot-tall gates stood wide open. The name of the ranch, Arden, was spelled out in glowing lights.

"It looks a bit like Jurassic Park," said Cathy.

"Hopefully, there's nothing here that will try to eat us."

"What time is it?" Cathy asked.

"About one o'clock. Let's see if anyone is up." Linda followed the road up the hill. It twisted and turned through the trees, offering them tantalizing glimpses of a broad river gleaming in the moonlight. As they climbed up the hill a bit more, they began to see RVs parked here and there, next to trees or along the river. And then finally, on the top of the highest hill, they saw a large building.

Cathy said, "That must be the ranch house. I see lights; someone's awake in there. I think we're fine knocking."

Linda steered the RV into a parking/registration spot near the front door. Cathy got out and walked up the wide wooden steps. The door was open, but the screen door was latched.

Cathy knocked and called out, "Hello? Hello?" There was no response for a few minutes, then a distinguished gentleman in his seventies came to the door.

He smiled pleasantly at Cathy. "Good evening. Can I help you?"

"We were told you have a veterinarian camping here. We found an injured dog on the road about twenty miles from here and hope she can take a look at him."

The gentleman was seemingly not too surprised at such a late-night request. "You must be the women Peter called about. If you follow this road down the hill, you'll see several RVs. The third one on the right is Alfreda's. If there are lights on, she is awake. Even if the lights aren't on, since this is urgent, knock anyway. Actually, I think I'll show you the way since it is so late."

Cathy said, "We also need a campsite for the night. Do you have one available?"

"Yes, absolutely. I'm Ben Arden. I own Arden RV Park." He started strolling down the drive. Cathy hesitated and then walked quickly and caught up with him. She turned and waved to Linda to follow in the camper.

"It's just about a five-minute walk," he said.

"The night sky here is unbelievable." Cathy was awestruck by the sheer number of stars.

Ben gazed upward, "I never get tired of looking at it, and I've lived here all my life."

They reached a row of parked RVs. Most of them were dark. Ben pointed to one that looked like someone was watching television. A bright light flickered behind the window shades.

"She's awake," he said. "I can introduce you if you would be more comfortable with me knocking on the door."

Cathy thought about this for a moment. "Yes, I think that would work best since we don't know her, and it is the middle of the night."

Ben stepped up to the door of the RV and knocked. Immediately there was an outburst of barking in response.

"Shhhh, doggies, it is just me," he said.

The door abruptly swung open, and a woman in her seventies, wearing sweatpants and a Howard University sweatshirt, peered out.

"What's up, Ben? I assume you know what time it is."

"Alfreda, you know that normally I wouldn't bother you at this hour, except these women found an injured dog on the road, and they were hoping you would take a look at it."

Alfreda's gaze shifted to Cathy. "I am Dr. Alfreda Tyson. What's the story?"

Cathy took a deep breath. "Hi, I'm Cathy Rosen. About twenty miles from here, we found a small dog with an arrow in his side. We were able to get him into a crate we borrowed from a police officer who stopped by to see what was going on. We think he must be in terrible pain. It looks infected. And so here we are, hoping you can help us."

Alfreda asked, "Can you bring him inside?"

"Yes," said Cathy. She walked to the door of the RV and, with Linda, carefully picked up the dog crate and began to move it. Betsy drowsily called out from her bedroom to see if they needed help.

"We're good," answered Cathy. "Thanks."

They carried the crate into Alfreda's RV, trying not to bump into anything. The dog had awakened and was calmly watching everything that was going on. Alfreda led them to a back bedroom that had been retrofitted as a vet's office. They put the crate on the floor and lifted the dog, still bundled in the blanket to stabilize the arrow, onto the examination table.

Alfreda leaned over the dog. "First, I'll check his vitals, then give him a pain killer and IV antibiotics." The little dog's eyes were focused on Alfreda's face, watching her every move. She gently stroked the dog's head and checked his mouth, eyes, and ears. She then took the dog's temperature, and while he didn't like it, he remained calm. "What a good dog," murmured Alfreda. "Not surprising, he has a fever. It looks like the arrow is not in very deep. Judging by the tissue around the wound, it has been there for a while. I'll operate tomorrow morning, depending on how he does tonight. I want the medicine to have a chance to get into his system." She washed her hands and turned to the two women. "Have you named him yet?"

"Frankie," said Cathy.

Linda looked at her, surprised since there had been no discussion whatsoever about a possible name.

Cathy looked at Linda somewhat sheepishly. "He just looks like a Frankie."

Linda smiled. "Then Frankie, it is."

Alfreda finished inserting the IV drip and secured it with tape.

"Okay, he is good for the night. The pain medicine will help him rest. I'll probably operate around nine. Stop by around ten thirty to see how he is doing. I take it you will be at a campsite here at the ranch?"

Cathy nodded. "Yes, but I'm not sure where yet."

"Ben will get you squared away."

Cathy and Linda said goodnight to Alfreda and returned to their RV. They found Betsy and Ben inside, chatting over cups of mint tea. Cathy updated them on the dog's condition, including his new name.

"Frankie," said Betsy thoughtfully. "I like it."

Ben stood up, "Let me show you where your campsite is, and then you can get settled in and relax for the evening. Or what's left of it."

Linda slid into the driver's seat and started the engine. Ben pointed it out. "It is just two campsites down here on your left. Number 35. It is a full utility site and is available for the next seven days."

They drove between two trees, and there it was—a beautiful campsite on a slight bluff overlooking the river. The river gleamed in the moonlight while ripples in the water set sparkles of light dancing across the waves.

"Oh my God," said Cathy. "This is gorgeous." There was a moment of total silence as everyone drank in the incredible view.

Ben opened the door and stepped down from the RV. "The power pedestal with your electrical, water, and sewage connections is right over here. We do offer breakfast from 6 – 9 at the ranch house. It's family-style—lots of great food and great company. Have a good night, ladies." With that, he strolled away into the darkness.

CHAPTER 3

The women immediately went around opening windows to let in the cooling breeze and soothing sound of the river as it rolled by.

Cathy said, "I know it's incredibly late at night, but we need to connect to the electrical outlet and water source on the power pedestal, so we're all set for tomorrow."

"Can't we just run everything off the generator," asked Linda, "since it is so late?"

"I know we're exhausted, but if we run the generator all night, we would have to charge it as soon as possible tomorrow morning. Speaking for myself, I'd rather just take it easy tomorrow morning and be able to relax and not have to run around trying to connect powerlines and things like that."

Linda sighed. "Okay, let's get it done and over with. Hopefully, it shouldn't take too long."

"In case we need guidance." Cathy held up a well-used, dog-eared book on the basics of RVing. Each of the three women had her own research methodology, and the book was a testament to their diverse styles. In addition to being heavily dog-eared, it was stuffed full of sticky notes and boasted a rainbow of bright highlighter colors on every page.

Telling Betsy to rest and take it easy, Cathy and Linda turned on the outside lights and put on headlamps and work gloves. They walked outside and over to the power pedestal. Everything was clearly marked, in good repair, and exceptionally clean. Linda opened the outside storage space behind the driver's side door and pulled out the electrical cable while Cathy got out the hose to connect the water. They quickly connected them, then moved on to the sewage hose. Once they got that connected, they put wooden chucks around the wheels to doubly secure the vehicle. Finally, they climbed back into the camper.

Their rental RV was an older model. The exterior was somewhat dated, but it was very comfortably appointed inside. It had two slideouts that added five feet to the width, soft leather seating, plush carpet, and panoramic windows. There was plenty of room for the three women to spread out and have their own space. The sleeping arrangements included an oversized queen bed and thick, comfortable cushions that transformed the dining table and sofa into two additional full-size beds. They had agreed that Betsy would have the queen size bed since she often took a nap during the day. The large bathroom had a spa shower. Next to that was a closet with a stacked washer/dryer. The kitchen had a double sink, microwave, and five-burner stove/oven. The dining table had banquet seating, which faced two club chairs and a couch. There was a large flat-screen TV, DVD player, and stereo speakers throughout. An additional loft bed over the driver area had a ladder for access. But none of the women wanted to risk going up and down the ladder, especially at night, so they used it for storage.

Linda and Cathy quickly transformed the couch into a bed. Then they lowered the dining table level with the bench seats bracketing it. They moved the customized cushions into place on the tabletop, so it too was now a comfortable bed. They murmured good night to each other, crawled into their respective beds, and immediately fell asleep.

With sunrise came a fantastic groundswell of birdsong. Cathy lay in her bed, listening to a variety of sounds—from melodic trills to whistles, cackles, and hoots.

Linda stretched, looking over at Cathy. "Wow. You don't need an alarm clock here, for sure. What time is it?"

Cathy stood up. "It's six thirty. I'll put the water on. Does anyone want to go up to the ranch house for breakfast?"

In her bedroom, Betsy sat up and reached for her medicines. She called out, "That sounds good, but I just took my medications, and I need about half an hour before they begin to really kick in."

Linda called back, "Betsy, how many times a day do you take medicine?"

"Six times, maybe more if it's not a good day."

"Wow, that's a heavy schedule," commented Linda.

"It's a pain. I feel like I am always taking medicine, about to take medicine, or waiting for it to kick in. That's the toughest time for me when I'm in the off-cycle—my last dose of medicine is no longer working, and I'm not quite ready for the next dose. I get very stiff and slow. It's difficult to keep my balance or use my hands. Sometimes even talking can be a challenge."

Betsy slowly walked down the hallway toward Cathy, who put her arm around her and said, "I'm so sorry. I don't know much about Parkinson's, but it sounds like it absolutely sucks. I'm glad you're here with us."

"I'm glad too. But I also want you to know, Cathy, what this is going to look like since we are living in close quarters. I'm not going to be able to hide from you where I am with things."

"We don't want you to worry about anything, Betsy. We want you to just be yourself—however you are feeling."

Gradually the women began fully waking up, chatting, stretching, and getting ready for the day. Linda and Cathy opened the RV's exterior storage space and pulled out a folding table and chairs. Then, Linda brought out a thermos of coffee and one of tea, along with leftover pastries from the day before. The women sat at the table with their morning mugs. They relaxed, drinking in the remarkable scenery and wonderful bird sounds as they savored the soft breeze coming off the river.

"What a beautiful way to start the day," commented Betsy while she sipped her cup of Irish Breakfast Tea. Her hands were still very stiff, and tremors made it difficult for her to hold a mug. Linda leaned in to help, stirring some honey into Betsy's tea and then adding a little bit of half-and-half. Betsy appreciated Linda's thoughtfulness, though she preferred doing things for herself; it helped her self-confidence to know that she could take care of herself.

But now she just smiled and said, "Thank you," as she warmed her hands on the mug of tea. She chuckled, "I just have to tell you guys this. This morning I was talking to Hugh … " Hugh was Betsy's Australian-voiced Siri entity, whom she called Hugh after her favorite actor, Hugh Jackman. The first morning they spent in the camper together, Cathy and Linda had been startled and then greatly amused to hear a male voice with an Australian accent coming from Betsy's bedroom. "I asked him how much battery I had on my iPhone. He told me I had 90%. But then he said"—Betsy started laughing harder at this—"he advised me 'to go forth and conquer.' Now where did that come from? Has my Hugh gone rogue? Does Apple know about this? I've never heard him say that before." By now, Cathy and Linda were laughing along with Betsy.

"All I ever do is ask for the time and weather," said Linda. "I'll have to start talking to him more often and see what else he has to say. I definitely need to select a different accent. Maybe Irish if they have it."

The women were quiet for a while, sipping their morning drinks and relishing the peace and serenity of their campsite.

"I wonder how Frankie is doing," said Cathy.

"He has got to be feeling better, what with the painkiller and antibiotics on board," said Linda.

Cathy sipped the last of her coffee. "Alfreda said to check in with her about ten thirty?"

"Yes."

Cathy smiled as she watched Linda pour another cup of coffee. Linda was notorious for brewing the strongest coffee around. Cathy kidded Linda that she once took a sip of her coffee by accident and was awake for two weeks straight.

"You know, Betsy," Linda mentioned, "I would be willing to try drinking tea if you show me how you make it. You always seem to enjoy it so much." She added, "I usually drink coffee because I want that jolt of caffeine in the morning, and of course, coffee also has that wonderful aroma."

"I would be glad to introduce you to the wonders of tea," said Betsy. "Tea has an aroma, too, but it's more subtle." She took a sip. "And you are right, I do derive a lot of comfort from having a nice 'cuppa.' The remarkable thing is that it has become so much easier to get a good cup of tea now. Used to be when I visited friends and they'd ask if I'd like some tea, I always hesitated to say yes because then they would root around in their utility drawer for about ten minutes, trying to find a single, dusty teabag that they bought back in the '70s." She made a face and then laughed. "It is different now. So many more people drink tea. I have all kinds for you to try and see if there is one you like."

Cathy stood up and stretched. "Well, I'm ready for some

breakfast. Want to head up to the ranch house?"

"Sounds good to me," said Betsy.

Everyone pitched in to clean up and stow things back in the RV.

"This is like being on a sailboat," Linda commented. "It is designed so well. Everything has its place and there is a lot of storage space. I love the efficiency and convenience. Plus, the independence you get by staying in a camper. I understand now why so many people with disabilities choose to go RVing for their vacation."

The women gathered by the front door to go up to the ranch house together. Betsy had her walker, to help her get up and down the hill easier. As they began strolling up the driveway, they saw others heading toward the ranch house too. Everyone they met smiled or said hello.

"They seem friendly enough." Cathy waved back at a couple with an elderly Labrador.

"Now if this was a Stephen King novel..." said Betsy.

The three women cracked up.

Ben was on the porch and greeted them as they approached. "Good morning, campers. I hope you had a good night."

"Good morning, Ben," they chorused back in unison.

Cathy said, "Thanks Ben for a great campsite. I usually have trouble sleeping but last night was so peaceful, I got a really good night's sleep."

"So did I," said Linda.

Betsy chimed in, "Me too."

"Glad to hear that. I hope you're hungry because we

have a wonderful breakfast set up inside. Lots of goodies." Ben grabbed some bright orange flyers, passing them to the women. "Here is today's schedule of activities and classes. We get a lot of retired teachers, musicians, artists, writers, photographers…and they love to discuss subjects they are passionate about. For instance, today, you can attend a talk on the real history of the Western US, learn how to meditate, or get some tips for winning at chess."

"Wow," said Betsy.

"Indeed. But first, come inside and have some breakfast." Ben led them into the ranch house, which was filled with light, laughter, and people. Large round tables were set up around the room and loaded with pastries, egg dishes, fresh fruits, and hot and cold cereals.

"This looks fantastic," said Betsy. "By the way, thanks for helping us out with Alfreda."

The rest of the women nodded.

Ben looked a bit embarrassed. "No problem. I hope your dog is doing better. I guess you'll find out this morning how the surgery went."

Cathy clarified, "Well, technically, he's not actually our dog. At least not yet. But he is a sweetie. I think we're trying to figure out what to do with him, whether to take him back east with us or not."

Ben said, "Speaking of dogs… we have a senior basset hound who showed up a few days ago. No license, no chip. He has been sitting near the porch out front there. Nobody seems to know where he came from or if, indeed, he belongs to anyone at all. If anyone mentions anything to you about missing a basset hound, please let me know. Alfreda estimates he is about 10-12 years old. He's a real character. We've nicknamed him Charlie."

Before leaving, Ben showed them to a big table overlooking the front porch and the river.

They looked at each other and grinned. "This is excellent," said Cathy.

"I don't know if I will ever want to leave this place," Betsy sat back and gazed around at their surroundings. "It is so beautiful here. I feel my blood pressure dropping already."

Linda stretched out in her chair, feeling the sun warm her face. As she closed her eyes, the external busy sounds around her stopped being a distraction. She began to slowly relax, something that was usually difficult for her. Linda did a yoga body scan, consciously tightening and then loosening muscles throughout her body. She started with her head and neck, then down to her shoulders, arms, hands, core muscles, legs, ankles, and feet. She even arched and stretched her toes. As she let go of bodily tension, she sank deeper and deeper into her chair. She felt totally relaxed.

Ben suddenly reappeared at the table. He glanced over at Linda and lowered his voice. "Alfreda called. She wanted you to know that the dog is doing fine. You can stop in anytime to see him."

"Great," said Cathy. "Thank you, Ben."

The women enjoyed a leisurely breakfast. The food was fresh and delicious. When they finished, they decided it was a good time to go visit Frankie. They walked back down the hill and found their way to Alfreda's RV. Cathy knocked on the door.

Alfreda swung it wide open. "Ahhh, it is my midnight visitors." She smiled. "Come in, come in."

"Good morning," Linda greeted her. "How is the patient?"

"See for yourself." Alfreda led them back to the exam room. There was Frankie, lying on his side in a padded cage. Even with an IV in his leg, he seemed to be resting more comfortably. When the women entered the room, Frankie stirred slightly and opened his eyes. When he saw them, he wagged his tail feebly.

"How is he?" asked Betsy.

"He is still coming out of the anesthesia, so he is pretty woozy," Alfreda explained. "The operation went smoothly. I got all of the arrow out of him and cleaned up the infection. It wasn't as bad as I thought it would be. It helps that he is younger than I originally thought. He is about three or five years old judging by the condition of his teeth. That is when dogs start showing tartar buildup or yellowing of their teeth. He is a sweet dog," Alfreda added as she washed her hands with sanitizer. "He let me do whatever I needed to—injections, stitches, x-rays—and didn't raise a fuss at all. I did find him to be seriously underweight. In addition, his right front leg was broken at some point and never set properly. He can walk, and I don't believe he is in any pain from it, but he does have a limp. So, my question to you is, what do you want to do now?"

"What do you mean?" asked Cathy.

"Well, do you plan on keeping him or adopting him out?" Alfreda dried her hands and stroked Frankie's head. "There are a couple of good rescue groups in the area. They are not all no-kill, but I can find out which ones you can count on to take care of the dog, no matter what." Even though it was not chilly in the RV, Betsy found herself shivering. She glanced over at the little dog who was gazing directly at her. She was surprised by the dog's intensity.

Linda asked, "What more does he need in terms of medical care?"

Alfreda snagged a piece of paper from her desk and read from it. "Two more days in the ICU. Antibiotics for another week, painkillers as needed."

"Well, that is not too bad," Linda replied.

"True," said Cathy. "But then what will we do with the dog? Are we going to keep him? We flew to Phoenix from Philly. I'm not sure about taking a dog we barely know back home on a plane. In which case we would probably have to return the RV to the place we rented it from in Phoenix and rent a car to drive from Phoenix to Philadelphia. And then there's the question of who actually gets to keep the dog, or do we share custody?"

There was a long silence. Each of the women was thinking about what had been said while they considered the dog who kept staring at them. Betsy could swear he had a worried look in his eyes, as if he understood that it was his future being discussed.

"First things first," said Cathy. "He needs to stay here for a few days to recover from his surgery. Is that a problem, Alfreda?"

"No."

"Then let's also confirm with Ben that we are staying for a few days, so we don't lose that beautiful campsite," said Linda.

They thanked Alfreda and paid her for the surgery. Then the women split up: Linda and Betsy heading back to the RV, and Cathy preparing to walk back up to the ranch house. Cathy had barely started on her way when she ran into Ben. He was slowly motoring along in a golf cart, greeting campers as they walked along the drive.

"Hi, Ben. I wanted to talk to you about staying here for a bit longer. The dog we rescued, Frankie, is going to need some follow-up care, and we want to make sure Alfreda is able to keep an eye on him for a few days." Cathy added, "We really love that campsite and would like to stay for the week."

"No problem, Cathy. I'll drop by the rental agreement this afternoon. Glad to hear the dog is doing well." He drove off.

Her task of securing the campsite for the week completed, Cathy started back to the RV. Her thoughts were filled with Frankie, and she wondered what they would end up deciding to do about him. She already had a suspicion what the outcome would be.

CHAPTER 4

As Linda and Betsy got closer to the RV, Betsy asked Linda, "What is that sitting on our front step?"

Linda peered ahead and then laughed. "This must be the year of the dog. I am fairly sure that is Charlie, the dog Ben told us about. He looks a little woebegone right now," she added, noticing his droopy posture and bowed head. She whistled and called "Charlie!" He immediately perked up and ambled over to them.

Linda smiled down at him. "There is something about basset hounds that gets to me. They are such nice, easy-going dogs." Charlie leaned against her leg and gazed up at her. She laughed and reached down, stroking his head and long ears. He made a low humming noise and closed his eyes.

Just then, Cathy walked around the RV, saw Charlie, and came to a standstill. He glanced at her and then slid down Linda's leg into a relaxed heap at her feet. Squatting down beside him, she continued to pet him. Cathy and Betsy exchanged glances.

"What?" said Linda. "What does that look mean?"

"It's just that we've never really seen you with a dog before."

"I like dogs," said Linda defensively. "There are just some dogs I like more than others." Betsy started to say something but then thought better of it and said nothing.

"Well," said Cathy, "the good news is that we have this campsite for a week."

"Yea," Betsy cheered. "I just want to sit and look out over the river and relax. I love the peace and quiet here."

"Sounds good to me," said Linda. Just then Charlie rolled onto his back and lay there with all four legs in the air. He started snoring loudly almost immediately.

Betsy asked, "Did someone mention peace and quiet?"

The women were soon settled in a semicircle, their chairs once again overlooking the river. Charlie came and joined them. Initially, Linda had determined not to pay a lot of attention or do anything special for Charlie. She didn't want him to become dependent or too focused on her. After all, she had no interest in taking care of a dog. But after she watched him twist and turn a bit on the gravel driveway, trying to get comfortable, she went inside the RV and brought out a big bath towel. She folded it carefully and placed it on the ground, next to her chair. Charlie watched the entire process with great interest, ambling over to her as she finished arranging it. He lay down on it with a contented sigh, wiggled a few times, and soon nodded off. Linda found herself looking down at him and smiling.

Betsy was reading over the schedule of activities for the day. "Wow, there's a lot here. I think I'll check out the meditation class this afternoon. Anybody else interested?"

Linda said, "I might be."

"I am thinking about taking a walk up to the ranch house," said Cathy, "and seeing where we can buy supplies. We are getting low on some basics like coffee, tea, milk, and honey."

"Do you want us to go with you?" asked Betsy.

"No, I'm fine going by myself," answered Cathy. "I will be back in a few."

"I have a feeling that we will be sitting here in exactly the same positions when you get back," laughed Linda.

Cathy grabbed a water bottle and started up the driveway. Linda and Betsy relaxed in the sunshine and listened to the birds.

At the ranch house, Ben explained to Cathy, "We have a camp store with basic camping supplies, a small deli counter, locally produced fresh milk and eggs, and some simple meals. We have a baker who comes in every morning and makes all kinds of breads, muffins, and cakes. If you want a more extensive selection, you will have to drive about twenty miles to the town of Candor, which has a substantial grocery store."

"Thanks, Ben," said Cathy. "We don't really want to go off campus if we can avoid it. We would just like to hang out here and relax and take in the beautiful views."

Ben smiled, "I'm glad you are enjoying your stay here." He excused himself, turning to help another camper with a question.

Cathy found her way to the camp store. It was located on the lower level of the ranch house and had a good supply of foodstuffs and baked goods. She was especially delighted to find Häagen-Dazs in the freezer. "This is just what I was in the mood for," she said, holding up a pint of vanilla ice cream.

A woman passing by said, "Ah, I see they carry one of the necessities of life." The two women smiled at one another in perfect understanding. Cathy grabbed a shopping cart, filled it to the brim, and paid for all the groceries. As she was heading out of the ranch house back to the campsite, she saw Ben by the front desk. He looked worried.

"I'm glad I ran into you again," Ben said. "I just found out there is a severe weather forecast for tonight. There is already a tornado watch up for this area."

Cathy asked, "What do people do here when there is bad weather?"

"If it's really bad, many of the campers will come up to the ranch house. Some people, of course, just hunker down and ride out the storm in their RVs."

"When is the bad weather due to hit?"

"After nine tonight. There is a tornado siren if one touches down near here. If you hear that siren go off, immediately seek shelter. Make sure you secure anything that's loose around the outside of your RV. Anything that can blow away will blow away." Someone called his name. Ben excused himself and hurried away.

'Yikes,' thought Cathy.

Back at the campsite, Linda moved her chair closer to Betsy, who was now in a totally relaxed posture with her eyes closed.

Linda asked her, "How are you feeling?"

"All right. A little tired but really doing all right now. Just relaxing. It is so beautiful here."

Linda nodded and looked down at Charlie, who was lying there beside her.

She hesitated and then asked, "Betsy, how do you manage having Parkinson's? I had a great aunt who had it, and I've been trying to remember how she dealt with it. Of course, the medications were quite limited at that time."

There was a long pause before Betsy answered thoughtfully. "The middle of the night is especially tough for me. I have trouble sleeping anyway and usually wake up at about two or three, and then I'm awake for a couple of hours. That's when the 'what if's' really get to me."

Linda nodded again and dropped her head a little bit as she listened.

Betsy continued, "If I'm not careful, I can talk myself into a major panic attack. I start imagining all kinds of things that can launch me quickly into a very dark place if I'm not careful. I try to forestall that by distracting myself somehow. I get out of bed and turn on the television. I start reading or cleaning up, focusing on anything that will get me out of my own head. When my ex was still my husband a few years ago, I had a greater sense of confidence that I'd be able to handle anything that came along. I have my doubts now, and sometimes it really scares me."

"What happened?" asked Linda. "Why the divorce?"

Betsy answered ruefully, "He couldn't deal with the Parkinson's." She paused for a moment. "Have you ever been married?"

Linda shook her head. "I had a few proposals. I said 'no' to all but one. Thank God he got cold feet at the last minute. Marrying him would have been a monumental mistake." She shuddered. "I thought he was the answer to all my worries and insecurities."

Betsy stretched her legs, "That's what I thought too until the day he walked out."

"Face it, Betsy, he was a schmuck. He didn't deserve you."

"Right back at you. Neither did yours."

Betsy and Linda sat quietly for a while, listening to the birdsongs around them.

Betsy said, "Let's agree to make this a schmuck-free zone."

Linda laughed, "Done." They shook hands on it.

A short time later, as Cathy headed down the road to the campsite with a bag of groceries, she saw Alfreda doing some weeding outside her RV. "Hey Alfreda, is it okay if I stop in and say hi to Frankie?"

"Of course," said Alfreda.

The little dog was greatly improved, standing up on his hind legs to greet her and wagging his tail furiously. "He looks great!" said Cathy. She fussed over him for a while as he wiggled all over with excitement. "How is he doing?"

"Well, he has a slight fever, which I'm not happy

about. But it is not unexpected after everything he's been through. We'll see how he's doing in twenty-four hours. He may be able to go home tomorrow with you, or maybe he can stay here for another day. We'll see how it goes."

"Thanks, Alfreda." Cathy started to leave, then stopped. "Have you heard that there is a severe storm alert for tonight?"

"Yes, Ben always keeps me informed of that kind of thing."

Cathy asked curiously, "How long have you known him?"

Alfreda answered, "I've taken care of his dogs for many years, and we've become good friends. When I started thinking about letting go of my practice, I wasn't sure what I wanted to do, and then I found out about his RV park. It's a perfect fit."

Cathy said goodbye to Alfreda and started for home.

After she arrived at the RV, she began unpacking the supplies and putting them away while she talked to Betsy and Linda about the tornado watch. She mentioned that Ben had suggested going up to the ranch house and sheltering there.

Betsy said, "I really do not want to be in an RV during bad weather."

"I'm with you," said Cathy. "Whenever they show storm damage on the news, they always show mobile homes that have been tossed around."

"And you can't get much more mobile than an RV," Betsy said.

"I think we should go up to the ranch house," suggested Linda. "We don't have anything to prove by going through severe weather in the camper."

All the women agreed.

"Ben said we need to secure anything on or around the RV that could fly away,"

"Let's take care of that now," Linda urged, getting to her feet, and heading for the door. Cathy followed her.

Once outside, the two women checked to see what needed to be secured. Bicycles, which they had taken out of storage in anticipation of doing some riding around the campground's bike trails, were put back into the storage compartment. Meanwhile, Betsy was in the RV, finishing up putting away the supplies that Cathy had purchased. Once she was done with that, she also stored dishes, mugs, cooking utensils, and anything else that could be easily tossed around or broken.

Then she joined Linda and Cathy outside helping to tie down whatever else needed to be protected.

Linda said to the two women, "I'm going to run up, check on Alfreda and see if there's anything she needs help with getting her RV ready before the storm."

The other women agreed and went back inside. Linda trotted quickly up the driveway, toward Alfreda's. Charlie had disappeared a while ago. Linda assumed he was off in search of food or a quieter place to sleep. She worried that he might get caught in the oncoming storm and hoped he had a safe place to shelter.

However, as she approached Alfreda's RV, she caught a

glimpse of movement out of the corner of her eye. It was Charlie. He appeared out of nowhere and was now right by her side, keeping up with her nicely. She knocked on the vet's door. Alfreda opened the door and welcomed Linda into the RV. Charlie scooted in behind her.

"What can I do to help you get ready for the bad weather coming tonight?" Linda asked.

"I would really appreciate some help. I have a couple of dogs here in ICU, and I need to make sure they are secure in their crates. I also need to make sure the windows are all closed and sealed and that my equipment is safe."

Linda said. "I'm glad to help, just point me in the right direction."

They immediately got to work securing crates and boxes with bungee cords and tie-downs.

Charlie was dogging Linda's steps around the RV. "Is it okay if he is here with me? He is following me everywhere now."

Alfreda looked down at Charlie and smiled. "I am very fond of the old boy. He is a sweet dog."

"Do you have any idea if anybody around here knows him? I'm worried about where he will be during the storm."

Alfreda thought about it for a moment and then said, "Nobody knows where he came from. He just showed up one day. I suspect he was dumped on the highway. We get all these older dogs left there. People just don't want to take care of them as they get older. Maybe because they now need costly medicines or help going up and down the stairs, or they start having accidents, or maybe simply because they just are not as cute as a brand-new puppy. All horrible reasons to get rid of an older dog but people do. Of course, the dog doesn't understand why after years of being loved as part of the family, they are suddenly being left by the side of the road. It's awful but it happens."

Alfreda looked over at Linda. "I'm sorry. This is one of those issues that drives me crazy. I just hate to see older animals being discarded like yesterday's newspapers." She then laughed. "I guess that is an outmoded expression now, isn't it?"

Linda looked down at Charlie who was sitting by her side with one of his feet resting on one of her feet. She reached down and petted him. "It's hard to believe he made it all the way from the highway to here."

Alfreda got a biscuit out of the treat box and tossed it to Charlie who, with a mighty effort, surged up from a sitting position and caught it in midair. Linda and Alfreda applauded and cheered.

Alfreda said, "I suspect Charlie has many hidden talents that helped him to survive."

Alfreda and Linda worked easily together securing the RV. Linda noticed a row of photographs, including some featuring well-known politicians.

"Alfreda, this picture of this woman standing here with the President, is this your mom? She looks so much like you."

"Yes. that's my mother. She passed away a few years ago. She was a mathematics professor at Howard University.

She was a phenomenal teacher and researcher. All the top universities and colleges wanted her. But she thought she would have the most positive impact at Howard so that's where she spent her career. That picture was taken when she had just created an innovative curriculum to help elementary school students to learn math in a fun and engaging way."

"Wow. You must be tremendously proud of her."

Alfreda smiled wistfully. "Yes, I am proud of her accomplishments. But even more, I miss her terribly. We were close, and I loved spending time with her. She was from Jamaica and had this wonderful accent. I really miss picking up the phone and hearing her voice. Whenever I heard that accent, this feeling of comfort and well-being would just sweep over me." She turned away and focused on moving a big pile of papers into a secure location.

After putting in an hour of preparation, Alfreda pronounced herself satisfied that everything was in good shape. She felt ready to take on the storm. She hugged Linda "Thank you so much for helping me. It made a world of difference."

Linda said goodbye to Frankie and Charlie. When she left, Charlie tried to follow her. Alfreda blocked him with the door, keeping him inside with her. She promised him that he would see Linda again soon. Then she closed the door and sank down on a kitchen chair, out of sheer exhaustion.

CHAPTER 5

Back at the women's RV, everything that needed to be secured had been. Cathy, Linda, and Betsy sat at the table, relaxing for the moment, and talked about what they should make for dinner.

Betsy said, "Do you realize we talk about food more than any other subject combined?"

Linda and Cathy looked at each other. "Do we?"

Cathy said, "Yes, I actually think we do."

Linda laughed. "That is fine with me. I like food and I like eating. Now, let's make some sandwiches."

As they ate dinner and chatted, dark clouds piled up across the sky. None of them addressed it directly, but each of them began to feel anxious.

Linda suggested, "We should take some blankets and pillows up to the ranch house, in case we have to spend the entire night there."

"Good idea" said Cathy. "By the way, where's Charlie?"

Linda responded, "He's with Alfreda. He'll stay there during the storm."

The wind began picking up, creating little whirlwinds of leaves, grass, and dust.

Cathy said, "Okay. I think it's time to batten down the hatches and head to the ranch house. It looks like the severe weather is moving in faster than expected. I do not like the look of that sky." There was a distant crash of thunder. They took a last look around their campsite. There was another rumble of thunder.

They started up the driveway. Betsy was tired and decided to bring her walker with her for extra support. Cathy and Linda walked beside her, carrying blankets and pillows.

As they neared the ranch house, they saw more and more people heading in the same direction.

"Thank goodness we are not the only ones," said Betsy. "At least I don't feel like a total wuss."

The night was almost totally black by now. A brilliant flash of lightning split the sky and streaked earthward.

"Yikes," said Betsy quietly. She could feel herself getting increasingly jittery. She tried doing kind of a walking meditation, taking long breaths to calm down. Another huge lightning bolt flashed across the sky. This time the thunder was closer and louder.

Ben stood on the front porch and waved at the small groups of campers headed his way. "Hi, guys. Glad to see you. Come on in, just follow the crowd to the community room downstairs. Make yourselves at home."

Focusing on the sky overhead, Betsy tripped on the porch step. Ben rushed forward to help her.

"I'm fine. Really. But thank you anyway," Betsy reassured Ben.

There was another flash of lightning followed by thunder, much louder this time. A big gust of wind swept across the driveway. Overhead, massive tree branches were beginning to sway back and forth, creaking loudly.

"OK, everybody, it's time to go inside now," said Ben. He cast worried looks at the branches and promised himself that he would get them trimmed after the storm. He began urging people along faster to get into the building.

Cathy asked, "Is everything all right, Ben?"

"The storm is coming faster than expected, and it looks to be even more severe. I want to get everybody inside as quickly as possible." He then asked for volunteers to help round up people who were taking their time getting to the ranch house. A number of people volunteered and quickly spread out to encourage people to pick up the pace.

The community room was a medium-size room that could hold up to fifty people comfortably. It felt secure because there were no windows in the room, and it was half underground. People were chatting and talking and putting down sleeping bags. Although, on the surface it seemed like an easygoing atmosphere, there was an underlying sense of unease and nervousness.

The storm was building. Lights flickered, went out and came back on again. Ben got on the PA system and told everybody that there was a generator that covered the building, so they would not be without power.

While Linda and Cathy chatted with other campers,

Betsy found herself getting more anxious. She pulled her blanket tight around her head to help block some of the storm's fury. Closing her eyes, she tried to meditate, focusing on her breath. But Betsy was finding it difficult to breathe evenly, her anxiety was causing her to hyperventilate. Linda looked down at her and realized that she was having a tough time. She nudged Cathy and put her blanket down next to Betsy. Linda laid down next to her and put her arms around her as Cathy did the same from the other side. They made a cozy little nest for themselves. They could feel Betsy trembling and gulping for air.

"What's going on Betsy?" asked Cathy.

"Panic attack," said Betsy shortly, sounding like she was physically having to force out the words, her jaw was clenched so tight.

Linda said, "I know it's scary, but we're all here together and you're not alone."

Betsy took in Linda's words and held on to them. The warmth of their hugs comforted her and helped her to let go of some of the anxiety. She could feel her tension easing and felt a little better.

Cathy whispered to Linda, "It looks like a big pajama party right now." Linda laughed.

As they nestled in their blankets next to each other, the three women started sharing travel stories.

Cathy said, "It's funny, whenever I'm away from home, I need to take a walk or a drive right off so that I feel centered. I like knowing where local landmarks are, what's around me, where I am in relation to my surroundings. I guess it gives me a sense of being grounded. When Richard, my husband, and I would travel together, it frustrated him that the first thing I would do after we arrived somewhere was to head out the door and start walking, whereas he liked to unpack everything, put his clothes away, take his time, and settle into the room. It took quite a few arguments, but we eventually accepted that this was the way it was for each of us—what we needed to do to feel at home. He needed to nest, and I wanted to be outside getting a bird's-eye view."

Betsy was curious. "How long were you and Richard married?"

"Fifteen years."

There was a pause, and then Betsy asked, "What happened?"

"Cancer," Cathy said in a short tone, clearly not wanting to talk about it. "I still have his sneakers that he always wore when we went on trips. I couldn't bear to throw them away." Blinking rapidly, she looked away.

Noting all the people who had their dogs with them, Linda whispered to Betsy, "I could have brought Charlie." Betsy looked at her for a moment.

Linda said, "What?"

"You are really bonding with that dog."

"I enjoy him, but I wouldn't say I'm bonding with him."

"Hmm," murmured Betsy.

There was suddenly a loud crack of thunder. Almost everybody in the room jumped. A few people laughed nervously. The lights flickered but then stayed on. It was now possible to hear the wind howling outside the building. Every once in a while, there was a loud crack, as another tree branch came down. The thunder picked up in frequency and in severity.

"Thank God there are no windows in this room. Lightning scares me," Cathy admitted ruefully.

"Me too," the woman next to them said. "My husband went to check on our dogs, and I thought he would be back by now." She looked away, worry lines creasing her forehead.

Suddenly someone in the crowd called out, "Hey, Ben, how about some music to take our minds off the storm."

Ben replied. "I don't know that we will hear the music over the storm but I'll try."

He walked over to an upright piano tucked away in a corner and pushed it to the center of the room.

"There's some guitars and banjos, and I think some tambourines. Anyone else want to join in and play?" Ben quickly tuned up his guitar and strummed a few chords. He began singing, "I feel the earth move under my feet…"

Laughter rippled through the room as people began picking up on what Ben was playing. There was almost a palpable release of tension, as other musicians picked up instruments to play along while Ben moved from one song to the next. A woman with flowing red hair strode over to the piano, sat down, and immediately began harmonizing along with Ben on Carole King and James Taylor songs. The music was doing its magic, soothing jangled nerves. Most people were either singing or humming to the music.

Even with the storm raging outside, it felt cozy and warm in the community room.

The three women were curled up in their blankets and pillows, leaning against each other and drowsily singing along.

Another huge crack of thunder that sounded like it was right on top of them startled everyone. The lights blinked on and off for a few minutes and then stayed on. The wind dropped precipitously. There was an eerie silence, causing people to look around in confusion. Then the wind came back with a vengeance. It was howling so strongly that people's ears popped. Ben realized he had lost his audience and put his guitar away. Yet another huge crash of thunder soon followed.

Cathy got up and walked over to Ben, who was drinking a glass of wine. He smiled at her as she approached. "Ben," she said quietly, "the woman next to us hasn't seen her husband since he went to check on their dogs right before the storm hit."

"Shit." Ben sighed. "There is nothing we can do right now. It's too dangerous to go outside. As soon as it lets up, I'll go check on him."

"Thanks," said Cathy. Ben walked back with her to the group of women. He went over to the woman whose husband was missing in action and speaking quietly he explained the situation. She looked frightened and was twisting her hands tightly together.

Ben walked back to the PA system. "Hey, everyone, may I have your attention." The crowd quieted, turning toward him. "No one is to go outside at this point. There is a lot of debris flying around, and I don't want anyone to get hurt. I will let you know when it is safe to go back to your RVs." He then walked around, talking to people, and answering questions.

Linda pulled a blanket up around her shoulders and leaned against the wall. "I hope Alfreda and the dogs are all right."

"We'll check on her first thing," Cathy promised.

Linda nodded and closed her eyes wearily. Betsy was curled up in her blanket fast asleep in spite of the storm raging outside.

Cathy felt antsy and got up to wander around and stretch her legs. She found a table with urns of hot coffee and hot water, along with an assortment of teas. Cathy chose chamomile to help her relax and get some sleep. She poured hot water over the teabag, added a teaspoon of honey, and let it steep for a few minutes. She breathed in its calming fragrance and felt herself relax a bit. Standing there, sipping her tea, she looked out over the room. She could hear the quiet hum of voices, punctuated by howling gusts of wind and the terrifying crack of tree branches along with resounding thuds as the branches hit the ground.

The woman whose husband was out in the storm came up to Cathy. "I wanted to introduce myself. My name is Sharon Knowden."

Cathy smiled at her. "I'm Cathy Rosen."

"I wanted to thank you and your friends for helping

me deal with my husband, George, having gone AWOL."

Cathy sipped her tea. "I would have had the same reaction if someone I loved was out in this storm."

Sharon turned away for a moment to blow her nose. Ben spotted them and came up behind Sharon. "It won't be long now before we can get outside and look around," he told her reassuringly. "The storm is beginning to move away. I checked the radar."

"That's good to hear, " said Cathy.

"Thank you." Sharon poured a cup of coffee, added sugar and cream, and went back to her sleeping bag.

"When do you think we can check on him?" Cathy asked Ben.

"I want to wait until dawn. Until there is a little light at least."

Cathy returned to her blanket. She felt a wave of exhaustion sweep over her, so much so that she staggered for a moment and then had to reach out and steady herself. She sat down, wrapped the blanket around her and leaned back against the wall. Within a few moments, she was fast asleep.

CHAPTER 6

It was the silence that awakened Cathy. Half asleep, she rolled over and sat up. She had a moment of confusion, not sure where she was or what time of day it was. The lights in the big community room were dimmed but still offered enough illumination for her to see that people were beginning to stir. It was quiet outside, no earsplitting crashes of thunder or deep rumbling of falling tree branches. She spotted Ben putting big canisters of coffee and hot water out on catering tables. She got up awkwardly—she was stiff from lying on the floor. First thing she needed was a bathroom. Ben looked over and saw her standing up and stretching. He pointed down the corridor.

"Mind-reader," muttered Cathy as she picked her way carefully through rows of still sleeping people.

Entering the darkened bathroom, she switched on the light. "Awkkk." She peered at herself in the mirror. She had clearly slept on something that had left a large red imprint on her cheek. "Looks like my flashlight." She laughed. "Well, that's attractive." Her hair was sticking out in clumps and her teeth felt fuzzy. She sighed, used the toilet, washed her hands, and headed back out in search of caffeine.

Cathy headed toward Ben but saw he was talking earnestly with someone. The person suddenly turned around, and Cathy recognized the police chief from the night when they had found Frankie. He looked at her and waved. She smiled at him, then remembered what she looked like.

"Oh, the hell with it," Cathy said to herself and walked toward the two men.

"Good morning," Ben greeted her. "Coffee?"

"That would be awesome," said Cathy gratefully. "Thank you."

"So, how's the dog?" asked the police chief.

"He is doing well, thanks to you, Ben here, and Alfreda the vet. She operated on him yesterday morning and was able to extract the arrow. There is some residual infection, but she thinks the antibiotics will take care of that. Frankie, that's what we named him, is taking it easy for the next few days and recovering from his wound."

"Good," said the police chief.

Cathy hesitated before saying, "I'm sorry, I don't remember your name, Officer."

"Peter." He held out his hand. She shook hands with him and introduced herself again.

Ben interjected, "Peter lives not too far from here and decided to stop by and see how we were doing after the storm."

"The tornado, an F-2, touched down about five miles

from here and stayed on the ground for a short distance. Luckily, it is mostly pastureland around here, not a lot of development, so it did not do much structural damage," Peter explained.

"Is it safe to go outside now?" asked Cathy. "I want to check up on Alfreda and also on the husband of the woman over there who went to see to their dogs and hasn't been back."

"I'll take you. Let's go," said Peter.

"Their RV is three campsites beyond Alfreda's," said Ben. "Number 45. I need to stay here for a little longer then I'll come down and help you look."

"Better grab a jacket," Peter told Cathy.

She walked quickly to her blanket and put on the bright yellow rain jacket she had brought with her.

Betsy opened her eyes blearily and asked, "Where are you going?"

"Just checking out storm damage and to see if anyone needs assistance."

"What time is it?" murmured Betsy.

Cathy answered, "It's only 6 a.m., go back to sleep."

"Okey dokey," Betsy pulled her pillow over her head, blocking out sound and light. She slipped back into sleep. Next to her, Linda was still fast asleep, totally cocooned in her blanket.

Peter handed Cathy her coffee as they stepped out onto the front porch of the ranch house. "Don't forget your morning dose of caffeine," he said.

Cathy started to thank him, when she got a good look

at the destruction from the storm. The words died on her lips. Aghast, Cathy looked around her at the large number of branches littering the ground. Several large trees had been uprooted. "I can't believe there is so much damage."

"It is going to take some time to clean this mess up." He walked over to an ATV and climbed on. "Let's head down into the campground." Cathy hesitated and then climbed on behind him. She wrapped her arms around his waist.

"Ready?" he asked.

"As I'll ever be," she answered.

Peter drove slowly down the hill, carefully avoiding all the debris from the storm. At the bottom of the hill, he turned right toward Alfreda's RV. Even from a distance, it was easy to see that her trailer had sustained damage. They pulled up next to it and saw the door was half off the hinges. "Oh no," said Cathy.

CHAPTER 7

Cathy climbed off the ATV and ran to the door. "Alfreda!"

"I'm here. I'm okay," cried a muffled voice. The storm had pushed the RV around, and it was now leaning at a slight angle, making it difficult to gain entry.

"Where are you?" Peter pulled at the door.

He and Cathy were finally able to scramble inside. It was a mess. Some of the shelves and cabinets had been knocked open, their contents strewn about the floor.

"Back here in the ICU."

Peter pushed his way through, clearing a path. They found Alfreda on the floor. She looked up at them and Cathy gasped. She was sporting an enormous black eye, which was already turning a dramatic deep purple.

"Are you okay?" asked Cathy, squatting down beside Alfreda. She realized even as she asked it that it was a nonsensical question. Clearly she was not all right. Cathy put her arm around the older woman and felt her tremble. She looked up at Peter with a worried expression.

"We need to get her checked out," she said to Peter.

He asked Alfreda, "Other than that award-winning shiner, is there anything else going on with you, any pain anywhere? You know you are going to have to get checked out at the hospital for possible concussion."

Alfreda shook her head, wincing at the movement. "I don't want to go. I have a couple of dogs to take care of, including Frankie." She groaned a little as she rubbed her shoulder. "The wind really shook the camper. Worse than I've ever experienced. I lost my balance and slammed my head against a cabinet. I got a little woozy after that, I'm not sure how I ended up on the floor. You're right. I probably should go and get checked out." She slowly started moving her arms and legs, "Cathy, could you help out with the dogs?"

"Of course," Cathy reassured her.

"I taped a piece of paper to each dog crate, explaining the diagnosis, what they need in terms of medicine, and what they need in terms of food. There are only three dogs back there right now, including Frankie. Oh, Charlie's back there too."

"No worries," said Cathy, "we will take care of everything. Linda's a retired nurse, so she can take care of the dogs in the ICU and make sure everybody's okay."

Alfreda sighed, closing her eyes. "That's a relief. Thank you."

To keep her awake and talking, Cathy asked "How was Frankie during the storm?"

Alfreda smiled. "He was no problem at all. In fact, he

was so calm he helped the rest of us calm down too."

Cathy got up and walked around the ICU, looking for Frankie. She spotted him in a corner, inside a covered crate. She bent over the crate to say hi to him, and he immediately struggled to his feet, jumped up, and tried to kiss her face. She giggled and hugged him.

Peter helped Alfreda carefully stand up. She wrapped her arms around his waist, and they walked slowly to the front door of the RV. Grabbing a folding chair, Cathy placed it outside for Alfreda to sit on.

Peter walked out of earshot and called Ben, "The wind knocked Alfreda's RV around quite a bit and she hit her head. She is conscious and lucid but we need to get her to the hospital." Peter heard Ben take a sharp intake of breath.

"I'm calling for an ambulance right now and I'll be down." Ben disconnected.

Cathy went back inside to find a blanket to wrap around Alfreda to keep her warm and safeguard her from shock. She also started to heat some water for tea.

Soon, Ben drove up in his golf cart with Linda riding shotgun. Piling out of the cart, they went over to Alfreda. Ben gave her a gentle hug. Linda was concerned by how pale she was, and unobtrusively started checking her over.

Ben said, "The ambulance crew is on their way. They should be here in about ten minutes."

Cathy exited the RV with the cup of tea balanced precariously on the blanket. Linda carefully lifted the cup off the blanket, and Cathy gently draped the blanket around

Alfreda, while Linda handed her the tea. Alfreda wrapped her hands around the steaming hot cup of tea, giving Linda and Cathy an appreciative smile.

Turning to the others, she said, "I feel so chilled."

Peter said, "Well you were lying on a non-heated linoleum floor for God knows how long, no wonder you're feeling chilled. The tea will help."

Alfreda took a sip and made a face. "Wow, that's super sweet."

Cathy explained, "I purposely made it that sweet for an energy boost."

"It's also good for preventing shock," murmured Linda.

"That too," agreed Cathy.

Linda continued her gentle examination. She paused upon feeling Alfreda's right wrist. "I don't know. This may be sprained, I can't tell. I don't think it's broken."

Alfreda winced and growled. "I hope to hell it's just sprained. I want to spend as little time in the hospital as possible."

Ben agreed, "That's right because you're such a good patient and so cooperative." Alfreda turned and bared her teeth at him. He grinned back at her. At the same time, he felt a sense of relief. It told him that she was feeling her oats and slowly getting back to normal. He gently patted her shoulder. "We'll break you out of there in no time."

"I'm counting on you to do that," she said.

Peter and Cathy glanced at each other, and Peter quirked an eyebrow at Cathy, who stifled a laugh.

"I lost track of Charlie during the storm," Alfreda

looked up at Linda. "I think he is somewhere back in the ICU, but I'm not sure exactly where. Can you look for me to make sure he's okay?"

"Of course. I'll go and look now."

"Thank you." Alfreda relaxed a bit as she was able to let go of her worry for Charlie.

Ben asked Peter and Cathy, "Did you by any chance come across Sharon's husband, George?"

"No," Peter replied, "We came straight to Alfreda's RV."

"Would you mind if after the ambulance crew takes Alfreda to the hospital, walking around to see if you can track him down?"

"Of course."

"Good. Thank you for doing that, Peter." Ben then turned to Alfreda. "Did you see anybody outside here on the driveway right before the storm hit?"

"No. When it started really getting bad, I moved away from the windows and into the back where it was safer. I didn't see anybody."

The ambulance crew arrived, driving slowly down the driveway. After they exited the vehicle, they quickly rushed to Alfreda's side, and began checking her out.

The EMT team leader came over to Ben. "Hi, Ben. We're taking her to St. Luke's. Given that she is seventy-three, I think they will probably want to keep her at least overnight for observation."

Ben asked, "When you bring her into the emergency room, make sure you list me as her contact. I'll call St. Luke's in a bit and go from there, but I also want you to give them my contact information. I don't know how much of a problem I will have gaining access to her information, given I am not a family member."

The EMT agreed. "I'll try to smooth the way for you. But no guarantees." He turned to his team. "Let's get going."

As the ambulance backed slowly out of the driveway, Cathy turned to Linda and asked, "How is Betsy doing?"

"She is not doing too well this morning, so she is sleeping in. The stress of the storm last night exacerbated her Parkinson's and she is feeling pretty stiff. I think she wants to wait until most of the crowd is gone from the community room before she begins to try to move around."

Ben overheard them and said, "She's doing well but seems tired out. There are a number of people still up at the ranch house. They will keep an eye on her and make sure she doesn't need for anything. We do have some people here with Parkinson's. They are an invaluable support system for each other. I'm sure they will welcome her with open arms."

"That's good to know, Ben," said Cathy.

Peter turned to the women. "I'm going to go look for George."

Cathy started to pick up papers that had been scattered by the wind, "We'll stay here for a bit, take care of the dogs, do some cleaning up, and make sure everything's in tip-top shape for when Alfreda comes home."

Linda climbed into the RV, "I'm going to see if Charlie is in the back." She made her way into the ICU, calling out,

"Charlie." At first, she couldn't hear anything. She called again. This time she heard a slight movement, and then a whimper but she couldn't tell where it was coming from. "Cathy, can you come help me?"

Upon entering the room, Cathy saw stacks of crates that had been knocked over by the storm rocking the RV. In addition to the upset crates, there were boxes leaning haphazardly against the wall. She desperately hoped that Charlie was not underneath all that.

The two women began moving the boxes away from the wall. Linda was worried about shifting the wrong box, causing an avalanche that would bring all the boxes down on them. But bit by bit, taking their time, they were able to move them out of their way.

Cathy muttered, "This is like playing Jenga."

Linda said, "Only with bigger consequences."

Finally, they had removed enough boxes for Linda to see that there was a cavity, a cubbyhole, way back against the wall. Very carefully, she pulled the final boxes away from the wall. And there was Charlie. Curled up in a space that was a bit too small to be comfortable. There was only one crate left blocking his exit. Linda dragged it aside and again called his name. When he saw Linda, he leapt to his feet, tail wagging furiously. He launched himself at her. She caught him in midleap and hugged him to her. Unexpectedly her eyes filled with tears. As she held him, she told Cathy, "I don't know why I feel so strongly about this dog. I barely know him."

Cathy smiled. "Alfreda said it happens that way sometimes. It's just an instant connection. He chooses you; you choose him."

"Should I think about adopting him?" asked Linda.

Cathy laughed. "I think it's kind of a moot point. You've already adopted each other... on an emotional level at least."

Linda tried to make a joke out of it, but she just couldn't do it. She looked Charlie over quickly, but he seemed to be okay. He gazed up at her as she stroked his long silky ears. When she looked down into his soft brown eyes, she felt a rush of warmth.

Finally, Linda got to her feet. "I am going to check and see who needs medicine and who needs food."

Cathy asked, "Do you want help?"

"I think I'm fine with this. If I need help, I'll give you a call." Linda glanced at Charlie who was now lying full-out across her feet. "I think he just might be my number-one fan."

Meanwhile, Peter had jumped on the ATV and driven to the next couple of campsites down. He knocked on the door of the camper where the husband was supposed to be. It was in surprisingly decent shape, with little obvious damage from the storm. Peter knocked again. He could hear dogs barking inside.

He called out, "Is anybody in there?" Nobody answered. He started walking back toward the ATV, when an older woman in the RV next door opened the door.

"Are you looking for someone?" she asked.

Peter responded, "Hello, ma'am. I'm Officer Jones. We were just checking to make sure everyone was okay and didn't need any help. Also, we are looking for a man in his forties called George. He came down to check on his dogs in the RV next to yours right before the storm hit. Unfortunately, the storm came in bigger and faster than expected, and he didn't make it back to the ranch house last night. His wife is understandably worried."

"Well, you've come to the right place," the woman replied. "He stayed with my husband and me last night. He just left a short while ago to go to the ranch house."

"Thank you." Peter felt relieved that George was alive and well.

The woman introduced herself, "My name is Isadora Doyle but everyone calls me Izzy. It was a blessing having him here. We had been going to head up to the ranch house, but then the storm got so bad that we were afraid to be out in it. We are both in our eighties and were worried about what we would do if one of us got hurt during the storm. Having him here made us feel safe. Luckily, our camper didn't sustain any damage."

"I'm glad for your sakes that it worked out." Peter smiled and waved at her and the older gentleman who had appeared in a window during their conversation. He then climbed on his ATV and headed back up to the ranch house.

When he walked into the main entrance, he saw Ben talking to a man in his forties. Looking up, Ben's eyes met Peter's, and he quickly waved him over.

As he approached, Ben said, "I want to introduce you to George. He is the gentleman that we've been looking for, the missing husband."

Peter shook George's hand. "I was just talking with the older couple where you spent the night. They said they appreciated how much more secure and safe they felt having you there with them."

George commented, "They are really nice people. I also felt more comfortable knowing that I wasn't alone. I think we helped each other."

"Have you seen your wife yet?"

"Yes, I just saw her. I wish she wouldn't worry so much."

"It seems to me, in this case, she had reason to worry."

George shrugged his shoulders somewhat irritably. "Yeah, yeah. She's already put me through the ringer about last night and how much of a risk I took. I knew what I was doing."

"So, are you just being an asshole because you realize you made a stupid decision by going out in the storm? And, by the way, are incredibly lucky it didn't turn out worse. Or are you just basically an asshole?" Peter stared George down. Ben snorted with laughter.

George looked at Peter for a long moment and then slowly grinned. "I guess I am pretty much just basically an asshole. I do appreciate you looking for me. I realize how lucky I am to have a woman that cares for me so much that she worries about me even when I do something stupid. I'd better go find my wife, apologize again, and head for home."

"Good idea," said Peter. George set off to find his wife. Peter turned to Ben. "Do you know where Betsy is?"

"Last I saw her she was getting a cup of tea."

"I'm going to see if she needs a ride back to the RV." He walked over and spotted Betsy right away. She sat on a chair, with her walker by her side, looking pale but smiling and chatting with fellow campers as they came up to get tea or coffee.

"Hi," Betsy said, "you look familiar, but I'm sorry, I don't remember your name."

"You might remember me better if I was wearing my police officer uniform."

Her eyes lit up. "I've got it now. Your name, I think, is…Paul?" He shook his head. "George?" He shook his head again. "Ringo?" she asked with a glint of mischief in her eyes.

He grinned. "Nope. Peter. I'm here to see if you want a ride to your camper."

"That would be great. Thank you so much. Is everybody back there? I checked my phone for messages but, as usual, it's dead. I can never seem to keep it charged."

"Smartphones are amazing, but boy do they suck up the juice."

Betsy started to get up. Peter watched her closely before holding out a hand for her to steady herself. He helped her out of her chair and set up her walker. Together they walked down the ranch house steps.

"Would you rather ride on the ATV or in my police cruiser?" Peter asked.

"I have never ridden an ATV. I think it'd be fun to try. But I have my walker with me. I don't know how that will fit."

"We can strap that on the back; that's no problem at all."

Peter helped Betsy onto the back of the ATV and made sure she was secure and balanced. He climbed on and told her to put her arms around his waist. They started off very slowly.

As they picked up speed coming down the hill, Betsy leaned forward. "This is great fun. Thank you." She sighed, "I tend to be pretty cautious these days."

Peter heard the sadness in her voice.

Betsy and Peter arrived back at the RV as Cathy, who had just returned from Alfreda's, was straightening up. Fortunately, there was minor damage to the exterior. Inside, a couple of things had been knocked off shelves but that was all. She was pleased to see Betsy up and about and gave her a quick hug.

Linda came around the front of the RV, Charlie trotting happily by her side.

Betsy turned to Peter. "Thank you, Peter, for everything you've done for us. You have been a tremendous help."

Peter smiled. "You're very welcome. Now I have to be on my way. I need to get ready for the evening shift."

Cathy said, "I can't believe you are scheduled for tonight after working all day, helping all of us."

"Well, since I do the scheduling, I have no one else to blame," Peter said. "I don't know if I will see you again before you leave, so I want to say it has been great meeting all of you. Take care of yourselves." He went to Betsy and gave her a hug. Linda was next. Then it was Cathy's turn and suddenly she found herself wrapped in Peter's arms. She felt the welcome solidness of him and inhaled the masculine essence of him—an intoxicating mix of leather, soap, and clean mountain air. She felt his heart beating, steady and strong. Then he let go of her. For a long moment, he looked down at her. She raised her head, looking straight back at him. When her gaze met his, she felt a jolt of electricity. He took a breath, nodded, and stepped back. He waved at the other women and got on his ATV, disappearing up the driveway.

The moment Peter was out of sight, Cathy felt like howling. She didn't know why. She was not even sure what she was feeling, only that it was a strong emotion that almost knocked her off her feet. It had been literally years since she had felt such a powerful attraction to a man.

CHAPTER 8

Cathy was used to taking care of herself regardless of the circumstances. She realized that when Peter had hugged her, she had felt a remarkable sense of comfort and safety while in his arms. And now it was over. He was gone.

She excused herself and went into the camper. Staring at herself in the mirror over the bathroom sink, she took a breath. "Pull yourself together, Catherine. It didn't mean a thing. It was just a friendly hug. Settle down." She stuck her tongue out at herself and went back out to join Linda and Betsy.

"Linda was just telling me she'll join us for dinner, but she will be staying at Alfreda's," explained Betsy. "She'll take care of the dogs and make sure everything is okay."

"There are only a couple of dogs in the ICU," clarified Linda, "and they don't seem to have serious issues. Two are recovering from being spayed, and the other one had a skin infection that is pretty much cleared up at this point. Only one dog is still in recovery mode, and that of course is Frankie. He is still on antibiotics and has a slight fever."

"Yes," said Betsy. "Frankie. What about Frankie? What are we going to do with him?"

Cathy said hesitantly, "If it is okay with both of you, I would like to adopt him."

"What made you decide to do that?" Betsy asked.

Cathy explained, "The poor guy has had a rough life so far. Yet he's happy and joyful as all get out. Whenever I see him, he wags his tail like crazy and tries to kiss me. He makes me smile. I can use that in my life. I live alone. I really don't have any family to speak of. I think he'd be a wonderful companion."

Betsy said, "I rather hoped that you might look on us as family."

There was a long pause before Cathy finally said, "Betsy, you will never know how much what you just said means to me. Knowing I have people in my life who consider me family means the world to me." She continued, "Who knew that when I joined the book club six months ago, how my life would change because of it, because of both of you."

"Hear, hear," said Betsy, "I feel the same. There I was living a predictable, somewhat boring life. And now here I am. With new friends, new places, new things to see and do. I'm testing the limits of my Parkinson's, and I only feel safe doing that because I know I have your support and care."

Linda looked out over the river. "I'm not sure I want to go back to my old routine. You start getting older, and the days and years just fly by. I don't want to waste any more time. I want to make the most of each day that I have." Linda looked at Betsy and smiled. "I have an idea I've been mulling over. We could start a nonprofit for abandoned senior dogs."

Betsy looked at her thoughtfully. "That sounds like an interesting possibility."

The women sat and watched the sun sink into the horizon. Other than the occasional murmur or quiet laugh, they were silent. Cathy and Linda sipped wine while Betsy nursed a glass of sparkling water. They listened to the birds, insects, and peepers—some revving up for the night, others slowing down, preparing for sleep.

"It's hard to believe," said Cathy, "after the violence of last night and all that terrible weather, and here it is so peaceful and calm today."

They discussed possibilities for dinner but without any real enthusiasm. Finally, Linda said, "I wonder if we could order pizza from somewhere. Let's call Ben and find out."

"Brilliant," said Betsy. "I could really go for some pizza." Linda pulled her phone out of her jeans pocket, got Ben's number from Cathy, and called him. She asked about pizza, and there was a long pause as she listened to his response. She thanked him, clicked off, and started laughing.

"What?" the other women demanded to know.

"Our timing is perfect. It's pizza night at the ranch house. We can call and order ahead." For some reason, after everything they had been through, this slice of normal life struck them all as hysterically funny.

The next day Peter drove Alfreda home from the hospital. She received a hero's welcome for staying with her hospital patients during the storm. People waved and cheered as she was driven to her RV. Ben got out of the back seat and put an arm around her waist to help steady her as she emerged from the car. She did a mock bow to her gathered fans and then entered her camper.

Linda was waiting for her inside. "Alfreda, do you want anything to eat or drink?"

Alfreda sank gratefully onto the couch "You know, I'd love a cup of tea. And then I think I'll take a nap. I am never able to sleep in a hospital."

"Did you have a concussion?"

"They took a number of tests and found out I had a mild concussion and a strained, not sprained, wrist."

While Linda busied herself making the tea for Alfreda, Peter worked on repairing the front door, which was still difficult to open and close.

Linda put the hot tea in front of Alfreda. "What would you like in it?"

"Well," said Alfreda, "I am from Vermont originally. So, I put maple syrup into everything I possibly can put it into. There is some in the fridge."

"You know, Alfreda, I'd be glad to stay here overnight to take care of the dogs and make sure you have everything you need. I am uncomfortable with you being here by yourself after a concussion, even a mild one."

"I would really appreciate that, Linda. I would feel more

comfortable having you here too. Though I have to say, all I want to do right now is just go to sleep. I'm so tired." She thought for a moment. "In fact, it would be great if you could get the dogs' files back in the ICU. Look up their owners' numbers and give them a call. Let them know their dogs are doing well and are ready for pickup. Find out when they plan on stopping by to get them. That would be a tremendous help to me right now."

"I'd be glad to do that. Let me go and get the files now."

About an hour later, Linda walked around the corner of the RV with Charlie by her side. "Hi, guys," she called out. Betsy and Cathy had been straightening up. Now, they looked up when they heard Linda. "I wanted you to know I'll be staying with Alfreda for a day or so to make sure she's okay. Peter is with her right now."

Cathy commented, "It's kind of you to do that." Linda blushed.

"Really, Linda, it's a nice thing to do," Betsy said. "Even if she doesn't admit it, Alfreda must be feeling some trepidation about being alone after getting injured in the storm and then being in the hospital last night." Betsy paused and then added, "I know I always feel better when there's someone in the house with me. Even if they're not there specifically to take care of me, I feel better knowing that if I fall or I have some other medical issue, there is someone to help me or call for help." This revelation by Betsy surprised both Cathy and Linda because she rarely talked about being anxious or fearful.

The three of them sat down in their chairs, facing the

river, and talked about what to do for upcoming meals. Betsy and Cathy suggested making a potluck dinner and bringing it over to Alfreda's for all of them to enjoy together.

"I remember seeing some rotisserie chickens for sale at the ranch house," said Cathy. "I am going to call and see if they have any available. Then we can make either stir fry or a chef salad, something simple."

"Good idea," said Linda.

Cathy went inside to make the call. A moment later she popped her head out the door. "Yeah, they have a couple that they will hold for us. I'll look around and get some fresh lettuce and possibly some dessert if they have anything."

Betsy chimed in, "Ice cream sundaes are always good."

"That sounds great," Linda said. "I am going to head back to Alfreda's to let her know what the plan is." Linda stood up and stretched. She nudged Charlie, who was fast asleep as usual. He rolled onto his feet, gave a shake, and was ready to go.

Cathy laughed. "He is such a character." She looked at Charlie fondly.

"He is a wonderful companion too. See you guys in a bit." She and Charlie started walking toward Alfreda's RV.

"Betsy," asked Cathy, "do you want to come with me to the ranch house, or do you just want to stay here and hang out?"

"I think I will just stay here and rest," answered Betsy.

Cathy grabbed her purse and a tote bag and headed up

to the ranch house. When she walked through the front door of the ranch house, she noticed a feeling of tension in the air. Usually, the employees called out a welcome when someone entered the store and joked easily with one another. Today they seemed quieter, more intense. There was no good-natured bantering. She glanced around for Ben. She enjoyed his calm, confident, and reassuring manner. Cathy spotted him across the room talking to a man in his fifties. She smiled and waved at him. He nodded at her but did not return the wave or smile. She faltered for a moment, unsure of herself and then walked down the stairs to the camp store. The two employees behind the counter were absorbed in their conversation. Cathy walked to the counter. The workers immediately stopped talking and asked if they could help her. She gave her order for the two rotisserie chickens. While she was waiting, she browsed around, picking up different side dishes to add to the meal.

She thanked the cashier, took her purchases, and started to leave. But then she stopped and turned around, walking back to the counter. "Is there something wrong? I noticed all the workers seem a little tense. Is something going on?"

The cashier paused for a moment, then seemed to make up her mind and said, "There was a break-in and a robbery at a house a couple of miles from here during the storm, and the homeowner was beaten."

"Oh no," exclaimed Cathy. "Is the homeowner all right?"

"He's going to be okay. But things like that just don't happen around here, so it's got everybody on edge."

"What about your police chief?" asked Cathy, "Is he any good?" She noticed the employee looking over her shoulder. Suddenly, she got the feeling she knew who was going to be standing there before she even turned around.

"Checking up on me?" Peter asked.

Embarrassed, Cathy felt her face turning red. "I am really sorry," she apologized. "I know that was a rude thing to ask but I was curious."

Peter leaned over her and said to the cashier, "Go ahead, Annie, tell her what you think of me and be honest."

The cashier, a young woman in her twenties, giggled. "It's hard for me to be objective about Chief Peter. He taught me how to drive a stick shift when nobody else in my family could or would. It opened up a whole new world for me. I was able to take the family car and go to school at the local community college. He is known for doing stuff like that all the time."

Peter added, "I also catch bad guys on occasion. And we'll get this bad guy, too, sooner rather than later." He looked at Cathy's bags crammed with groceries. "Would you like a ride back to your RV?"

She replied, "That would be great. Thank you very much."

Peter took the bags from her and carried them out to his cruiser, putting them in the back seat. Cathy settled into the front seat. Peter started the SUV and drove slowly down the driveway.

"It is beautiful here. Did you grow up in this area?" Cathy asked.

"Yes, I was born and raised here. After my mother and father got divorced, when I was in my teens, my mother moved out to San Diego with my two younger sisters. My older brother and I stayed here with my father. I was able to visit my mother and sisters a couple of times a year."

"That must've been tough on you," said Cathy, "not being with your mom and your sisters full time."

"It was. The plus side," said Peter, smiling, "was that I had my dog Addie with me, and she was my best friend when I was a teenager. She was a beautiful golden retriever."

"You know, Peter, I also had a dog when I was a teenager, and she was my best friend too. Whenever I was upset, she picked up on it and comforted me. She would lean against me and put her head against mine. She was a great dog."

"What was her name?" asked Peter.

"Juno. My best friend from childhood gave her to me when she moved out of the area and couldn't take her. We always used to kid that Juno was a combination of a springer spaniel and a great big white dog." Cathy smiled, thinking about her. "When I was in college, I would call home—a long distance collect call, mind you—and tell my mother I wanted to talk to Juno. I'm sure she really appreciated that." They both laughed.

Peter said, "Did she put Juno on the phone?"

"Yes, yes, she did. As you can imagine it was a pretty

one-sided conversation." She mused, "Do they even have collect calls anymore?"

"Don't know. That was another time, another era. Here we are." He pulled up to the RV.

Cathy swung open her door and got out. "Thank you, Peter," she said as she got her bags out of the back seat. "I really enjoyed talking with you."

"I enjoyed talking with you, too. Do you need help with the bags?" Peter started to open his door.

"No problem," said Cathy, "I got this. Thank you." She climbed into the RV with a bemused smile on her face.

The women had a peaceful evening. They shared a meal with Alfreda and visited with Frankie and Charlie. They chatted long into the night about a wide range of subjects, including past relationships.

"Did you ever want to get married?" Betsy asked Linda.

Linda was sitting cross-legged on the floor, playing with Charlie's ears. "My dad divorced my mom when I was five, and he pretty much cut me out of his life. That kind of rejection from a parent is hard to work through. Luckily, I had a great therapist. But trust is still a hot button for me."

Cathy murmured, "I can understand why."

Linda rubbed her hands over her face. "You know we get all these images and happily-ever-after stories from books and movies, and we start to believe there is a great love of our lives out there for us. It's hard to accept when it doesn't happen. Movies like *Sleepless in Seattle* and *You've got Mail*…" Linda surprised herself by tearing up.

"You know Tom Hanks has a lot to answer for." She smiled abashedly at the three women and quickly brushed the tears away. "You think you have all the time in the world to find someone to love and share your life with…then one day you look in the mirror and realize that you are halfway through your life, doors are closing and you don't have a lot of options left. I have a very good life," she stated firmly. "I have nothing to be sad about."

Betsy put her hand gently on Linda's arm as Cathy gave her a hug.

Alfreda said, "Even if we do understand it on an intellectual level, it is still hard to accept when our hopes for a loving partner go unrealized."

Betsy chimed in, "As my British ancestors would say at a moment like this, how about a nice cup of tea?"

"Sounds great," said Linda with a sigh of relief. She rarely if ever opened up about herself and her feelings and felt uneasy allowing herself to be that vulnerable. But she felt surprisingly comforted by the women's caring responses.

Alfreda and Linda returned to Alfreda's RV. In the middle of the night, there was a heavy downpour. It woke up Linda, who was asleep on Alfreda's couch. She pulled the blanket up over her head and went back to sleep.

Early the next morning, Ben stopped by to talk with the three women. "There is a flash flood warning, due to heavy storms overnight in the mountains ringing the ranch. I don't think floodwaters would overflow your campsite, but I'm not willing to take that chance. I want you to temporarily move your RV to another site that is further away from the river but still very nice. Then when the water goes down, you can move back here if you want."

The women all looked at each other. Linda said, "Sure, no problem Ben. We'll move this morning."

After Ben left, they walked down to the river to take a look and were shocked at the difference. The broad shallow river that they had grown to love was now a different type of beast altogether pounding against the earth, pulling small trees and branches into the brutish current, scraping boulders against the riverbank. The sound and fury of the river was scary and the women backed away. "We are definitely moving the RV," said Cathy. Linda saw how close Charlie was to the riverbank. Feeling a rush of fear, she called his name. He looked up, wagged his tail, and turned to amble back to her. She smiled at him.

CHAPTER 9

Without warning, the edge of the riverbank where Charlie was standing gave way. He dropped into the water with a terrified yelp. Paddling frantically, he tried to keep his head above water. But he was not a natural swimmer and was pulled under by the water, again and again. The river picked him up, whirling him away downstream. He quickly disappeared.

Linda screamed a wild, ragged sound full of anguish. She raced for the edge of the river. Cathy raced after her. Once she reached Linda, she tried to grab her arm.

Linda yelled, "Let me go!"

Cathy yelled back, "No! You'll drown!"

Betsy appeared at their side and grabbed Linda's other arm, pleading with her. "It's too late!"

With all her strength, Linda pulled her arms free from both of them, raced to the water's edge, and jumped.

"No!" screamed Cathy and Betsy.

"Jesus Christ!" Cathy grabbed Betsy, "I am going to run along the river and see if I can spot them. Here's my phone. Call Ben. His number's in there, so is Alfreda's and Peter's. Call them. Call 911. Get help." With that Cathy spun on her heel and raced off toward the river.

The last few moments of extreme stress had triggered Betsy's Parkinson's. Her hands began shaking so violently that she dropped her phone twice before she could hold it securely enough to bring up Siri. She instructed Siri to call Ben. Ben wasn't answering, so she left a message. She then called Alfreda and, again, had to leave a message. Finally, when she called Peter, he picked up. He started to greet her pleasantly. She cut him off, relayed what had just happened and that they desperately needed help. He told her he was at the ranch house and would be right down.

While Betsy was waiting for Peter, she noticed something shiny and metallic in the bunch of weeds right by the river. She went over and pulled the weeds aside. It was an old aluminum rowboat. Lots of dents but no holes and, better yet, two oars. She began pulling it out of the weeds, pushing it toward the river. "You can do this," she told herself, even as she shook with fear. She was about to push off, when powerful arms grabbed her around the waist and lifted her away from the boat.

"What the hell do you think you're doing?" Peter yelled.

"I'm going to save my friends!"

"The best thing you can do for them right now is to stay put. Ben will be here in a few minutes. Tell him I am going after Linda and Charlie in a rowboat."

Peter pushed the boat out into the river. The moment he hit the main current, the river lifted the rowboat and virtually hurled it downstream. He held on tight during the wild ride, fending off tree branches and other debris with the oars.

Meanwhile downstream, Linda was clinging desperately to a boulder jutting out of the water. She felt a sharp pain in her side and suspected she had a broken rib. The flood waters kept slamming into her, and she realized that she was losing her grip on the rock. Desperately she tried shifting her handholds but felt herself slipping down the face of the boulder.

She had managed to catch up with Charlie for a brief moment, holding on to him by grabbing his harness. But then a log slammed into both of them, causing her to lose her grip, and he was swept away again. She realized he probably did not have much time left. He was so exhausted when she saw him that he was barely able to paddle. She pressed her face into the side of the rock and wept. Feeling her hands slip again, she scrambled to hold on to the rock, knowing she, too, would not last for much longer.

Further down river, Charlie was fading fast. He had fetched up against a big pile of debris that had accumulated by a bridge spanning the river. He lay panting heavily, battered by the river's current, unable to move and entangled in tree branches and debris. After a few moments, with all his strength, he tried one last time to pull himself up and out of the water, further up onto the debris pile. But it was no good, he was too weak. Charlie let out a quiet whimper. Then he closed his eyes and felt himself drift away.

Cathy ran along the path, next to the river. She kept glancing over to see if she could spot anybody in the water. She tripped over a root, twisting her left wrist as she put her hands down to break her fall. In spite of the pain, she was quickly up and moving again, cradling her wrist as she ran. The path opened up ahead of her, and she could see that it led across a bridge. She raced to the middle of the bridge hoping to see Linda.

Linda's hands slipped once more and she began to slide into the water. She hadn't prayed in years, but she prayed now as hard as she could—for her friends, for herself, for Charlie. She tried to lunge out of the river to get a higher handhold on the boulder. But her hands were too cold to get a good grasp. She fell back into the river and became fully submerged. She fought her way back up, toward what she hoped was the surface. Tree branches caught at her clothes. She felt like she was losing her breath, and she began to panic.

Peter rocketed along in the current. A couple of times the rowboat was hit broadside by debris, almost knocking him into the water. But he found a way of bracing himself low in the boat, keeping his balance so he could steer. Suddenly, off the port bow, he spotted an unusual color in the water. It was a bright purple, just like a sweater he had seen on Linda. He started calling her name.

Exhausted, Linda gave a final push and she surfaced. She heard a voice say her name and she turned her head. A rowboat shot by her with inches to spare. Hearing her name again, she looked up and saw Peter's face looking down at her. He said something, but her hearing was muffled.

"Peter!" Desperately she thrust her hand at him and he grabbed it. He wrapped his fingers around her wrist and with all his strength pulled her back against the current and over to the boat.

She tried to latch on to the gunwale with her other hand, but she was too weak and could not hold on.

"I've got you" said Peter, leaning precariously over the edge of the boat. "I'm not letting you go." Peter gripped her other hand and pulled her halfway into the boat. Then he reached down and grabbed the waistband of her jeans and yanked her all the way in.

Linda lay in the bottom of the boat—sobbing, shivering, cold, and wet.

Peter said, "Stay low so you don't get hurt." She nodded and curled into a ball. He added, "There is a bridge around this bend. I'm hoping we can spot Cathy and maybe Charlie once we get down here a bit further."

"Cathy?"

"She has been running along the river, trying to spot either you or Charlie. There is the bridge. Jesus, look at all that debris. We've got to move out of this current, or we'll get slammed into it and sink for sure." Peter glanced at the bridge again and said disbelievingly, "I think I see somebody up there."

Linda knelt in the bottom of the boat beside him and peered over the edge. "I see somebody too."

"My God, that's Cathy!" Peter pulled back on the oars

with all his strength to bring the boat in sideways to the debris pile. "She's pointing over there."

Linda looked and cried out, "Charlie!"

Peter rowed hard to get the boat closer to where the dog lay. Then he looked up and saw that Cathy was gesturing frantically at them. He looked where she was indicating and saw a group of people standing next to a pullout ramp. They were yelling and waving.

He steered the rowboat to where Charlie lay motionless. Peter and Linda called Charlie's name. There was no movement.

"Linda..." Peter began to say.

She shouted hoarsely, "He is not dead!"

Peter nodded. "Okay, let's get him into the boat then." He moved the boat closer to Charlie, and he and Linda grabbed on to the dog and tried to move him into the boat. But for some reason, they couldn't move him. He was caught on something—they couldn't see exactly what.

Cathy, standing on the bridge, saw what was coming and became terrified. Approaching the curve and moving fast in the raging river current was a fishing cabin that had been pushed off its moorings by the flood. It was coming straight toward the bridge and straight toward Peter and Linda in the rowboat.

Cathy realized that Peter and Linda could not see the cabin that was just now approaching the curve, and they could not hear her over the roaring water. She made a fast decision and climbed over the edge of the bridge, starting down the debris pile. Cathy went down as fast as she could, slipping and sliding the whole way. Her hands were quickly bloodied by cuts and gashes from the debris.

Linda had just started to say something to Peter when he saw her expression change. He whipped around, and there was Cathy stumbling over the debris toward them. She was yelling to them, "Go! You've got to go now! There's a cabin off its moorings coming down the river. It's heading here. Right now."

Linda wailed, "We have to get Charlie in the boat."

Cathy slid the last few yards to Charlie's side. Peter said to her, "He's stuck on something."

Cathy ran her hands over his back. "It's his harness, it's caught on a branch behind him." Peter quickly pulled out his utility knife and sliced the harness in half. He immediately lifted Charlie into the boat. Linda took the dog and cradled him in her arms. She put her face close to his face and murmured in his ears. His eyes remained closed.

Shaking with fear, Cathy half climbed, half fell into the boat as the still intact cabin was slamming around the bend in the river. All three of them could now see it. From Peter's perspective on his knees in the rowboat, it looked like the Empire State Building was coming right toward them.

The people on the riverbank were yelling at them, urging them to move. Several of them were now standing in the water, waiting to grab onto the rowboat to pull it out of danger. Cathy could see Ben, Alfreda, and Betsy in the small crowd. The cabin was now past the bend in the river and heading straight toward the bridge. Peter was pulling on the oars as powerfully as he could. It wasn't enough. The rowboat was not breaking free of the current.

Peter had his eye on the cabin moving toward them. He said to the two women, "I want you to get as low as you can in the boat."

Cathy shook her head. "If I'm going down, I'm going down fighting." She knelt by the side of the boat and plunged her arms into the water and used all her strength to paddle. Linda knelt by her side of the boat and did the same. The sharp pain in her side made her gasp but she kept paddling.

The cabin was almost on top of them, there was virtually no time left. Peter gritted his teeth and pulled ferociously at the oars. He started saying the only prayer he could think of, the Lord's prayer, under his breath.

Suddenly the rowboat began to move inch by inch away from the debris pile. Peter leaned heavily back in the boat, again and again, using his weight to power the oars through the current. Slowly, agonizingly, the boat pulled free.

One foot...two feet...three feet... They were getting closer to the people standing in the water at the access ramp.

"Link your arms!" Ben yelled to the crowd standing beside him. Quickly the group linked their arms and formed a human chain.

Peter strained against the oars as the women poured all their strength into paddling. The crowd stretched out to them, desperately reaching for the boat.

Suddenly the boat broke free of the current and shot toward the access ramp. The human chain grabbed the gunwale and quickly pulled it up onto the sand. The crowd didn't waste time helping the boat's passengers to evacuate one by one. Instead, they grabbed the sides of the boat and used all their strength to pull it higher up onto the bridge path. When they got to the top of the path and safety, they all turned to look. At that very moment, the cabin slammed into the bridge. There was a massive crunch and the ground shook. At first, it looked like the bridge would hold. Then in slow motion, the bridge tilted and toppled into the river. The bridge, the cabin, and debris were swept away by a monstrous wave. The river roared past, twisting, and turning, with whitecapped waves cutting across the still powerful current.

Linda was carefully holding Charlie. Alfreda came running up to her with a young volunteer in tow. She did a quick check of Charlie's gums and said urgently, "He is in shock. I need to get him to the infirmary now." Linda handed him over to her. Wrapping Charlie in her jacket, Alfreda passed him to the volunteer. They took off at a run.

Another volunteer yelled to Alfreda, "I'll take you! It's the first golf cart in line there. The blue-and-white one." Alfreda slid into the passenger seat, while the volunteer holding Charlie climbed into the back. The driver sent the cart flying up the pathway.

Linda stood there looking lost. Betsy and Cathy came over and put their arms around her, trying to comfort her. Peter came up behind them and put his arms around all of them. They stood there silently for a long, long moment, drawing warmth and comfort from each other.

"I don't know how to thank you," Linda said, starting to weep. "I could have died. You all could have died. I am so sorry to have put you at risk like that. When I saw Charlie go in, I just lost it."

Peter murmured, "It's all right. We survived. We made it through." Linda leaned against him and cried harder.

Ben came over to them with blankets. As he and Betsy helped wrap them around Cathy, Peter and Linda, Ben said, "The paramedics are here. They want to take a look at you."

Peter said, "Linda needs to go to the hospital; she has serious pain in her right side and may have a broken rib."

Cathy hesitated. "I fell and tried to catch myself, but I landed full on my right wrist. I don't know if it's broken…"

Tony, the EMT, came over and stared down at her still bloodied hands. "You have some deep lacerations there."

Cathy said, "It's really beginning to hurt."

Then the EMT turned to Peter. "You have a very nasty cut on your forehead. We need to take care of that."

Peter looked startled. "I do?" He put his hand up to his head, and when he took it away, it was covered with blood. He took a step back as he turned a ghastly white and then started to collapse.

Tony shouted, "Dave!" while reaching forward to catch Peter. Cathy and Ben leaped to help, just as another EMT appeared by their side. The four of them got Peter onto a gurney and into the ambulance. Ben and Cathy stepped back as Tony and Dave secured Peter for the ride to the hospital and hooked him up to monitors to keep an eye on his vitals. They placed an oxygen mask on him and did the same for Linda. Dave helped Cathy up into the ambulance and had her sit on the jump seat where the EMTs usually rode. She was also draped with monitor leads.

Tony climbed into the driver's seat. "All set?"

Dave responded as he handed Cathy an ice pack for her wrist. "We're all set back here. Everybody is stable."

Ben leaned into the back of the ambulance. "Hey, guys, I'm going to follow you in my car, so I'll see you soon at the hospital."

Ben carefully closed the door to the ambulance. As the ambulance began its slow, torturous journey out to the main road, Linda and Peter simultaneously heaved huge sighs of relief. Within minutes they were both sound asleep. Cathy relaxed, closing her eyes.

An hour later, Ben and Betsy joined Cathy in Linda's hospital room. The moment Linda saw them, she immediately asked, "How is Charlie?" Ben walked over to her bed and reached for her hand. Linda shot him a frightened glance.

She stammered "Oh no don't tell me…"

CHAPTER 10

Ben shook his head. "No, it's not that. Charlie is still with us, but he's struggling. Alfreda thinks he may be able to pull out of this with a lot of care. He swallowed quite a bit of water and was chilled to the bone. But he doesn't seem to have any broken bones or anything like that. It's hypothermia and shock that are causing him problems."

Linda nodded and put her head back on the pillow. She closed her eyes, and a couple of tears slowly streaked down her cheeks.

At that moment, the ER doctor entered the room. She glanced over at Linda, saw that she was crying, and shot a sharp glance at Ben.

"What's going on?" she asked.

"No secrets here, Doctor," said Ben. "We were just talking about Linda's dog and how he is doing."

"I'm Dr Horton, and I don't want anyone upsetting my patients. Got that?"

Ben started to explain, "Look, I'm sorry but she asked…"

The doctor interrupted him "I don't care what your explanation is, stop upsetting my patients."

"Got it," said Ben with an apologetic shrug.

"OK, then. Cathy, here's a prescription for antibiotics, and one for painkillers. I gave you a tetanus shot and some intravenous antibiotics to get things started to take care of any possible infection from the cuts you sustained. A couple of the lacerations did require a few stitches, but not too many. You're in good shape other than that. I do have a follow-up care plan for you but you can go home tonight."

Dr. Horton turned to Linda. "You have more serious injuries. You have a head injury that is worrisome. That's why we are going to keep you for at least two nights."

Linda responded, "I really don't think I need to be admitted to the hospital."

"I'm sorry there's no negotiation on this." The doctor told her. "You have a couple of bruised ribs but nothing broken. It will be a little difficult for you to breathe for the next couple of days. And since the pain will probably inhibit your breathing, I want you to practice breathing deeply. Even if it hurts. I'm going to show you some exercises to do to keep your lungs clear. We don't want any complications from asthma or bronchitis."

The doctor said "Now for my next patient…"

At that moment two police officers peeked in the door. "Looking for the Chief," one said. "They told us he was in here."

"Wrong room, he's next door." The doctor promised Linda, "I'll be back in a bit to check up on you."

Following the police officers into Peter's room, the doctor made her way to his bedside.

Pale and exhausted, Peter asked her, "I have never fainted before. Do you know what was going on? Why did that happen?"

The doctor explained, "I heard what you did. How you saved lives. It's pretty amazing. In terms of your fainting, I think it's probably from a rare occurrence that brought about a confluence of events. Exposure, exhaustion, hypothermia, stress, they worked together to dramatically lower your blood pressure. Luckily, there were people there who were able to get to you fast enough so that you didn't crash to the ground."

"I understand. I just don't want to have it happen again."

"We'll keep an eye on you for at least two nights and monitor your heart rate, blood pressure, and oxygen levels. We will make sure you are in good shape before we let you go." She smiled at him, patting his arm before leaving the room.

Ben pushed open Peter's door and leaned in, "I think we are going to head back to the ranch. Is there anything you need before we leave?"

Linda called from the other room, "Ice cream and magazines. In that order."

Peter cracked up and added, "What she said. That sounds excellent."

"OK, then we're on a mission," said Ben. "We'll hunt down ice cream and magazines for you, and then I'll be back to pick you up when you are okayed to leave."

A short while later, having left Peter and Linda happily eating their ice cream, and browsing through magazines, Ben, Cathy, and Betsy climbed into Ben's Range Rover. They headed back to the ranch. Cathy asked Ben to drop them off at Alfreda's RV. Both Cathy and Betsy were exhausted but wanted to see how Charlie was doing. However, Betsy was really having trouble keeping her balance, so Cathy suggested she head back to their camper and rest while she checked on Charlie. A pale and shaky Betsy readily agreed. She took Cathy's arm, and they walked slowly, arm in arm, to their RV. With a sigh of relief, Betsy sank down onto the couch cushions and closed her eyes. Cathy made her a cup of lemon-ginger tea with a dollop of honey and then headed over to Alfreda's.

Once she arrived, she noticed there were a couple of lights on. She knocked on the door. Alfreda called out, "Just a moment!" She opened the door and when she saw who it was, she smiled a big smile of welcome. "I am so glad you stopped by. I can't wait for you to see how the old man is doing."

Cathy smiled back at her. "It sounds like the old man is doing well."

"Very well, indeed," said Alfreda. "Thank goodness. I'd hate to be the one to have to tell Linda that he did not make it. Come with me."

They walked back, to the ICU and Cathy saw Charlie curled up and sleeping in a crate that was being fed with fresh oxygen. He had an IV going into one of his legs.

She told Alfreda, "I'm amazed at how good he looks given everything he's been through."

"Yes, I'm very pleased. I really didn't think he was going to make it. But I have to say, once I got him back here and pumped some meds into him, his blood pressure and heart rate stabilized. I felt much more hopeful. Frankly, I think he has a strong will to live because of Linda."

Cathy looked skeptical. "Do you really think Charlie's connection with Linda made that much of a difference to help bring him back from the edge?"

Alfreda was surprised by Cathy's question. "I've seen countless dogs beat seemingly impossible odds when they heard their owner's voice or felt their touch. Love is powerful medicine."

Cathy looked down at the still sleeping Charlie. "Maybe there is something to that," she murmured.

Alfreda added, "If you have ever been around service dogs and their human partners, especially medical alert service dogs, you'll see a relationship built almost totally on nonverbal communication and deep abiding trust. It is truly remarkable."

Cathy looked around for Frankie.

Alfreda saw her searching for the little dog and said, "He's in my bedroom with the door closed. We were watching a movie together."

Cathy laughed. "Shall I take him off your hands?"

"Why don't you leave him here while you get things squared away on your end. I don't mind. He's good company. How are you doing, by the way?"

"Actually, I'm not doing too badly. I'm exhausted of course and achy and my hands hurt, but other than that, I'm doing pretty well."

"I am very glad to hear that."

Cathy thanked her and walked down the drive to the RV.

Betsy had already turned in. Cathy checked on her and was pleased to see her sleeping peacefully. As she started to transform the kitchen table into her bed, exhaustion overwhelmed Cathy. She finished putting the bed together and then just sank down onto it. The emotion of the day hit her when she was least expecting it, and she burst into tears. The realization of how close they had come to dying swept over her like a tidal wave. She buried her face in her pillow, so she would not wake Betsy and just sobbed.

CHAPTER 11

Nestled deep in her bedsheets, Cathy slowly became aware of an irritating noise. It took her a moment to recognize what it was. Someone was knocking loudly on the RV door. And they were not going away. She reluctantly opened her eyes, still puffy from last night's crying binge and realized how very bright it was. It had to be way past dawn. She heard grumbling and mild cursing in Betsy's room.

She called, "Good morning, Betsy."

"Good morning," Betsy called back.

"There is someone at the door. I'll get it."

"Thanks," Betsy responded, "I was so tired last night that I didn't set my alarm, so I missed my first dose this morning. I am pretty stiff, but I should be better in about half an hour."

"No worries, Betsy, don't bother getting up. Just lie there and relax. Is there anything you want right now? Water? A cup of tea?"

"A cup of tea would be fantastic right now. Irish

Breakfast if we still have it."

"What do you want in it?"

"Some half-and-half and a teaspoon of honey."

Cathy said "Coming right up. Let me just see who's at the door first."

Ben was standing there with a tray of homemade pastries and fresh squeezed OJ. "I thought you could use a special treat this morning," he said as Cathy let him in.

Betsy emerged from her bedroom, clad in pj's and robe. "That looks awesome. Ben, will you join us for breakfast?"

"Thank you, I'd like that."

"Good," said Cathy. "How about a cup of tea?"

"Excellent," he replied.

Betsy set about making tea for all of them, getting out her teapot and pouring hot water over loose tea leaves. She put out a small pitcher of warmed half-and-half and a small pot of local honey from the camp store.

Ben asked, "What kind of teapot is that, Betsy?"

She smiled and held it up for him to see. "It's called a Brown Betty. A friend of mine brought it back from London for me. It has been handmade in a town called Stoke-on-Trent since the 1600s. The shape is supposed to be perfect for making tea."

"I had no idea there was so much history behind that teapot," exclaimed Cathy.

"Kind of amazing, isn't it?" Betsy poured another cup of tea for Ben.

"Have you heard anything from the hospital?" Cathy asked.

"Peter and Linda are both doing well. They're going to keep them for another night for observation. I'll pick them up tomorrow and bring them back here."

"Good news," said Cathy.

Betsy chimed in, "Definitely."

"I did want to ask you," said Ben, "if you would prefer to move to another campsite. After everything that happened here yesterday, I want to make sure you're comfortable. I do have another site available. It's not on the riverbank, but it does have a pleasant view."

Betsy and Cathy looked at each other. "We are only going to be here a few more days," said Cathy.

"I think we are fine," Betsy agreed.

"But thank you for thinking of us and making that offer." Cathy said.

After Ben left, both Betsy and Cathy decided to take it easy and just hang out for the day—sitting in the sun, reading, doing crossword puzzles, playing Scrabble, and taking naps. At the end of the day, they shared a quiet spaghetti dinner with Alfreda.

"I really needed a peaceful day, especially after yesterday," Betsy said.

"Me too," said Cathy.

Alfreda yawned and stretched, "Time for me to head home. Thank you for dinner."

The next morning Cathy's cell phone rang. It was Ben. She held it up so Betsy could hear him too.

"We're up here at the ranch house!" he yelled into the phone, trying to be heard over a considerable amount of background noise. "Come and join us. Peter and Linda are here." Cathy looked at Betsy with a question in her eyes. Betsy smiled and mouthed the word 'yes.'

Cathy said into the phone, "We'll be up as soon as we can." They quickly finished getting ready and walked up to the ranch house.

As they got closer, they could see there were grills and smokers going gangbusters outside the ranch house. A group of male campers had commandeered the grills and were busy flipping burgers and hot dogs. Even though it was still morning, a number of the backyard chefs were tossing down beers. One of them offered a beer to Cathy. She declined.

She whispered to Betsy, "I haven't even had my morning tea yet." Betsy laughed.

Suddenly Cathy looked up, and there was Peter standing on the top step of the ranch house. He smiled down at her. Even with a large bandage covering part of his forehead, Cathy thought she had never seen a more welcome sight. She smiled and waved to him, and when he waved back, she felt her heart begin to be beat faster. He came down the steps and hugged first her and then Betsy.

"It's good to see you looking good," stammered Cathy, feeling her face flush. "I meant to say that you look like you're doing well. You look good." She heard Betsy next to her laughing. She elbowed her in the ribs. "How are you feeling?" she asked Peter.

"Very grateful just to be alive. Come and join the party."

They walked up the steps together. The ranch house

was overflowing with music, people, and laughter. Ben spotted them and walked over.

"What is this all about?" asked Cathy.

"Well," answered Ben, "This crew is always up for a party. Early this morning they got together and decided to have a celebration-of-life party."

Sharon and George appeared behind Ben. Sharon said, "Hi guys, this is my husband, George, who was missing in action during the intense storm. It turns out he stayed with our next door neighbors in their RV during the worst of it. George, these are the women I told you about who were so supportive."

George smiled and shook their hands. "Thanks for helping my wife."

"It's good to meet you," said Cathy.

"Can I get you something to eat or drink?" asked George.

"Not for me," said Cathy.

Betsy piped up, "I'll take a bagel with a schmear."

George looked confused. "Not sure what that is."

Betsy explained, "It's a bagel spread with cream cheese."

"Got it," he said and went off on a mission to find a bagel.

Ben looked after him with amusement. "He's going to be gone for a while. I'm quite sure we don't have any bagels. In fact, I'm pretty sure there aren't any bagels within twenty miles of here."

Betsy said, "Thank God I didn't ask him for lox."

"What's lox?" asked Sharon.

Betsy grinned and said, "Come with me while I find some tea, and I'll explain the wonders of a bagel with lox and a schmear."

Alfreda walked up as Ben turned to Cathy. "I presume you're looking for Linda?"

"Yes," answered Cathy.

"She is a little slow moving today," said Peter. "She got pretty banged up on the rocks yesterday, and she's definitely feeling it. Last I saw her, she was sitting by one of the windows. Let's find her." He reached his hand out to Cathy. Startled, she looked up at him and hesitated. He quickly dropped his hand. "I think I saw her over here." He started walking through the crowd. Cathy paused and then followed.

Alfreda and Ben watched Peter and Cathy walk away. Alfreda looked at Ben. "What was all that about?"

"I wish I knew," answered Ben. "That's the first woman I've seen Peter interested in a long time. Anyway, how are you feeling this morning?"

"Exhausted," Alfreda replied.

"Me too," he said.

"Did you think about what we discussed?" Alfreda asked.

"Yes," said Ben. "I think it is a good idea. I've already emailed my son, Luke, to see if he'll come and stay with me for a spell. Thanks for the suggestion." Alfreda put her arm around his waist and gave him a gentle hug. He put his arm around her shoulders and pulled her close.

Having secured a cup of tea, Betsy turned and saw Alfreda and Ben.

She looked at Sharon with a raised eyebrow. "Well, that's interesting."

Sharon stammered, "I-I had no idea."

Linda was sitting at a table by herself as Peter and Cathy approached. The table had a gorgeous view of the campground and river. A volunteer carried Linda's tray of food and set it down carefully in front of her. She thanked him and turned to Cathy who caught sight of her face covered with purplish bruises and gasped. Betsy joined them at the table and was also shocked to see Linda's bruises.

She smiled stiffly. "Pretty bad, huh?"

Betsy and Cathy exchanged quick glances and decided to be honest in their responses. "It looks like it really hurts," Cathy said sympathetically.

Linda shrugged awkwardly. "It does, but they gave me some pretty strong pain pills." She yawned and stretched. "I think I'm going to head back to the RV and just take it easy for the rest of the day."

Betsy said, "Good idea."

Peter's phone rang. He excused himself and walked outside.

Betsy glanced at Cathy. "What's up? You seem kind of out of it."

Cathy hesitated, then decided not to say anything about her recent encounter with Peter. "I'm too old for this nonsense," she muttered.

Betsy focused on her with razor-sharp intensity. "Are you talking about Peter?" Embarrassed, Cathy nodded.

Linda leaned forward. "What do you want to happen?"

Cathy took a sip of tea and picked at the bandages on her hands. "I don't know. I'm very confused." She hesitated and then took the plunge. "I haven't felt this way about someone in a long time. But we're only here for another day or two. What happens after that? I don't want to put myself out there just to get hurt."

"What if you don't get hurt?" asked Linda. "What happens if this is the beginning of a whole new chapter in your life? Maybe it's like riding a bike."

"Bad analogy," said Cathy. "The problem is, if you're a little kid and learning to ride a bike and you fall, it hurts but it's not a big deal. But if you're an adult and you fall, it can be a very big deal. A broken hip, an ACL injury."

"But what if—" Betsy started to say.

Cathy interrupted her. "I have a comfortable life back in Pennsylvania. I have good friends, a nice home, my life is predictable. I have an even keel life. I know that might sound boring. But do I really want to take a chance on the unpredictable, my emotions zooming up and down? It was exhausting when I was in my twenties and thirties, and I was more resilient then."

Linda stared down into her tea. "I get it. I understand what you're saying."

Betsy nodded. "Whatever you decide, we're behind you one hundred percent."

Cathy said, "Thank you."

They sat quietly, watching all the action going on in the ranch house, each caught up in their own thoughts. Alfreda walked over to the table. The women were delighted to see her and greeted her warmly. They asked her to join them as they had something to talk to her about.

"That sounds serious," she said looking at the three of them.

Betsy responded, "First of all, we want to thank you for everything you've done for us, for Frankie and Charlie. It is only because of your efforts that they are both still with us and doing well."

Cathy chimed in, "We want you to know we are all agreed on this." She took a deep breath and continued. "You once said a dog adopts you as much as you adopt him or her. We see that connection between you and Frankie."

Linda continued, "So, we've, all of us, decided we want you to have Frankie."

Alfreda teared up. "Are you sure?" she asked.

Linda said, "Absolutely. I think the clincher was when you told me you were watching a movie together. That's when I knew. That's when we all knew."

Alfreda smiled through her tears. "You have no idea how much I've been dreading saying goodbye to him. I absolutely adore that little dog. This is fantastic. Thank you so much." She hugged each of the women.

CHAPTER 12

On a nearby hill, overlooking the ranch house, two men in their twenties were watching the celebration through binoculars.

"What do you think?" asked Smithy, the shorter and cleaner of the two.

His partner—a tall, thin heavily tattooed man named Sullivan—shook his head. "Too much going on right now. Let's come back later, when it's dark, and take a look around. We'll pick out the weakest of the bunch."

Smithy bit his lip as he listened to Sullivan. "I don't like it. I don't like anything about this."

Sullivan sighed. "Look, this is easy pickings. Most of these people are too old to fight back. Plus, they've got tons of money. I saw this old woman at the truck stop yesterday getting gas. She pulled out this huge wad of cash. I was going to just grab it and run, but they have cameras there now, so I followed her and she pulled into this RV park here." He lit a cigarette with tobacco-stained fingers and inhaled deeply. "You know, if you don't need the money, I can always get someone else."

Smithy hesitated. "Nah, I'm good."

Sullivan said, "We just need to keep a low profile so no one can ID us."

Smithy glanced at him and thought to himself, 'Yeah, right,' as he eyed Sullivan's large, garishly designed confederate flag tattoo on his left arm and confederate flag T-shirt.

The two men packed up their gear and hiked out to where they had left Smithy's pickup hidden under camouflage nets and loose branches.

Back at the ranch house, the party was beginning to wind down. Cathy, Betsy, and Linda started making their way back to their RV, chatting with other campers on the way.

"I'm exhausted," said Betsy. "I'm going to lie down for a while."

Linda glanced over at her with concern. "Are you all right?"

"Yes, just wiped out."

Linda sighed. "Me too."

Cathy nodded. "Definitely time for a nap."

They arrived at the RV and quickly transitioned the dining area into a bedroom.

"Anybody want to set an alarm?" asked Linda.

Cathy said, "I think we should just sleep until we wake up. After the past few days, we need to take it easy."

"Agreed," said Betsy. The three of them quickly dropped into a deep sleep once they hit their pillows.

About an hour later, Linda started tossing and turning and began gradually waking up. Quietly she got dressed, left a brief note, and headed to Alfreda's. She knocked on the door. Alfreda opened it with a welcoming smile. "Here to see Charlie?"

"Yes. How is he doing?"

"Very well, indeed. I am really pleased with his progress. Let me call him. Charlie!" They heard a quiet bark from the back of the RV, followed by a muted crash.

Alfreda grinned. "He is not the most graceful dog, that's for sure."

Linda started to respond when Charlie appeared in the doorway. If ever a dog looked ecstatically happy to see someone, it was Charlie, followed by Frankie. Linda went down on her knees. He bounced over to her and was immediately wrapped up in her arms. Tears ran down her face as she hugged him close. He licked her face until she started giggling. Frankie was prancing about, trying to get in to say 'hi' to Linda. But Charlie effectively blocked him.

Alfreda laughed and grabbed Frankie, "He is such a character. Charlie is ready to go with you now. I just have some antibiotics he needs to take a little bit longer. But other than that, he's good to go."

"Amazing," said Linda.

Alfreda agreed. "I thought we were going to lose him there for a bit. But he has a great amount of willpower, and that pulled him through. Plus, he knows he has you. And that was probably better medicine for him than anything I could give him."

Linda said, "Speaking of that, I want to take care of his medical bill."

Alfreda tried to brush that off, saying, "There is no need. Thank goodness everyone ended up okay. It all worked out."

Linda was adamant, "You saved his life. The least I can do is compensate you for the cost of the medicines you used."

"All right," Alfreda agreed.

After everything Charlie had been through, Linda decided to take him on a relaxing stroll before heading back to the RV. As they walked, a number of fellow campers greeted him warmly. He was clearly well-known throughout the park. Linda felt like she was in the company of a celebrity.

Betsy woke up shortly after Linda left. She got up from her bed, staggering a bit, went to the bathroom, and splashed cold water on her face. She read Linda's note and woke up Cathy.

"She's gone to check on Charlie," Betsy told her.

Half awake, Cathy asked, "Is he coming home?"

"I don't know. Maybe." Betsy was checking her phone. "Wait a minute. I just got a text from Linda. Yes, Alfreda released him from the hospital. He's coming home! We have to celebrate."

"How about a welcome home banner in the shape of a dog biscuit?" suggested Cathy.

"Perfect!" Betsy laughed. "I have paper and a couple of sharpies in different colors."

Quickly they went to work.

An hour later, Linda and Charlie returned home after their walk. The sun was beginning to paint everything with a warm, golden glow. It was very peaceful. Birds were calling back and forth to each other, winding down the day. A couple of bullfrogs were tuning up for an evening concert on the riverbank.

As they got closer to the RV, Linda noticed something fluttering in the wind. A few more steps and she was finally able to see that it was a banner:

Welcome Home Charlie!

Cathy and Betty had been watching for them. Now they swung open the door and yelled out, "Welcome home, Charlie!"

Charlie seemed a little startled at the effusive greeting and pressed close to Linda. She laughed and reached down to pet him. Immediately he calmed down and went over to greet Cathy and Betsy. They petted him and made a fuss over him, giving him treats.

The three friends got out their chairs and arranged them so they could look out over the water and watch the sun go down. Linda made sure she had a leash on Charlie and had him secured to her, so he wouldn't go anywhere near the water's edge.

Cathy said, "Well as usual we need to talk about our favorite topic. What are we going to have for dinner tonight?"

"We have the fixings for a chef salad, how about that?" Linda suggested.

Betsy said, "That sounds great. I'm in the mood for something light."

Cathy reluctantly added, "We also have to start talking about our plans to leave and head to the Ghost Ranch to spread Alice's ashes."

"Let's go inside," suggested Betsy, "and check out Google Maps for the best way to get there."

The women spent the evening planning their visit to the Ghost Ranch. They debated stopping in Santa Fe, with Betsy campaigning strongly for that option. But they ended up deciding the trip was running much longer than they had originally planned. They mapped out a route to get them to their destination as quickly as possible from their present location.

The next morning Linda surprised Betsy and Cathy by baking blueberry muffins. The muffins were a perfect addition to their breakfast. They lounged in their camp chairs, sipped tea, ate muffins, and watched the sun come up.

As they cleaned up the breakfast dishes, Linda said, "You know we need to get some provisions. I think the camp store has most of what we need, but I'm not sure if they have any dog food."

Charlie wagged his tail at the words 'dog food.'

Betsy asked, "You don't think he knows what that means, do you?"

Linda laughed. "With him I have no idea. Anything is possible."

Betsy said, "I think we should begin packing up today if we want to get on the road first thing tomorrow morning."

Cathy nodded. "We need to say some goodbyes too."

For a moment, the women were quiet, reflecting on their experiences at the campground.

"I'm sad to leave," commented Betsy. "At the same time, I'll be happy to get home again."

The other women murmured in agreement. They began clearing their dishes, washing, and putting them away.

Betsy suddenly announced, "There are three pairs of reading glasses on the dining table. Will the owners of the reading glasses please step up and claim them."

Linda laughed, "We should label them to avoid confusion." Each woman grabbed her pair of glasses and tucked them away.

"Cathy, where are your red glasses?" asked Linda.

Cathy answered, "Oh, I just use them for driving."

"Now that's straightened out," said Betsy, "I'm going to do a laundry. Does anyone else need things washed?"

"I have a couple of things," said Cathy.

"Me too," piped up Linda. "If you wouldn't mind, that would be great."

"No problem," said Betsy.

Suddenly there was a knock on the door. Cathy was closest, so she just leaned over and opened it. Peter was standing there. Startled she took a step back and tripped over Charlie, who was lying there contentedly in the midst of everything. Peter quickly stepped through the doorway and grabbed her arm, keeping her from falling.

"Th-thanks," she stammered.

"Hello, everybody," Peter warmly greeted them.

Linda and Betsy chorused, "Hello, Peter."

He grinned at them. "I want to borrow Cathy for a bit. Would you like to go for a ride, Cathy?"

She looked at him before saying, "Well, we're just getting ready—"

"That would be fine," Linda interrupted her.

Cathy started to say, "But—"

"That's a great idea," Betsy cut her off. Cathy gave her a frustrated look.

"Go have fun," said Linda. She handed Cathy her windbreaker and shoulder bag. Peter mouthed the word "thanks" to Linda.

Before she knew what was happening, Cathy found herself getting into Peter's SUV.

"You have really good friends," said Peter as he slid into the driver's seat. "It's obvious they care a lot about you."

"I feel the same way about them," said Cathy.

Inside the RV, Linda and Betsy were laughing and high fiving each other, delighted that Cathy and Peter were spending time together. After a while, they calmed down enough to continue cleaning up the RV. Then they did a load of laundry and decided to walk up to the ranch house to see if there was anything they could buy for dinner.

Meanwhile Peter had turned off the main highway onto a narrow paved road, telling Cathy that where they were going was a surprise. Realizing she was going to have to be content with that, she relaxed and sat back, enjoying the scenery.

Peter talked about his childhood. He shared how his

family was split apart by divorce when he was a teenager. After high school, Peter took classes in criminal justice at a nearby college, graduating with honors and then joining the local police force. Unfortunately, shortly after that, his father and stepmother died in a car accident. A year later his mother passed away.

He decided to run for police chief after becoming aware of the police department's pressing need for better training, communication, and salary structure. Before he took over, at least half the police department was working second jobs, usually construction, to help pay bills. It didn't take long for the members of the police department to learn to trust him, understanding that he meant what he said and was 100% behind them.

Cathy was impressed by his commitment to his department.

"How long have you been police chief?" she asked.

"Fifteen years."

Now came the question that Cathy was the most curious about and wanted to know the answer to. "Have you ever been married?" She asked with some trepidation, unsure what his answer might be.

"Yes," he glanced over at her. "I was married for about twelve years. We had a good marriage, but the life of a police chief is twenty-four hours, seven days a week. That begins to wear away at your relationship. Lots of plans get canceled at the last minute. Lots of missed special events." He took a deep breath and continued, "I have two daughters—Jeanne and Ellen. When we got divorced, my wife moved out to San Diego and took the girls with her. It made sense at the time, given my crazy schedule. But I miss them terribly. I try to get to see them when I can. Thank God for Facetime. They are both in college right now. Jeanne wants to be a teacher, and Ellen wants to be a civil rights attorney. I am immensely proud of them."

Cathy asked, "Did you ever consider moving out there?"

"Yes, but at the time I was caught up in a political battle with a corrupt official who wanted to get me fired. I was torn between my commitment to my family and my commitment to my department. At one point the entire department came to me and asked me to stay. Honestly, I don't know if I made the right choice or not. But I made the choice that I thought I had to make."

"It sounds like that decision still bothers you a lot."

"Yes, it still does." Peter turned onto a private road. "Turnabout is fair play. Have you ever been married?"

"Yes, for about fifteen years. He got cancer and died. He was a good man but…" she hesitated.

"What?" asked Peter.

"I always felt like there was a part of him that was totally shut off from me. Billy Joel has a song about a room in his heart being closed and losing a relationship because of it. I felt ashamed that I wanted more. I had friends who were upset because their husbands were cheating on them. There was nothing like that with my husband. It just felt like we were more good friends than anything else. I thought it was me."

"Maybe it was him." Peter looked at Cathy for a long moment.

She nodded. "Maybe it was him. That would be a relief for me. I wouldn't feel like I had failed him somehow."

She looked out the window as they came around a curve, and there was a beautiful log cabin gleaming in the afternoon sun. It was on the side of a hill, overlooking a valley that had a river running through it. The house looked like it had grown naturally out of the hillside and was now ready to take flight.

Cathy realized she had been holding her breath. She let out a long sigh. "What a beautiful house."

"Thank you," responded Peter. "I built it."

"You built this?" exclaimed Cathy. "What a gorgeous place."

"I'm glad you think so." Peter pulled up in front of the house. When Cathy got out of the vehicle, she could hear dogs barking. She looked at Peter, questioningly.

He reassured her. "They're fine. They're very friendly dogs. Apollo is a border collie, and Pippin is a small mixed breed. My daughters got Pippin from a local shelter. They kept saying, "Look at her paws, look at her paws. She's going to be about fifty, sixty pounds. Well, so much for the big paw theory; she only weighs about eleven pounds. But in terms of personality, she's the size of a Saint Bernard."

He opened the door to the house and was immediately rushed by the dogs. Peter knelt down to say hello. He put his arms around them while they excitedly licked his face. He laughed and told them what good dogs they were. He then introduced Cathy to them by having them sit and shake hands with her. Trailed by the dogs, Peter took

Cathy on a tour of the house. She was impressed by the overall design and thoughtfulness that had gone into it.

The living room was built around a circular natural stone fireplace. Surrounding the fireplace were comfortable sofas and chairs crafted from repurposed wood that had been sanded and polished to a satiny finish. Plush cushions with rich colors and intricate Native American designs were positioned throughout the room.

Four bedrooms opened out from the living room like the spokes of a wheel. Each room had a hand-crafted four poster bed, dresser, rocker, original artwork on the walls and a large picture window.

The four bathrooms had walk-in showers with multi-level, multi-head rainforest shower heads and built-in seats.

The kitchen was a cook's dream. A state-of-the-art stove, oven, and refrigerator were surrounded by artfully designed work and storage spaces featuring polished granite surfaces. Gleaming copper pots and pans, along with bouquets of dried herbs, hung from overhead ceiling panels. Best of all was the view. French doors opened out onto a deck that overlooked the valley and river.

Peter opened the doors, and the dogs raced out onto the deck and then down a flight of stairs. He explained to Cathy that he had an enclosed run for them below the deck where they could exercise but also be protected from any predators.

He asked her, "Would you like something to drink? I have homemade lemonade."

"That sounds great. Thank you." Cathy walked out onto the deck and stood by the railing looking out. "Is this all your land?" she asked.

"About 140 acres, pretty much everything you see stretching down to the river. The other side of the river is a family farm that was donated to a land stewardship project run by the state. That land can never be developed. I'm thinking I will probably do the same thing with my land. I'm looking at retirement soon, and I have to decide what I'm going to do—if I'm going to stay here or move closer to my daughters in San Diego. I'd like to be closer to them, but they don't want to move back here."

He shook his head. "I'm sorry to be laying all this on you. There are not a lot of people I can talk to about it."

Cathy gazed out at the landscape, "Talking about retirement before you are actually ready to retire can be tricky, especially if you are a public servant."

Peter looked at her curiously. "Were you ready to retire?"

Cathy answered thoughtfully, "Yes and no. I was ready to try something new, but at the same time I was worried about all the unknowns—would I have enough money, would I be lonely, would I feel adrift without a purpose? I didn't want to spend my retirement years playing round after round of golf." She put her hand over her mouth. "Oh, I am so sorry…do you like to golf?"

He smiled at her. "No. I tried it a few times as a way of networking and found it boring. But I understand the concerns about the unknowns."

He stood up, stretched, and asked if she wanted dinner.

"That would be great, how can I help?" asked Cathy.

"You can chop up veggies while I barbeque chicken and steam some rice."

They worked companionably together, making dinner, chatting, and laughing about favorite movies, music, books, and all kinds of things. They dined out on the deck under a full moon and a night sky studded with stars.

Back at the RV park, on the way to the camp store, Linda and Betsy had met up with Alfreda, who was walking Frankie. The little dog clearly felt at home. He looked happy and was super excited to see them, especially Charlie, who was, as usual, by Linda's side. Betsy asked Alfreda, "Would you like to come to dinner tonight? Frankie can come as your Plus One."

"Love to," exclaimed Alfreda. "Can I bring Ben?"

"Well, I don't know," said Betsy, "that's Plus Two. We'll have to check the rule book on that."

Linda chimed in, "Oh, let's toss the rule book just for tonight."

"You wild and crazy woman…okay just this once…" Betsy grinned at Alfreda, who was laughing, "bring Ben."

Alfreda turned back to her RV while Linda and Betsy continued to the camp store to find something for dinner. They ended up with barbeque rotisserie chicken, mac and cheese, and baked beans.

"You've got some big-time comfort food there," said Ben after running into them in the store.

"Actually, you are on the guest list for dinner courtesy

of Alfreda. Can you make it?"

"Absolutely, and I'll bring dessert."

Betsy and Linda were delighted. But as the two women were standing there talking to him, an elderly couple came up and asked to speak to him. They were upset, and Linda and Betsy moved away to give them space to talk to Ben.

"Look Ben, we've been coming here for years and have always had a good time and felt wonderfully safe," explained the woman, "But last night our car was keyed and we think some things are missing from our car and RV." She put her hand on his arm, "I'm sorry Ben, but we want our car repaired, hotel accommodations while we are waiting and a full refund of our camping fees."

Ben looked absolutely stunned by news of the vandalism. "Of course. I'll set that up for you right now. We'll get this taken care of as quickly as possible."

His sincerity went a long way to diminishing the older woman's frustration and fear. But she was still determined to leave.

At this point, Ben's reservations manager, Jim Swann, came up to him and asked if he could speak to him privately.

"Sorry to bother you, Ben," said Jim, "but a number of people have heard about this incident and are talking about cutting short their stays and getting a refund on their deposits. What do you want me to do?"

Ben answered, "Let them out of their reservations and absolutely refund their deposits. Meantime, I'm going to call the police and get them to come out and talk to people in that area to see if they heard or saw anything at all."

Ben walked over to Betsy and Linda and apologized. "I have to beg out of dinner tonight. I've got to care of this." He was clearly agitated, running his hand through his hair repeatedly.

"Anything we can do to help?" asked Linda.

"No, thank you. Nothing like this has ever happened here before," Ben said. "Excuse me." He hurried off.

Betsy and Linda carried their groceries back to the camper. "Do you think we should be worried at all?" Betsy asked Linda.

Linda responded, "Well Ben says it hasn't happened here before. So, I guess we go with that though of course things can and do change over time. I think we just need to be careful and aware. Keep an eye out for any strangers, keep an eye on each other, make sure we're all safe. We have Charlie who hopefully the bad guy will think is a vicious watchdog. A dog tends to make us look like not such an easy target."

CHAPTER 13

Peter and Cathy finished dinner. Afterwards, they were enjoying mugs of hot chocolate, when Peter got out an old guitar whose wooden curves were well burnished through use. "This is what I call my kitchen guitar," he explained, laughing. "It's the one I always pull out to play around with." He tuned the guitar and started strumming. "Do you play?"

Cathy laughed. "I've been teaching myself to play ukulele but... wait!" she called to Peter as he disappeared briefly into the house.

He reemerged, smiling, with a ukulele in his hands. "I bought each of my daughters one. I had visions of the three of us sitting out here jamming away into the night."

"And how did that work out for you?"

"Kids and expectations..." Peter sighed dramatically. They both laughed. "Jeanne loved it and Ellen didn't."

"Well," said Cathy, "all I know how to play is 'Happy Birthday'."

"Fine. You start with that and I'll harmonize."

A little self-consciously, Cathy started playing, and Peter strummed along. He began building an accompanying melody, chord by chord. His music swirled and soared around her simple version of "Happy Birthday," transforming it into a multi-layered improvisational piece. Cathy was surprised at how good their combined effort sounded.

As the song drew to a close, Cathy was listening to the final notes float away into the night, when Peter leaned over and kissed her. She closed her eyes and opened herself to the moment, letting herself experience the soft firmness of his lips. She leaned into him and kissed him back, opening her lips slightly, feeling him respond in kind. He lightly brushed his hand over her hair and then gently touched her face with his fingertips. Cathy shivered. Opening her eyes, she looked into his, seeing them deepen and darken with sudden intensity.

Without warning, Peter's dog Apollo dropped a tennis ball into his lap. They both laughed and the mood suddenly changed.

Cathy said, "It's getting late."

"Do you want to stay? I have a guestroom that is all set up. I could drive you home in the morning."

She hesitated. "I'm not really comfortable with that."

"I wasn't suggesting anything but I understand. Let me just clean up the kitchen a bit, and I'll drive you back."

As he put the kitchen to rights, whistling as he worked, Cathy wandered around the living room, looking at numerous pictures of him and his daughters smiling, laughing, and enjoying each other's company. She texted Betsy and

Linda and told them she would be home soon. Both immediately texted back.

Linda sent, "Take your time. It's a beautiful night. Enjoy the evening :-)."

Betsy texted, "Open yourself up to the experience. Seize the day (or chief in this case) ☺."

Cathy smiled, feeling a wave of affection for her friends.

She stood, looking out of the large living room window at the evening sky. She heard Peter walk into the room and come up behind her. He slid his arms around her and pulled her close. Cathy relaxed against him, closed her eyes, and sighed. He leaned down and softly kissed her neck, running his hands slowly down her body. She shivered and turned around to face him. They kissed long and lingeringly, starting softly, then building in intensity. His voice husky with arousal, Peter asked, "How far do you want to go?"

Cathy stepped back, putting a little physical distance between them. "I honestly don't know. I'm getting really excited here, but I don't want to make a snap decision based on my physical reaction to you."

He traced the curves of her face with his fingertips. "While I'm glad to know you have a physical reaction to me, I don't want you to feel bad about anything we do here. So, I think it's time to call it a night."

She looked up into his intensely blue eyes and said, "Regretfully."

He smiled at her. "Yes, regretfully."

Back at the women's RV, Alfreda, Betsy, and Linda were

enjoying homemade ice cream sundaes, when they received Cathy's text, informing them she was on her way home. Linda and Betsy proceeded to grill Alfreda about Peter.

Betsy asked, "How long have you known Peter?"

"About ten years."

Linda bluntly asked, "Is he a good guy?"

Alfreda turned to her. "Peter is the best—kind, caring, good-hearted. Why, do you think Peter and Cathy are interested in each other?"

"Yes," Linda and Betsy said at the same time. They laughed.

Betsy added, "There's been something—a spark, a connection—between them from almost the very beginning."

Alfreda commented, "I have to say it is pretty unusual for him to invite somebody out to see his house. In fact, this is the first time I know of him bringing a woman out there."

"That's encouraging," said Linda.

CHAPTER 14

About a quarter of a mile from the RV park, Sullivan and Smithy were planning their next move. Wearing camo gear and equipped with night goggles, they had hiked under the cover of darkness onto the property.

"What do you think?" asked Smithy.

Sullivan pointed to an expensive-looking RV a couple of campsites over. Through the windows, they could see an old man, who looked very frail, using a walker to get around. A woman with white hair, who looked pretty frail herself, was helping him walk.

"But no one gets hurt, right?" asked Smithy somewhat anxiously.

"Yeah," said Sullivan, "just a quick smash and grab—whatever they have of value. They'll be scared shitless. It will be a walk in the park."

They silently crept closer to the RV. The windows were open to let the breeze in. Through the blowing curtains, they were able to watch the woman doing dishes and talking quietly to the man, who was now seated at the table. His head was down, and he was just staring at his fingers.

"What's wrong with him?" asked Smithy.

"Shhhh!" warned Sullivan.

Smithy was feeling worse and worse about this whole thing. To add to his anxiety, the old woman looked familiar. He peered at her, trying to place her.

Next door, Sharon and George were getting ready for bed. They had already walked their two dogs for the evening, but noticed the dogs seemed unsettled and anxious.

"What do you think is going on with them?" asked Sharon. George shrugged; he was engrossed in watching the highlights of a Yankees game on the news. Sharon kept watching the dogs. She found she was getting anxious just from watching them being anxious. She tried to shake it off.

She turned to George. "I don't know what is with them. Could you take them out one last time?"

"I'll take them out in a minute. I just want to watch this."

Sharon said, "If one of them has an accident..."

George responded somewhat sharply, "I said I would take them out in just a minute."

Sharon waited for a few minutes before saying, "That's all right. I've got it." She shrugged her jacket on and grabbed the dogs' leashes. The two shelties did not seem that thrilled about going out. She was surprised at their behavior. Usually when she got the leashes in her hand, they got excited and started dancing around. This time she had the leashes in her hand, and the dogs just stood there quietly. Even after she put the leashes on them, they seemed hesitant. She almost had to drag them out the door. Once they got outside, they stood close by her legs and didn't make a sound. Again, this was totally unlike them. Usually, they wanted to explore right away. Sharon felt ill at ease. Their unusual behavior was freaking her out.

Sharon took a few steps away from the door and thought, 'I should've brought my flashlight.' She almost went back for it but hesitated and then thought, 'I'll just go a little bit further. And they can do their business.'

She took a few more steps, saying aloud to herself, "That's it, no more. I'll have George take them out if they need to go out again." She turned around at the same time a tall, dark figure stepped in front of her. She opened her mouth to scream, but the figure grabbed her and pulled her tightly against him. He crushed his hand over her mouth, stifling any noise she might try to make. He grabbed the dogs' leashes out of her hand and tossed them to another figure who appeared out of the darkness and caught them. The second figure then tied the dogs to a tree. The dogs started whimpering. Sharon tried to struggle.

The figure who held her captive said roughly into her ear, "Make any noise and you get hurt. And the dogs get hurt. Nod your head if you understand." Sharon nodded her head, all the while trying to think of how she could get loose. Suddenly the television set in the RV went dark. Sharon's heart dropped. She was terrified George would step out into this situation totally unprepared. And get hurt. Or worse. Sharon decided to try a move she had seen on YouTube, biting her captor's hand and at the same time stamping with all her might on his instep. She then heard George call her name. She got ready. The door to the RV opened with a squeal. Just as Sharon was about to bite down, a bright spotlight blinded all of them.

A fragile, yet firm, voice asked, "What's going on? Who is out here?" Sharon's eighty-five-year-old neighbor, Izzy, was standing there with a portable spotlight in one hand and a shotgun in the other.

Sullivan, who was holding Sharon, laughed, and said with a snarl, "Listen, you old hag, this doesn't concern you. Go inside if you don't want to get hurt." He tightened his grip on Sharon. At which point, Izzy angled the gun upward and fired.

Quickly she pumped another shell into the chamber and brought the gun down level, focusing on Sullivan. Izzy sternly said, "Let go of her and step back with your hands up."

Sullivan didn't move.

Meanwhile, Alfreda was heading back to her RV after dinner with Linda and Betsy. Carrying Frankie, who had fallen asleep from all the excitement, she saw the spotlight and heard the loud voices. Curious, she walked closer. Then she saw the gun. She ran to a nearby fire alarm box and pulled the lever.

Ben was going over the books in his office with Jim when he heard the alarm go off. He immediately pressed the buzzer that alerted the nearest fire station of an emergency. He and Jim ran downstairs.

In that moment, Peter was driving up the driveway with Cathy. He heard something and rolled his window down.

Cathy looked startled. "What is that?"

"A fire alarm," Peter answered grimly.

As he drove up to the ranch house, Ben and Jim came rushing out. Peter stopped, and they jumped into his SUV.

Ben said, "It's down by the campsites."

As he drove toward the alarm's location, Peter jammed an emergency light array onto the roof of his vehicle and got on the radio, calling in reinforcements. Coming around the curve in the driveway, they saw lights and a crowd of about fifteen people blocking the road.

"This is not a fire," said Peter.

They all got out of the vehicle and started hurrying toward the crowd. Ben saw Alfreda, along with Linda and Betsy, on the edge of the mass of people.

"What's going on?" asked Peter.

Alfreda turned. Seeing Peter, she said, "Thank God, you're here. It's a hostage situation."

"What?" exclaimed Ben, his face ashen with shock.

Peter said to Ben and Jim, "Start moving these people out of here; get them back."

Peter immediately started to work his way through the crowd to the front. "Shit," he said. Izzy had her shotgun trained on Sullivan, who was still holding Sharon as a shield against him.

Smithy was pleading with Sullivan to let her go. "This is not what I signed up for. Remember, we weren't gonna hurt anybody."

Sullivan looked over at Smithy with disgust. "Shut up!"

Peter stepped into the circle of light surrounding Sullivan and Sharon. He took a few steps closer.

"Hello, Sully," said Peter.

Cathy who had moved closer to the front of the crowd, along with Alfreda, Linda, and Betsy, watched with a mixture of terror and pride.

"Well, well, Chief Peter," said Sullivan. "When are those two lovely girls of yours going to be ready for a real man? Maybe the next time they visit, I'll take them out and show them a good time. One they will never forget." He laughed and spit on the ground.

Izzy said, "What a pig." She asked Peter, "Do you want me to shoot him for you? I doubt at my age that I would get charged for it. Be glad to do it."

Peter remained totally expressionless, "Thank you Izzy for the offer but I'd rather you didn't shoot him."

There was a distant sound of a siren. Sullivan flinched and jerked Sharon backward. She almost lost her balance.

Peter stepped forward and talked directly to Sullivan. "You have a choice here, Sullivan. You haven't used a weapon and so far you haven't hurt anybody. Give it up now, and you're facing a less serious charge."

"Really," sneered Sullivan, "you expect me to believe

that? You're going to put in a good word for me?"

While Sullivan was talking, George had crept around behind the RV and through the woods to where the dogs were tied. As he inched forward to untie them, he looked up and saw Smithy watching him. His blood froze as he waited for Smithy to alert Sullivan. Instead, Smithy shocked him by nodding and stepping to the other side of Sullivan. George reached forward and yanked the dogs' leashes free. They immediately raced toward Sullivan, barking and growling.

Sullivan kicked out at them, swearing, catching one of them in the ribs. The dog yelped but then renewed its attack. Sharon bit down hard on Sullivan's hand and stamped with all her might on his instep. He raised his fist to punch her face but Smithy grabbed his arm, twisting it and pulling Sullivan backward off balance. George charged in and tackled him around the knees, bringing him slamming to the ground. As Sullivan struggled, he tried to hold on to Sharon. Peter ran to help pull Sharon free. He used his body weight to force Sullivan to stay down, clamping his wrists together. Izzy moved in closer, keeping the shotgun trained on Sullivan.

She called out to Ben, "I've got some handcuffs in the utility drawer, next to the fridge." He spun on his heel and raced to get them.

Continuing to pin Sullivan, Peter said, "Izzy, I won't even ask what you are doing with handcuffs."

Ben came back with the handcuffs, tossing them to Peter, who caught them one-handed. He snapped them on

Sullivan. George strode over to Sharon, and they held each other tightly before reaching down to hug their dogs, who were leaping around them excitedly. Smithy continued to help Peter hold Sullivan down.

Izzy shone the spotlight in his face. "I know you. Bob Smith, isn't it? I taught you in elementary school art class." He nodded, ashamed, keeping his face averted. "You were so talented, I figured you'd go off to college to study art. What in God's name happened?"

At that moment two squad cars came roaring down the driveway, nearly rear-ending Peter's vehicle. Four police officers piled out of the squad cars and raced over to Peter. One of the police officers stood by Smithy. He had handcuffs at the ready, and he looked questioningly at Peter. He nodded, and the police officer snapped the handcuffs on Smithy.

Izzy said, "Wait a minute. Why are you arresting him?"

Peter responded, "Look he may have had a change of heart at the end, but he didn't start out that way, so I need to take him in. The judge will make a decision as to whether to take that into consideration."

Now that the situation was under control, Izzy lowered her shotgun, emptied it, and put the gun away. Peter had his officers take her statement, as well as Sharon's and George's, as to what had happened.

Cathy saw how upset Ben was. She walked over to him and quietly asked, "How are you doing, Ben?"

"Not too good," he replied. "Things like this have never happened here before. It has always been a safe place. Now violence is coming onto this property, and I don't know why. Maybe it's time for me to get out of this business…" His voice trailed off, he excused himself and walked over to Peter. They started talking.

Cathy saw Alfreda, Betsy, and Linda. She said to them, "I think it's time to head back to the RV." They nodded in agreement and started walking back up the hill.

"How is Ben doing?" asked Linda.

Cathy said, "Judging from the brief conversation we had just now, I don't think he's doing very well. He sounds like he's ready to throw in the towel and sell the place."

"Oh no," said Betsy, "that would really be a shame."

Peter finished talking to Ben and looked around for Cathy. He noticed that Betsy, Linda, Alfreda, and Cathy had all disappeared. It had been a long and stressful night, and he assumed they had headed back to their RVs. He wanted to stop and talk to Cathy but knew he had to head to the police station to conduct interviews with Sullivan and Smithy. With a muttered curse, he climbed into his vehicle, pulled a quick U-turn, and headed up the driveway.

When they got to her RV, Alfreda said good night to the three women and, still carrying Frankie, went inside. She had been on the lookout for Ben but did not see him as she was leaving. She had hoped to be able to talk to him and offer some comfort. She gave Frankie a treat and a hug and then sat down wearily at her table. There was a quiet knock at her door. She peered out. Immediately she unlocked the door and stepped back. Ben entered and with a deep sigh walked straight into her arms.

CHAPTER 15

The women climbed wearily into their RV. "I am wiped out," said Betsy. "But I do want some tea, and I need to talk a bit about what just happened. I have to decompress for a bit before I can go to sleep."

Linda said, "Me too," and Cathy nodded her agreement. While Betsy took out her teapot and prepared chamomile tea for all of them, Linda pulled out a Ziploc bag of chocolate chip cookies. Cathy and Betsy looked at her in surprise.

"Where did that come from?" Betsy asked.

"It is my emergency stash," said Linda. She repeated emphatically, "It's for emergencies only."

Cathy started laughing.

"I think that is a great idea," said Betsy.

Linda passed out cookies to Betsy and Cathy. "OK, what's the scoop?"

"To what are you referring?" Cathy asked in a very prim voice.

Betsy grinned. "Channeling *Downton Abbey* are we?"

Linda took over. "Well, things have gotten a bit confused, what with the hostage situation. But basically, we want to know how the date with Peter went."

Cathy sighed and looked at a cookie for a long moment. "It was wonderful. We had a fantastic dinner under the stars. We even played music together. And then he kissed me."

At that, Linda and Betsy reached for the same chocolate chip cookie at the same time. They looked at each other and laughed.

Wow," said Linda. "This just gets better and better."

Betsy asked, "So how are you feeling about him now, Cathy?"

Cathy took another cookie. "I really like him. If we lived in the same town, there would be no question I'd continue to see him. But we don't. We live thousands of miles from each other."

Betsy started to protest, "But you know there's Facetime and Zoom. There are all kinds of ways of keeping in touch now. Much more immediate and intimate than in the old days of writing letters, or even long-distance phone calls."

Cathy asked, "But do those things really help to maintain a long-distance relationship better than before?"

Betsy looked thoughtful. "You know, that's a good question. Let me Google that." She pulled out her laptop and asked Siri to look it up for her.

Cathy looked at her curiously. "What does Hugh have to say?"

"He says he's thinking," responded Betsy.

Linda smiled at her and said, "He's quite high maintenance, isn't he?"

"Oh, but he is so worth it," said Betsy.

Cathy looked at both of them before saying, "I'm exhausted. I'm going to head to bed."

Betsy closed her laptop. "I agree, it's time for bed. I will see what I can find out tomorrow."

Linda added, "I'm making this a trifecta and heading to bed too. Tomorrow is another day."

The women climbed wearily into their beds. Charlie sat next to Linda's bed, looking up at her hopefully. She tried to ignore him but finally she gave in. She patted the bed and said, "OK." Charlie tried to jump up but fell short. He tried another jump. Again, he fell short and slid back onto the floor. Linda giggled.

Cathy looked over from her bed. "Looks like he has too much ballast in his behind."

Linda leaned over, put her arms around him, and lifted him up. He immediately made himself at home and snuggled next to her. She patted his head, kissed him on the nose, and turned out the light.

Cathy commented, "I bet he snores."

Linda laughed. "Oh, without a doubt. But then so do I."

Meanwhile, at the police station, Peter poured a cup of coffee from the station's dilapidated coffee machine, ignoring the flap of duct tape holding the filter in place. The coffee was lukewarm and tasted like motor oil, but at least it was caffeine and he really needed that kick to get through the next few hours. He took a sip of the coffee and shuddered at its bitterness. His deputy, Tom, swung in through the open door.

He looked at Peter's expression with amusement. "That bad, huh?"

"Worse," answered Peter, rubbing his hands over his face. "How are our guests doing?"

Tom grabbed a swivel chair, swung it around, and sat on it. "Well, Smithy is not saying or doing anything. He is just sitting there with his head down. It is clear he really regrets ever getting involved with Sullivan. On the other hand, Sullivan seems ready to spark a revolution. Given half a chance, I think he'd try to break out of here."

Peter looked at him. "Who else is in there with him?"

"Three guys who got over-excited at a wedding reception and got into a fight. They just need to cool their heels for a while."

An elegantly attired man in his fifties appeared without warning in the doorway, with a cashmere overcoat draped loosely over his impeccably tailored suit, his silver hair styled with great care. He looked around the office with a sneer before his gaze finally alighted on Peter. "So, this is where you ended up. I have to say I expected more from you, but I am not surprised it's this much less."

Peter looked up at him resignedly. "Hello, Bennie." He indicated his deputy, "You know Tom McDonald." Benedict ignored the introduction.

"It's Benedict Samuels, as you well know," said the man with some asperity. "I use my full name now."

Peter sighed. "What are you doing here, Benn... Benedict?" he asked.

"I'm here to get my client out of jail."

As tired as he was, Peter felt a shot of adrenaline. "Who exactly is your client?"

"James Sullivan."

Peter took a long sip from his cup of coffee, ignoring the fact it was ice-cold. "Sullivan is your client?"

"He certainly is, and I want him out of jail now."

Peter said thoughtfully, "I am curious as to how you knew he was here at all."

Benedict looked down his nose at him. "I have my sources." He stalked from one end of the office to the other. "I want him up here now."

Peter said, "We are waiting for the judge to get back to us. We woke him out of a sound sleep."

Tom slipped out of the room.

"Tough," said Benedict. "Get him on the phone. He's a dinosaur; he should have been ousted years ago." Benedict shot his sleeves down, straightening his cuffs and then his tie. "I want to talk to my client now."

Tom came back into the room, followed by a woman who was dressed to the nines. Her sleek kimono-style silk coat softly rustled against the splintery wooden office door.

Peter looked up at her in shock. "Elizabeth." He stood up. "I thought you were in New York."

She smiled at him and put her hand on his arm. "I was, but I was feeling a little homesick, so I thought I would take a quick trip home. It's good to see you, Peter. You look as handsome as ever." She leaned forward and gave him a kiss on the cheek. "I know you and my brother have things to talk about. I'll be waiting outside in the car." She then nodded at Benedict. "Don't be too long."

Peter murmured something in response. Elizabeth swept out, trailing the faint scent of a very expensive perfume behind her.

Tom glanced at Peter, taking in the situation. "I have the judge on the line. Do you want me to put him through?"

"Yes," responded Peter.

Benedict interrupted firmly, "Put him through now." Peter shot a sharp glance at Benedict but then nodded to Tom, who disappeared into the outside office. Peter's phone rang, and he and Benedict reached for it at the same time. Peter was faster and put his hand up to stop Benedict from interfering. Peter began to talk with the judge about Sullivan.

Benedict prowled around the room and then stood facing Peter across the desk, trying to stare him down. Peter ignored him. After a brief conversation, Peter handed the phone to Benedict and then called Tom in. Benedict discussed bail with the judge, and they agreed on a figure. Benedict said he would personally guarantee it.

He hung up and turned to Peter. "OK. Let's get Sullivan out of here." Peter stood up without a word and headed out to the jail cell where Sullivan was being held.

Tom chased after him. "I can take care of this."

"I know, but I just felt the sudden need to get some fresh air." Peter ran a hand through his hair. "I don't want to leave Benedict in my office alone. I don't trust him. Get Sullivan and bring him up to my office."

He spun on his heel and went back to his office. Benedict, who had been looking at some of the papers on Peter's desk, stepped back hastily. "Well?" he asked.

"He's on his way up." Peter glanced at Benedict and then down at his desk. He debated whether or not to say anything to Benedict but then decided it wasn't worth it. Tom walked in with a surly Sullivan in handcuffs.

Benedict said, "He doesn't need handcuffs."

Tom glanced over at Peter.

Peter shrugged. "Take them off."

Sullivan pulled his wrists free from the handcuffs. Rubbing them, he said to Peter, "I could get you for police brutality, you know. You'll be sorry."

Frustrated and exhausted, Peter could feel his temper wearing thin. Benedict glanced at him and saw the anger building under the surface. He grabbed Sullivan by the arm and quickly pulled him out of the office. He said over his shoulder, "I'll be in touch."

Tom and Peter looked at each other.

Peter said, "There is something so much more going on here. How is he getting covered like that? What's in it for Benedict?"

"What do you want to do next?" Tom asked him.

Peter sat down heavily in his chair. "Nothing right now. It's been an exceedingly long day and night." He stood up, stretched, and pulled open a cabinet, taking out a blanket and pillow.

Tom asked, "You're going to sleep here?"

"Yes, I'm too tired to make the drive back home."

"Well, you are certainly welcome to stay over at my house if you want."

"Tom, you've got a brand-new baby. I'm sure your wife would be thrilled to see me on your doorstep. How long has she been without sleep now?"

Tom laughed. "Yeah, it's been a while. But she's hanging in there. You got to come over and meet the most beautiful baby ever."

Peter slapped him on the back. "I'll be over to see her soon. Sounds like from what you're saying, she's got your wife's looks."

Tom grinned. "Yeah, you got that right. Thank God." He paused for a moment and then added rather too innocently, "Elizabeth is looking good. Even better than when she was homecoming queen at the prom. And you were the homecoming king."

"Are you going somewhere with this?"

"Just saying," Tom grinned at Peter. "When she came in and found out that you were in your office, she was like a homing device. Homing right at you. She's still got the hots for you."

Peter laughed. "What are you in ninth grade still? Look, no matter what she thinks, I was never interested in her other than as a friend."

"Well perhaps you could bring Cathy with you to see the baby."

"I'd like to, but I think they are probably leaving the

area pretty soon."

"Well, that doesn't have to mean the end of the relationship."

"In my experience, long-distance relationships don't seem to work out too well. Even if both people want it."

"I'm sorry." Tom started heading out the office door and then turned back. "If you're hungry, there are sandwiches left over from lunch. I can't guarantee how fresh they are or how good, but at least it's something to put in your stomach if you need it."

"Thanks, Tom. See you tomorrow."

Early the next day, the three women woke up to a beautiful morning, the warm sun creeping over the horizon, a symphony of birds singing at the top of their lungs.

Cathy asked, "Linda, can I take Charlie for his morning walk. I just really enjoy his company. There is something about him. He has this remarkable calming effect on me."

"Sure, just keep him on leash."

"Thanks," Cathy leaned down to Charlie's level. "Ready to go for a walk?" Charlie gave a soft woof and wagged his tail. "We're ready. See you in a bit."

"Have fun," said Linda as Cathy and Charlie left.

Linda and Betsy started putting breakfast together, making tea and toast and taking out some homemade blueberry jam Alfreda had given them. Linda noticed that Betsy had a book tucked under her arm.

"What are you reading?" She asked curiously.

"It's Michael J. Fox's latest book."

"Is that the one about him getting hurt? I heard he had

a bad fall not too long ago."

"Yes," answered Betsy. "He wrote a book about it and about where he is with this disease. I am about halfway through. It's a good book, but it does make me think about things."

"Like what?"

"Like what if I were to have a bad fall, what would happen to me?" Betsy paused. "It is so easy to fall when you have Parkinson's. You just simply put your foot wrong and if your balance is off, which it often is with Parkinson's, you can go over very easily and break something. I'm afraid that if that were to happen to me, I might end up in a nursing home." Unexpectedly she teared up. Drying her eyes quickly with her sleeve, she started to turn away from Linda.

But Linda stopped Betsy and put her arms around her, giving her a big hug. "Betsy, so many people care about you. Don't even think about a nursing home." She smiled and added, "You can come and live with me anytime you want, or I'll come live with you. You know, we talked about starting a nonprofit that would offer a forever home for senior dogs. I'm extremely interested in following up on that, seeing if we can somehow make that happen."

"Seriously?" asked Betsy.

"Absolutely."

Betsy could feel the energy flowing through her at the thought. Since her retirement, she had felt adrift. The idea of having a purpose in her life and being involved in something of value that had a lasting impact was critically important to her. She hadn't realized quite how important it was to her until that very moment. She brightened up and smiled at Linda. "Let's do that. Let's seriously look into it."

"Agreed." Linda reached out to shake Betsy's hand on it.

CHAPTER 16

At the police station, a ratcheting up of the noise volume was enough to wake up Peter. Even with the door closed, he could tell there was a change in the tempo of daily activity. He stood up, got dressed in the clean clothes he kept in his office for emergencies, and opened the door. Tom who had been sitting at his desk doing some paperwork stood up and walked over with a steaming hot cup of coffee.

"You are a lifesaver, Tom," said Peter gratefully. He took a breath and inhaled the wonderful deep-roasted scent of coffee. "This can't be from our machine."

"No, I got it from the cafe down the street, along with a couple of donuts."

"Fantastic," murmured Peter as he took a sip.

"Smithy?" asked Tom.

"I have some ideas about that. Let's go into my office."

With the door closed, Peter relaxed back into his office chair. "OK, this is what I have in mind. I'm going to ask the judge for community service for Smithy. Thirty-five hours a week for three months. And I want him to report to you every Monday morning at 8:00 a.m. to get his assignment for the week."

Tom said, "Oh great."

"He needs contact with someone who's responsible and dependable. I think being around you will have a positive impact on him. He hasn't really had any kind of formal training and hasn't been around someone who had a responsible job before. Growing up, his father was out of the picture. His mother worked a lot of menial jobs, trying to support them. They ended up living in the family van for quite a while."

"Sounds like he's someone that could use a couple of positive breaks in his life."

Peter nodded. "Bring him up to the office, and we'll talk to him about it and see if he's willing to go along with the plan. If he is, I'm going take him out to the RV park and have him apologize to everyone and see if maybe we can get him started with Ben on community service. In the meantime, I also need to interview folks out there and make sure we have all the information we need on what happened last night."

At the other end of town, Elizabeth poured herself a cup of coffee, sat down on the couch, and started skimming her phone messages. She glanced up occasionally to look out the big windows at the meticulously manicured lawn. It was a beautiful home, and she was grateful to her brother and his wife, Joan, for letting her stay there while she was in the area. She heard noises from overhead and smiled.

Her brother sounded like he would be down shortly. She glanced over to see if there was enough coffee for him too. Within a few minutes, Benedict clattered down the stairs, at the same time fixing his tie.

"Good morning." He poured himself a cup of coffee and sat down near Elizabeth. He picked up a copy of the local paper lying on the table.

Elizabeth glanced over. "I can't believe they're still publishing that. Most places have shut down their papers altogether."

Benedict unfolded the paper. "Yeah, I know, but this paper serves as my connection to the community. I run an ad every week."

"Do you mean to tell me you get clients from newspaper ads?"

"No," said Benedict, "but I like the visibility. Plus, I always check and see if there are any property transfers I might be interested in."

For a while it was peaceful as they both checked their phones and drank their morning coffee.

Elizabeth said, "Oh, by the way, Joan said she'd see you later tonight. She was thinking maybe we could all go out for dinner."

Benedict looked up from his phone. "That sounds good. Except there's not a lot of decent places to eat around here. But I guess we can head over to the Country Club."

Elizabeth commented, "Really? Country clubs are so stuffy."

"Their customers are my demographic, and it's a good

way for me to make contacts."

"Speaking of contacts," said Elizabeth, "why in God's name are you representing Sullivan. He is such a lowlife."

Benedict put his cup of coffee down and looked at her with a faintly professorial look. "Everyone deserves decent and fair representation before the law."

She gazed at him for a long moment, then burst out laughing. "Look, little brother, could you sound any stuffier and more arrogant? I don't for a minute believe that you're doing this out of the kindness of your heart. Or your desire to provide fair and decent representation before the law. So, what's the real story? Why are you representing Sullivan?"

Benedict stared into his coffee for a few moments and then said, "This has to be just between you and me. Absolutely. You must promise." She nodded; her curiosity now aroused. He took a long breath. "About six months ago, I had an affair with Sullivan's sister."

Elizabeth stared at him. Whatever she was expecting, it wasn't this.

"It only lasted about four months," he continued. "It really didn't mean anything. But unfortunately, there are pictures. Sullivan has threatened to go to Joan with them if I don't help him."

Elizabeth closed her eyes for a moment. "And you don't have a prenup."

He nodded. "I could lose a lot of my assets."

Elizabeth got up and rinsed out her coffee cup in the sink. "Benedict, I really don't know what to say. Joan is a decent, good woman. I like her a lot. You've really screwed up here. If she finds out, she's going to want a divorce. And Benedict, make no mistake about it, she is going to find out somehow, somewhere."

Benedict protested, "But it didn't mean anything…"

Elizabeth slapped her hand hard against the counter, making Benedict jump. "I hate that. I hate it when men say that. If it didn't mean anything, then why the hell did you do it? Why couldn't you just keep your pants on?"

"Well, Joan was busy with launching her nonprofit and wasn't home much."

Elizabeth angrily retorted, "That's bullshit. Don't even go there; don't even try to tell me it's because she wasn't available to you. You're a big boy. You could have dealt with it. Instead, you betrayed her." She grabbed her coat and purse. "I've got to get out of here. I need fresh air. I'm taking your car."

"There's a jeep in the barn. The keys are in it."

"No, no jeep for me. I'm taking the Benz. I'll see you later."

Benedict started after her. "Remember, you promised."

Elizabeth turned and looked at him full in the face. "I wouldn't talk to me about broken promises if I were you." She slammed the door on the way out. Jumping into the Mercedes-Benz, she cranked the car up and spun out of the driveway, spitting gravel out from under the tires.

"Shit!" said Benedict. But as he got ready to leave the house for his office, he realized that he felt a sense of relief. Like a weight had been lifted.

Angry and upset, Elizabeth sped into town. She drove around for a while, trying to calm down. She wasn't sure what she was going to do. But she knew one thing. She needed to talk to Peter, someone she'd always trusted and respected, even when they had disagreed about their relationship.

She parked, got out of the car, and started walking. After a few blocks, she came across Joan's nonprofit, A Safe Place. The name was emblazoned across a door that featured a kaleidoscope of colors and images—all created by the children who came here to study, laugh, talk, daydream, and to feel safe. Snacks and drinks were always available, free of charge. Volunteers were on hand to help with homework assignments.

Elizabeth had already donated quite a bit of money to A Safe Place. When she walked in today, she was happy with how many children were there reading, working on projects, or quietly talking with one another. She waved to Joan who was in a meeting in the conference room. Elizabeth decided to hold off talking to her. Instead, she took out her checkbook, wrote a check for a few thousand dollars, and carefully folded it into the donation piggy bank on Joan's desk.

Waving to Joan again, she headed out down the street to the police station. Pushing open the door, she spotted Tom. "Hi, Tom. Where's Peter? I need to talk to him."

Tom hesitated, not sure what to tell her.

Exasperated, Elizabeth said, "Tom, this is nothing personal to do with Peter and me; it's police business regarding Sullivan. I really need to talk to him."

Tom replied, "Peter is out at the Arden RV Park right now and should be back in a few hours. Do you want me to get a message to him?"

Elizabeth made a quick decision. "Just tell him I was looking for him." She gave Tom her phone number and then decided to go back to A Safe Place and wait for a chance to talk to Joan. Elizabeth still hadn't made up her mind what to say yet if anything. She had some momentary guilt about breaking the promise she had made to Benedict. But his involvement with Sullivan was worrisome, and she was afraid that he might get hurt by that involvement, not just legally but physically.

CHAPTER 17

Back at the RV campsite, Linda was finishing up washing and drying their breakfast dishes. "I hate to bring this up again," she said.

Betsy nodded. "I know. We have to talk about the elephant in the room. We've got to get going to the Ghost Ranch to spread Alice's ashes. Though I guess I shouldn't really refer to her ashes as the elephant in the room."

Linda sighed. "It will be hard to leave here. The people are so nice and caring. I feel really at home here."

Betsy agreed. "I feel amazingly comfortable here too. And I usually don't feel comfortable in unfamiliar places."

Cathy arrived back with Charlie. They all sat down at the picnic table.

Linda said, "You know I've really enjoyed having breakfast outside. I'm going to miss this gorgeous scenery."

"I'm going to miss the people most of all," commented Betsy. She and Linda looked at each other.

Then Linda asked, "Are you going to miss Peter, Cathy?"

Cathy stood up abruptly. "I told you before, nothing is

going to happen between Peter and me. Leave it alone!" She started striding toward the RV. "Here I am having a wonderful breakfast and feeling very relaxed, and you have to go and ruin it by bringing up Peter."

Linda looked shocked at Cathy's response. "I am so sorry," she apologized. "I guess I just want to see you happy. I thought he made you happy."

Betsy started to say, "Cathy—"

But Cathy interrupted her, responding with considerable anger. "Enough already. There's not always a happily ever after. Leave it be." She pushed open the door to the RV and tried to slam it as she entered. Unfortunately, the door's spring was loose, causing it to slowly and gently close, undermining her efforts at making a dramatic exit.

"Damn it," Cathy said. Grabbing her purse, she headed back out. "I'm going up to the ranch house," she called out to Betsy and Linda, who were still sitting at the table, shocked by her outburst. Wiping away tears, Cathy headed up the road.

Betsy and Linda looked at each other.

"Well shit," said Betsy, "that did not go well."

Linda looked after Cathy as she walked away. "Are you OK here by yourself?" she asked Betsy.

"Oh, I'm fine. Just leave Charlie here to keep me company."

Linda ran after Cathy. She quickly caught up with her. Cathy tried to ignore her, picking up her pace as she walked.

But Linda grabbed her arm and stopped her dead in

her tracks. "Look, I'm sorry I said anything about Peter. It's just that your face lights up when you're around him. So, we kind of thought he made you happy. But if it's not going any further, then it's not going any further. We'll support you, whatever you want to do."

Cathy said, "All I want to do now is spread Alice's ashes at the Ghost Ranch and then go home and just think of this whole thing with Peter as a nice vacation memory."

"OK, then that is what we will do."

As they approached the ranch house, Linda and Cathy saw a huge Harley-Davidson motorcycle with a sidecar parked in front.

"Wow," said Cathy, "look at that."

They walked around the gleaming monster machine.

Cathy said admiringly, "That is one heavily tricked-out bike. Totally customized. Look at that stereo system."

Linda glanced at her. "How do you know so much about motorcycles?"

Cathy snorted with laughter. "My misbegotten youth."

"You?" stuttered Linda in disbelief.

"For a while there in high school, I had a penchant for bad boys. So, I got to know motorcycles pretty well. I still have my motorcycle license, even though I haven't driven one in years."

They went inside and saw Ben talking with a man with his back to them. He was holding a motorcycle helmet in one hand and the leash of a large yellow lab in the other. The dog was wearing a service dog harness and was sitting patiently by his side. The man was wearing faded jeans, cowboy boots, and a leather jacket.

Ben looked up. A bright smile broke out over his face when he saw them. "Hey, Linda and Cathy, I want to introduce you to someone. This is my son, Luke Arden, and his service dog, Harry." The man he was talking to turned around to meet them. Although he had a sweet smile as he said hello, Linda noticed there was a bleakness that haunted his eyes.

"I asked Luke to come and stay with me for a while, since we've had incidents of violence and vandalism here recently. I want to make sure I have enough coverage. He's a decorated marine vet who served in Afghanistan. Between the two of us, we should be able to tamp down whatever is going on and find out the reason behind it."

"It's a pleasure to meet you," Linda said to Luke while shaking his hand. "What a beautiful dog. Can I pet him?"

Luke shook his head. "Not now. He's working."

Linda looked startled by this.

Luke explained further, "He's a medical alert dog. He warns me when I'm about to have a seizure."

"That's amazing," said Cathy. "How did you teach him to do that?"

"I didn't. A service dog organization trained him. Actually, like some dogs, he already had the innate ability to sense impending seizures. What the trainers did was promote that behavior with click-and-treat training methods. He learned through treats and praise that alerting to an upcoming seizure was a good thing."

"What is an alert?" asked Linda, intrigued.

"It is our own special communication that we've worked out. He nudges me or puts his head on my leg or he'll paw at my arm. If I'm really not paying attention, he will actually sit on me to make sure I don't move until the danger is past. He can alert me up to twenty minutes ahead of a seizure so that I have plenty of time to sit or lie down."

"So, you don't fall and hit your head when a seizure strikes," Linda said knowledgeably. "That's incredible. What a difference that must make in your life."

Cathy said to Luke, "Linda is a retired ER nurse, so she is very familiar with different medical conditions."

Luke smiled at his dog, who looked up at him with the well-known, and much-loved Labrador smile. "I can't even put into words how much safer I feel with him by my side."

"I can totally understand that" said Linda. "I know of kids with epilepsy who can't take a shower without supervision, in case they have a seizure and fall and hurt themselves." Linda looked at Harry with a renewed respect.

Cathy turned to Ben, "Sorry to interrupt, but I'm glad we ran into you. We are planning on leaving sometime tomorrow, probably in the morning. We wanted to see what we need to do to check out. We also wanted to tell you how much we appreciate everything, all the courtesies you've shown us, and all the hospitality. You've been absolutely fantastic." Spontaneously Cathy hugged Ben, and Linda joined in, turning it into a group hug.

Ben looked shocked. "Of course, I knew that your stay was temporary. But you've become such an integral part of our community so quickly… really I consider you part of our family. It'll be difficult to see you leave."

Linda teared up at his words.

Ben added, "Let's at least have a farewell dinner for you. I'll invite people from the RV community to have dinner with us."

Linda said, "That would be absolutely wonderful. We would love the chance to say goodbye to all the friends we've made here."

Ben asked, "Does Peter know?"

Cathy mumbled something under her breath and then answered, "No. Not yet. We're just getting everything in order so that we can leave early tomorrow morning. I haven't spoken to him yet."

"How does seven o'clock sound?" Ben asked.

Cathy nodded. "That sounds good."

Linda said, "We'll see you then. Nice meeting you Luke, and Harry of course."

As they left, Cathy wondered how difficult the next 24 hours was going to be.

CHAPTER 18

Betsy was sitting on a chair outside the RV, looking out at the river. She had a book of poems by Mary Oliver on her lap, but she wasn't reading it. She was just gazing at the scenery.

Suddenly, she heard a voice calling, "Hello, hello!" She turned around, and there was Izzy coming toward her.

She stood up stiffly with the help of her cane, "Hi, how are you doing Izzy? Have you recovered from last night? Come sit by me." Izzy walked over to her and sat down with a sigh.

Betsy asked, "Would you like some tea or coffee, or would you rather have water?"

"No, nothing for me. Thanks anyway," Izzy looked down and saw the book that Betsy was holding. "Oh, I love Mary Oliver."

Betsy said, "I just discovered her poetry. I really like how she thinks about life, and about nature."

Izzy turned to Betsy. "And what will you do with your one wild and precious life?"

"I am still trying to figure that out. Though I think I may have found an answer." Betsy shared with Izzy, Linda's proposal to create a nonprofit sanctuary for senior dogs.

"Oh, I love that idea!" said Izzy, smiling at Charlie who was fast asleep at Betsy's feet.

Betsy looked at her curiously. "Is there something I can help you with?"

"I don't know if you're aware of this, but my husband has Alzheimer's."

"Oh, I'm so sorry." Betsy reached over and took Izzy's hand and held it gently. They sat quietly for a moment, listening to the sound of the river flowing by and the birds singing in the trees.

Izzy took a deep breath and then said, "Well, unfortunately, in addition to that, he has been diagnosed with Parkinson's."

Betsy started. "Oh, that is so unfair."

"That's exactly how I feel about it. I think there should be some kind of quota. If you have one chronic life-changing illness, you shouldn't have to deal with another one. But I guess it doesn't work that way." Izzy shook her head in frustration. "I hope you don't mind, but Alfreda told me you have Parkinson's. We are very new at dealing with this, and I was hoping to be able to ask you a couple of questions if you don't mind."

"I'd be glad to answer any questions you might have. We're leaving tomorrow, but anytime you need to talk, just give me a call, or text me. Are you comfortable using a computer?"

Izzy smiled at Betsy. "I'm on Twitter, Instagram, Facebook, TikTok, and YouTube."

Betsy grinned. "You're doing better than I am. It sounds like you could teach me a few things."

"When you have family and friends spread out across the country, it really helps to be able to connect with them digitally. I don't know what I would do without Facetime."

"Well, it certainly sounds like we'll be able to keep in touch easily. When was he diagnosed?"

"Just a couple of months ago. Because of his Alzheimer's, it's hard to tell sometimes when he's having difficulties and what he's feeling. It's also hard for me to see exactly what's going on."

"Why don't you give me your number, and I will look through my books and other resources and make a list for you of what I think would be most helpful."

"That would be great," said Izzy, "thank you so much."

Betsy stood up. "Come inside and I'll show you some of the books I have."

Back at the Arden RV Park ranch house, Peter pulled up in front and parked, with Smithy riding shotgun.

"I'm pretty nervous," said Smithy. "What if they all hate me?"

"Maybe some of them will," said Peter, "but that's what you have to deal with for doing what you did. Most of them are good people, so I don't think you'll have any trouble. I'm going to run in first and talk to Ben. I'll just be a few minutes, so stay here in the car and don't move. Do not move," Peter repeated firmly.

Smithy nodded and slunk down in his seat, out of sight.

As Peter trotted up the steps of the ranch house, he saw the beautiful motorcycle in front of the building. He let out a long whistle and walked slowly around the motorcycle. Looking at all the customizations on the bike, he was impressed. He whistled again. Then he glanced in the sidecar and saw it had a dog bed in it, a leash and harness, and a pair of dog goggles. He laughed and walked into the building, having a good idea who he was going to see when he got inside.

Ben was talking to a man with his back to him, a service dog at his side. Ben waved him over.

The man turned around, and Peter broke into a big grin and grabbed him in a ferocious hug. "Luke, how are you?"

Luke responded with a big hug of his own.

Peter said, "It's been too long. Last I heard you had re-upped."

"Yeah, I did," answered Luke. He paused and then placed his hand on his dog's head. "This is my service dog, Harry. I got hit with an IED and suffered a traumatic brain injury."

"Oh my God," said Peter.

"I spent quite a lot of time in rehab," said Luke, gently stroking Harry's ears. "I had to relearn how to walk and talk. Now the only real residual effect of that explosion is occasional seizures. That's why I have Harry here with me. He is a medical alert service dog. He can tell when a seizure is coming and he alerts me."

Peter said, "I've heard that some dogs can detect that.

Like bomb-sniffing dogs, I guess. So where will you be staying while you're here? You know you can always crash at my place."

"Thanks for the offer, but I'm going to stay here with Dad. The whole upper floor of the ranch house has been transformed into a family unit. There's plenty of room for me up there."

Ben said, "I'm thrilled to have him staying here with me. It's been a while since we've spent any time together."

Luke said, "It feels good to be home."

Ben put his arm around Luke and hugged him.

Peter said to Ben, "Actually, I'm here on police business."

Ben looked at him, startled. "Is it about last night?"

"Yes, I need to get your input on what happened." He turned to Luke. "I take it you know about last night?"

Luke nodded. "It was very upsetting to hear about that kind of violence taking place here. Though I understand that Izzy was one of the heroes of the night."

Peter grinned. "She definitely was that. You know Izzy?"

"Of course. Peter, don't you remember her from art class in elementary school? She was a great teacher."

Peter exclaimed, "Oh my God! Of course. I thought she looked familiar." He turned to Ben again. "I want you to know I have Smithy in the car with me."

Ben looked concerned. "Why did you bring him here? I don't want him on the grounds."

"Well, that is your prerogative, of course. But right

now, he is here to apologize. We're also trying to work something out so that he can make amends by doing community service. I have in mind three months, eight hours a day, supervised by deputy Tom. Would you be willing to consider him for any projects you have around here?"

Ben thought for a moment before saying, "There are a lot of older people in this RV Park. They come here for the peace and quiet and beauty—and for the community. They feel safe here. A number of them saw what happened the other night and have expressed to our staff how worried they are about the possibility of it happening again. I'll have to talk to them and get a sense of their feelings about having Smithy around. They may not feel safe, and their safety is my first priority."

"I can absolutely understand that. But I would ask you to at least meet with him, so he can apologize to you."

Ben said, "It's not just me. There's a lot of people he needs to apologize to."

Peter agreed. "We will get to them. I intend to take him around today and introduce him to the various people that were involved with last night. Starting with you, then Sharon, George, and Izzy."

"Well," said Ben, "he did stop Sharon from getting badly hurt by Sullivan, so maybe at least I can talk to him."

"Excellent. Thank you," Peter said.

Luke said to Peter, "I'm going to be sitting in on those meetings."

"Absolutely. I think that's a great idea."

Ben added, "Luke, people knowing that you are around will certainly make them feel safer." He then turned to Peter. "Bring Smithy up to my office when you have a moment. We'll get this over with now."

Peter nodded. "Thanks." He started to walk away.

Ben called after him, "Did you know that the women were leaving tomorrow morning?"

Peter spun around. "What?!"

"They told me a short while ago that they were planning on leaving early tomorrow morning."

"I had no idea. I need to talk to them. I need to talk to Cathy. Let me bring Smithy to talk to you, and then I'll track Cathy down." Peter strode out of the ranch house.

Luke looked at Ben. "Who's Cathy?"

"You just met her," said his father.

Smithy was still slumped down in the passenger side seat, chewing anxiously on a fingernail. Peter knocked on the window sharply, startling him. "OK, come on in. We've got to talk to Ben."

Smithy slowly extricated himself from the squad car, and they went into the ranch house together.

Ben stood in the middle of the main room, ramrod straight, his hands on his hips, looking very stern. Smithy looked at Peter hesitantly. Peter nodded.

Smithy walked over to Ben. "There's no way what I say will make any difference, or erase what happened last night," Smithy stammered, "I-I'm ashamed I was involved in all of that and that people were afraid because of something I did. I don't expect you to forgive me. I can understand if you don't, but I do want to just at least say that I'm sorry." Smithy stood quietly, waiting for Ben's response.

When he did respond, it was harsh. "What you did was pretty much unforgivable. People could have gotten seriously hurt."

Smithy nodded and dropped his head, staring at the ground.

Ben said, "Look at me when I'm talking to you."

Smithy looked up at him.

Ben continued, "As it was, they were terrified by *your* actions. Your only saving grace was at the end when you helped to resolve the conflict without bloodshed. Because of that, I'm willing to give you a second chance."

Both Peter and Smithy looked at Ben, startled. Knowing how angry Ben had been when talking to him earlier, Peter had honestly not expected this response.

Ben added, "I understand that Peter wants you to do three months of community service at thirty-five hours a week, eight hours a day. I can use you for two or three days a week so that will take care of that. Then I guess you can go around town and talk to other people about how you can help them. But at least you can get a start here. That will help people think positively about bringing you in for community service."

Smithy didn't respond for a moment. He was actually in shock. He wasn't expecting Ben to offer him hours. He stuttered, "Th-th-thank you. You won't regret giving me this chance."

"I'd better not." Looking at Smithy straight in the face, Ben then said, "There won't be another chance."

Smithy said, "I understand." He hesitated and then reached out his hand. There was a slight pause before Ben shook it.

Ben said, "Now it's time for you to go down to the campsite and apologize to Sharon, George, and Izzy. Peter will drive you down."

Luke had been standing quietly this entire time, with his arms folded, listening to what was going on. Now he nodded to Smithy. "I am Ben's son, Luke. You'd better believe I'll have my eye on you. We want you to know that we will hold you to this commitment."

Smithy replied, "I understand that. Thank you."

Peter turned to Smithy and said, "OK, let's get going."

Peter knocked on Izzy's door. She had just gotten back from her talk with Betsy and was looking at some of the books Betsy had given her. The unexpected knock on the door startled her. But then she glanced outside through the peephole and saw Peter. She opened the door with a bright smile and started to say something to him when she realized that Smithy was standing behind him. Her smile froze.

Then she got right in Smithy's face. "What the hell do you think you were doing last night? You scared the hell out of Sharon and George, and me for that matter. You could have gotten yourself shot. I don't understand it."

She was so angry she started shaking her finger at him. Smithy looked embarrassed. But beyond that, there was something else in his face. As he was listening to her, he realized that nobody had ever cared enough about him to scold him about anything, to take the time to try to help him be a better person. As Izzy reamed him out, he realized that she cared about him. Even more than that, she actually "saw" him, though he had tried hard all his life to be invisible. It was a shock to his system.

"I'll try to do better. I promise," he said, "I will prove to you that I can be a better person because you believe that I can be."

Izzy stopped in mid-rant and stared at him.

"I remember how much your class meant to me when I was in school. It was the high point of my week. I also recall there were times I didn't have anything to eat and you shared your lunch with me."

Peter stood there and watched the dynamics of this conversation with a bemused look on his face. He was thinking this idea just might work. He then said, "OK, well you got that out of your system, Izzy. I wanted to let you know Smithy has been assigned community service to make amends for what happened last night. Ben has some jobs here at the ranch but wants to make sure everybody is okay with having Smithy around. He will be under the supervision of my deputy. Are you comfortable with that?"

"I think I would be fine with that," said Izzy. "In fact, if you need some community service projects, he could probably help out at Joan's nonprofit. A lot of the kids spend their time in there doing artwork. He's a talented artist. I think he'd be good at that."

Peter said, "I'll keep that in mind and talk to Joan and see what she thinks."

Izzy added, "I could really use someone to take my husband back and forth to doctors' appointments too. That would be a tremendous help."

Peter said, "I think that can be arranged."

"Good," said Izzy. "Now I need to take a nap, so skedaddle."

As Pete and Smithy started to leave, Izzy touched Peter's sleeve. "I appreciate you stopping by and having him apologize."

Impulsively Peter reached over and hugged her. "I'm glad we stopped by too."

After saying goodbye to Izzy, Peter and Smithy moved on to Sharon and George. Peter warned Smithy that this might be a difficult visit, given the attack on Sharon. Peter stepped in front of Smithy to knock on the door. They heard dogs barking.

Smithy asked Peter, "Do you think those dogs will remember me and try to bite me?"

"I'd be more worried about George." Peter knocked on the door again.

George opened it, saw Smithy, and immediately got very angry. "What the fuck are you doing here?" He scowled, his hands curling into hard fists.

CHAPTER 19

Peter stood calmly in front of Smithy and faced George. "Smithy is here to apologize for last night—"

George interrupted him, "He can never apologize for last night. That's bullshit. You should see the bruises on Sharon. Her arms are all swollen and purple."

He tried to step around Peter to get to Smithy, but Peter adroitly blocked him. "We want to talk to you and Sharon."

"Sharon is in no condition to talk to anyone, especially you," he looked pointedly at Smithy.

"I would like to talk to him," said Sharon as she stepped up, beside George. "Come on in." George started to protest, but Sharon put her hand on his arm, "This is important to me; it'll help with the nightmares."

George hesitated and then stepped aside.

"You're having nightmares?" asked Peter, gently.

"Yes, horrible ones."

George added, "She woke up screaming a couple of times last night."

Peter winced. "I have the name of a great therapist in town who helps people who've been victims of violent crime."

"We don't need a therapist. We just need to get the hell out of here and go home." George scowled again.

Peter talked directly to Sharon. "Sometimes it takes more than just changing locations to get through it."

"I understand that. Please give me the name. If I'm not able to do it here, at least I can get a reference to someone in our hometown."

"Good idea I'll give you the name and number."

Both pointedly ignored George, who was sputtering in frustration.

Peter introduced Smithy to Sharon. "This is Smithy. He wants to talk to you about last night. He wants to make an apology."

George snorted, "Like that does a fucking lot of good. What difference does that make after the fact when he's already terrorized my wife. I could have lost her."

Sharon said, "Now, George, this is the guy who helped me last night. If you remember correctly, he didn't say anything when you let go of the dogs, and then he saved me when that other guy was about to hit me full in the face. This guy, Smithy is it? He grabbed his arm and stopped him. The least I can do is listen to what he has to say."

She nodded to Peter and Smithy and said, "Come on in."

They entered the RV. The dogs immediately raced up to them, sniffing them carefully and walking in circles around them. One of them growled softly.

"George," said Sharon, "please put Hansel and Gretel in the bedroom."

George looked at Sharon, Peter, and Smithy before saying, "I'll be right back."

Sharon replied, "I think we can count on that."

George disappeared into the back.

Sharon sighed. "Would you sit down? How about some coffee?"

"No thank you," said Peter.

"Don't mind George. He was absolutely terrified last night for me, as I was, to tell you the truth."

Peter said, "Your husband said that you were very bruised from last night. How are you feeling?"

"I am very stiff, and I definitely have some major bruises on my arms. With that said, however, it could have been much, much worse." She looked at Smithy calmly and waited for him to say something.

He glanced at Peter, then looked nervously around for George, who was still with the dogs in the back room.

He swallowed noisily and then focused on Sharon. "I don't know how to begin to tell you how sorry I am. I made a huge mistake. I got involved in something that was way beyond what I thought it was going to be. I stupidly didn't think about the people who were going to be affected by what we were planning—trying to steal some things that we could sell for cash. It was only when I saw Sullivan grab you…"

Peter, standing behind Smithy, saw Sharon's face twist

in pain as she jerked back slightly in her chair. He realized it was way too soon, for her to be talking about this.

He started to interrupt, but she put her hand up to stop him. "Go ahead, Smithy."

"I realized I couldn't go along with it. I had to stop it somehow. I had to jump in."

Sharon looked at Smithy. "I remember you very clearly stopping him from hitting me. I saw his fist go back, and I looked in his eyes and they were dead, like a shark's. And I was thinking this is going to be bad—really, really bad. Then all of a sudden, I saw you grab his arm and pull it back. And he was off me. You definitely saved me, and I'll never forget that."

Smithy looked embarrassed. "Peter was there, too, and of course Izzy."

Sharon nodded. "I know."

There was a moment of silence. Peter shifted his weight. "Smithy will be doing some community service for us over the next couple of months. I don't know what your situation is going to be. Whether you are going to be staying on for a while or leaving soon, but he will be available if you have any projects you need done. He'll be under the supervision of my deputy."

Having returned in the midst of the conversation, George jumped in, "Well I'm glad he'll be doing something to try to repay what he did. Community service is a beginning. I'd like to see him do some time too." He put his arm around Sharon. "What about the other guy?"

"He is out on bail right now," said Peter. He saw their

reaction to that news and reassured them that Sullivan's lawyer had him on a short leash, since he was financially responsible for him.

Peter thanked Sharon and George, and so did Smithy. They got in the car and started to head back toward the ranch house, when Peter saw Cathy and Linda puttering around their RV. He pulled over, told Smithy to stay put, and got out.

"Hello," he said, walking up to Linda and Cathy.

"Hi, Peter," exclaimed Linda, glancing over at Cathy.

"Hello," said Cathy, feeling a bit awkward.

"Ben told me that you're leaving tomorrow morning?"

Cathy said, "Yes, we need to get on the road. We still need to spread our friend's ashes up at the Ghost Ranch before we head back east."

"Do you think we could take a walk right now, just a short walk? I want to talk to you about some things."

Cathy replied, "Well this is not really a good time for me. We have to get a lot of things together to get ready to hit the road early tomorrow morning."

Linda cut in, "I think we have things pretty much under control here. In fact, I'm going to go inside in a few minutes and have a cup of tea with Betsy. So why don't you two take a walk. Take your time and enjoy this beautiful day. We'll see you in a bit." Before Cathy could protest, Linda disappeared into the RV, where she quickly updated Betsy on what was going on.

"Cathy," said Peter as they strolled toward the river, "we have only known each other for a week or so. But on some level, I feel like I have already known you for much longer. I have that kind of comfort with you. I'm able to truly be myself with you. I'm not able to do that with many people. I feel an extraordinarily strong connection to you." He turned to face her and took her hands in his.

A slight breeze tousled Cathy's curls. She looked at him. "Peter, I live across the country from you. Flying back and forth is just not really a doable thing for me—financially, emotionally, physically." She sighed. "I lost my husband to cancer. I really don't want to feel pain like that again. I'm sorry. I like you a lot, too, and I feel very comfortable with you, but I just don't think this thing between us is something I want to pursue. I am content with my life as it is right now." She started to head back to the camper as her eyes filled up a bit.

He asked gently, "Then why are you crying?"

"It's the wind," she said, hurriedly wiping her eyes.

He softly touched her face. "I've told you how I feel about you. But you don't want to take a chance to see if there's something better on the other side for us? Life is just too short to let it go when someone crosses your path with whom you feel this kind of connection. It just doesn't happen that often. You know where I live. You know how to get in touch with me. Call me, text me, email me, skywrite me if you ever change your mind." Peter kissed her cheek and then turned and walked away.

Cathy stared after him. She wanted to call out to him, to tell him to come back. But her emotions felt so jumbled up. She wasn't sure whether she wanted to do it because she was so hurt and sad or because he was the best thing in her life and he was walking away, out of her life. She stood there for a long time, looking after him even though he'd gone out of sight.

CHAPTER 20

Inside the RV Betsy and Linda, who had only heard the last part of the conversation, were stunned. They stared at each other.

Linda asked Betsy, "What do we do? Is there some way we can help?"

Betsy answered, "I don't think we should interfere. I mean, after all, this is her decision. I think we should respect her feelings, try to understand what she's going through, and let it go."

Linda said sadly, "Maybe you're right. I hate to see something like this that has so much potential fall apart. But it is her life, after all."

They sat down at the dining room table. "Well, this sucks," said Betsy.

"You're not kidding. I was getting my rom-com needs met by watching those two. I thought for sure there was going to be a happy ending. He's such a good guy." Linda looked very sad.

They heard a slight noise outside the door. Cathy

climbed slowly into the RV, saw them sitting there, and burst into tears. Betsy and Linda quickly got up and put their arms around her. They held her tightly as she sobbed.

"Wh-what am I doing?" she stammered as she gulped her tears down. "Did you hear what he said to me?"

Betsy answered, "Only the very last part."

"He said he's never met anyone who affected him like me. I feel the same way. But I'm so afraid of it. I'm afraid of him."

Startled, Linda asked, "What do you mean you're afraid of him?"

"No, not in the way you think. I'm afraid because I feel like I could really fall deeply in love with him, and then what if it ends? What happens if we're together for years and then he dies? How do I deal with that kind of pain?"

Betsy said, "Cathy, I think you're getting a little bit ahead of yourself when you're talking about him dying."

Linda said thoughtfully, "It must have been very painful for you when your husband died."

"It was." Cathy wiped her eyes. "Look at me. I'm sixty-three. I shouldn't be dealing with these kinds of emotions when I'm this old."

Betsy said gently, "I don't think there's an age cutoff for falling in love."

"I barely know Peter, but I already feel a powerful connection to him," murmured Cathy. "What if how I'm feeling is not real but just some biochemical physical reaction to him?"

"Well," commented Linda, "you really won't know

unless you give it a chance. But one of the advantages of being our age is that we've been through a lot. A lot of experiences, a lot of emotions. There's a wisdom that comes with our years."

"If you've been paying attention," threw in Betsy.

Linda smiled at her. "Yes, if you've been paying attention to your life, hopefully you will have the information to know what is real and what isn't real."

"How did you leave it?" asked Betsy.

"Well, basically I said there was no future. That I was going home and that would be it." Cathy burst into fresh tears.

Betsy said, "Well you know you can always contact him. It's not like going home to West Chester is falling off the ends of the earth."

Half laughing and half crying, Cathy added, "He said I could skywrite him if I wanted to get in contact with him."

"There you go," said Linda. "He certainly is leaving the door open, or at least the sky. That's a good sign."

"I just don't know," said Cathy. "I feel so confused right now."

Betsy said, "Go take a shower, and afterward we'll head up to the ranch house, have a nice dinner, and say goodbye to everybody."

Charlie who had managed to get up on Linda's bed was sleeping quietly. Now he slipped off the bed and walked up to Cathy and put his head on her leg, looking up at her with soft brown eyes. He stared at her until she smiled at him and stroked his ears.

"He's such a good boy," she said. "How could anybody have dumped this wonderful dog in the middle of nowhere?"

Linda said, "I can't even think about that and what he went through. I get too upset."

Cathy nodded sadly before going to take a shower.

CHAPTER 21

On the outskirts of town, Benedict pulled up in front of Sullivan's house. As he got out of his car, he nearly tripped over an empty six-pack of beer. He kicked it to one side and knocked on the door.

A gruff voice inside called, "What the fuck do you want?"

Benedict called back, "Sullivan, I need to talk to you."

Sullivan's shadowy figure appeared behind the screen door. Bleary eyed, he kicked the door open for Benedict. "This better be good."

As Benedict entered the house, he was unnerved to see that Sullivan had a gun shoved in his waistband. "What's that for?"

"What do you think?" sneered Sullivan.

"Look," said Benedict, "you're out on bail right now—bail I posted for you. If you get caught with a gun, that's it; you go straight to jail. I won't be able to help you then."

Sullivan said, "Then me and your wife will have to have a little talk."

Benedict looked around for some place clean to sit but did not see anything remotely sanitary, so he remained standing. "It is no use threatening me. I've already talked to her about everything, and she knows the whole story."

"Really? She knows the whole story? Has she seen the pictures?"

Benedict felt sick to his stomach but kept all expression off his face. "She knows the whole story," he repeated firmly.

Sullivan smiled nastily. "Well, we'll see." He took a swig from a half-empty bottle of Southern Comfort. He swished it around his mouth and then spit into the sink.

Benedict said, "I think it's better if you left this town and never came back."

Sullivan grinned. "Now why would I do that?"

"Because I'm going to give you a lot of money to do just that. To take the money and go, and never come back. If you do that, that's it—we have no more dealings. You don't go to jail, nothing happens to you, you go free, but you never come back here. If you do come back, you go immediately to jail and you'll serve the full sentence for what you did the other night."

Sullivan took another swig. "Is the judge on board with this?"

"Let's just say he owes me a couple of favors and I'm calling them in. So, yes, he's on board with this."

"How much?"

"$10,000."

"Cash?"

"If that's the way you want it," said Benedict, "then that is the way you'll get it."

Sullivan stared at Benedict. "And I never have to come back to this shithole?"

"Nope, but this is a short-term deal. You say yes now and we have a deal. You wait even half an hour and this deal is off the table."

"Did you grow some balls overnight?" asked Sullivan.

Benedict ignored him.

"What about Smithy?" asked Sullivan.

"None of your concern. This deal is just for you. Do you want it or not?"

"I guess there's nothing really holding me here. Yeah, I'll take it."

Benedict added, "In addition, I get all the pictures."

Sullivan walked over to a beat-up dresser, yanked open a drawer, and took out a tattered envelope stuffed full of pictures. "Here you go. Enjoy yourself."

Benedict's hands were shaking slightly as he took the envelope. "I will have the money for you tomorrow morning. I'll drop it off here."

Sullivan squinted at Benedict. "You don't want anybody to see us together, right?"

"Right," answered Benedict sharply. "I'll be here at nine tomorrow morning. After we meet, I expect you to be on the road within the hour."

He turned to go out the door. Sullivan suddenly grabbed him and slapped him on the back almost knocking him over. "Thanks, Benny. You really came through for me. I won't forget it."

Benedict turned and looked at him seriously. "I want you to forget it. Forget we ever knew each other."

Sullivan looked startled. "I guess I can understand that. You got it." He clapped him on the back again, then turned back into the house. Benedict walked to his car feeling shaky, but also like a huge weight had been lifted off him. He jammed on the gas and then took off at high speed. He cranked up the stereo, feeling exhilarated and thinking it was all going to work out.

On the way back from the RV park, Smithy asked Peter if he could stay in one of the empty cells since he had nowhere to go other than sleeping on the street. Peter okayed his request, feeling it would also be a good way to keep an eye on Smithy to make sure he stayed on the straight and narrow.

After getting Smithy settled, Tom followed Peter into his office, saying nonchalantly, "I hear there's a party tonight."

Peter looked up from his computer. "You certainly have your ear to the ground. How did you know about the party?"

"Oh, you know I hear things." He looked out the window and added, "By the way, Elizabeth stopped by. She was looking for you. She said she had some information about Sullivan she thought you needed to hear."

Peter groaned. "What's your read on that?"

"I think she was legit. She seemed anxious and really wanted to talk to you."

"OK, I'm going to hold you to that assessment. What's her number?"

After Tom gave him the number, Peter called her, and she immediately picked up.

"Hi, Peter. We need to talk."

Peter said, "I understand you have some information about Sullivan? Why don't you come down to the station and we'll talk here?"

"No, I need someplace more private. How about the diner at the end of town, Miller's? They are never crowded and have plenty of booths."

"Fine. Half an hour?"

Elizabeth agreed and Peter disconnected. He said to Tom, "I want you with me as a witness."

"You got it."

By the time Peter and Tom got to the diner, Elizabeth was already there in a back booth. She stood up and gave both men a kiss on the cheek. A waitress wandered over, but Elizabeth just waved her off.

"So, what's up, Elizabeth?" asked Peter.

She looked down at the table for a moment, and Peter noticed that she was twisting her hands together tightly.

"I've thought long and hard about whether I should tell you this. But I thought you should have all the facts. I'm assuming that you're wondering why Benedict is representing Sullivan."

"Yes."

"Well," she continued, "he has something on Benedict. Something pretty big."

Peter and Tom glanced at each other.

"What does he have?" asked Peter.

"Will this have to come out?" asked Elizabeth.

"I won't lie to you," said Peter. "It might. I don't know exactly what you're talking about, but it may have to come out. We'll see."

"If it comes out, it'll ruin Benedict personally and probably professionally."

Peter waited for Elizabeth to go on. Suddenly she stood up quickly. "I can't do this. Not right now. I'm just not sure. I don't want to be responsible for ruining his life."'

"Elizabeth..." Peter stood up and reached out to her, but she was already on her way out of the restaurant.

"Damn it," said Peter. "What the hell was that about?" As they left the restaurant, he said to Tom, "It looks like we're going to have to pay a visit to Mr. Sullivan."

Tom nodded. "I'll call it in and get some backup."

A couple of miles away, Benedict had driven into town and was now parked near his wife's nonprofit. He walked in and spotted her in her office. He knocked on the door. She looked up in surprise.

"What are you doing here?" Joan asked.

It occurred to Benedict that he very rarely stopped by. Quite honestly, he pretty much ignored her work. Now as he glanced around, he saw little kids fingerpainting and reading. Some were eating snacks. Others looked like they were just dozing in comfortable kid-size chairs. He wished he had a place like this to escape to when he was growing up. His house had been filled with the loud voices and bitter words of his parents who argued constantly.

He turned to Joan. "I'm sorry to bother you but we need to talk."

Joan replied, "Elizabeth stopped by a little while ago."

Benedict felt a chill go down his spine and briefly considered lying about everything but then thought enough is enough. "Did she say anything to you?"

"No, but she seemed frazzled." She thought for a moment before saying, "Maybe anxious would be a better word for it. She played with the kids for a while and then left. She did make a sizeable donation before she left." Joan sat down at her desk. "What's going on, Benny?"

He winced at her use of his childhood name. She knew how much he hated it. The fact that she was using it showed there was anger rumbling beneath her calm demeanor. Joan indicated he should sit down in the chair facing her desk.

He hesitated. "Maybe we should go someplace more private to talk."

"That bad, huh? Is this about Sullivan's sister and you having an affair?"

Stunned, Benedict dropped into a chair and stared at her with his mouth open. "How did you know? Oh, I get it. It was Elizabeth. She told you."

"Nope, she didn't say a word. I've known for about a week. This is a small town, Benny. Sullivan's sister is a good friend of my hair stylist. I heard them talking when I was getting my hair done. The whole story came out." She looked down at her desk and then up again at Benedict.

"I've been dealing with the pain and trying to decide what to do."

For one of the few times in his life, Benedict felt shame. He put his head down in his hands and said, "I'm so sorry, Joan."

She stood up and put her hand on his shoulder. "I'm sorry, too, Benny, but you realize this is the end of the road for our relationship. I want a divorce."

He said slowly, almost under his breath, "I will make sure you're taken care of financially."

She laughed. "If you remember, we don't have a prenup. So, yes, I will be taken care of financially. I will make damn sure of that. Now I want you to leave. I have a lot of things I have to get done today. I need to talk to my lawyer. I also want you out of the house."

Benedict said in surprise, "It's my house."

"Not anymore," Joan shot back at him.

CHAPTER 22

Peter and Tom drove up the deeply rutted driveway. They parked out of sight of Sullivan's house.

"Backup is on the way," Tom said. "They're about ten minutes out."

"We'll wait for them," Peter said. "We've known Sullivan all his life. As much of a jerk as he is, he's never used a gun. But let's not take any chances." After getting an update that the team was now only a few minutes away, Peter ordered his team, "No sirens and come in on foot." He and Tom got out of the car. They unholstered their guns and switched their body cameras on. Peter waited to move until he saw a team member signaling from the woods next to Sullivan's house.

They approached the house carefully. As they got close, Peter called, "Sullivan! It's Chief Peter. We need to talk."

They saw a shadow moving inside the house. Tom felt his mouth go dry. He glanced over at Peter, who motioned that he should move away from him and into a flanking position.

Peter felt his radio vibrate, indicating backup was in position. "Sullivan!" He felt his adrenaline pounding in his veins. With his senses on high alert, he put his hand on his gun. He saw the shadow move suddenly to one side of the window. "Down!" he yelled at Tom, who hit the ground just as a bullet came through the window.

"Sullivan, don't be stupid," Peter shouted. "Throw the gun out of the front door and come out with your hands up."

"Fuck you," cursed Sullivan. He shot through the front door.

"Jesus Christ," Peter said. "We just wanted to talk. You are making this really difficult for yourself." Peter's team moved in closer to the house, creating a perimeter. Tom crept to the back of the house. There was a long silence. Peter started to call out his name again, when Sullivan suddenly came around the side of the house, taking Peter by surprise. He whipped around. Sullivan raised his gun and shot him.

Peter felt a powerful blow to his arm, then a searing, burning pain. Looking down, he saw the sleeve of his shirt quickly turning red, bright red. He had a moment of disbelief, and then he felt a surge of adrenaline. He looked up at Sullivan, and quickly tossed his gun from one hand to the other. He pointed it at Sullivan and ordered, "Drop your gun now!"

Sullivan just laughed, raising his gun again. Tom stepped out from behind the house and pressed his gun hard against Sullivan's back. "I wouldn't do that if I were you. Drop the gun."

Sullivan smirked, tossed his gun down and said to Peter, "Your playmate is sharper than I thought he was."

Peter's team surrounded Sullivan, cuffed him, and read him his rights.

Feeling a little weak, Peter leaned against the house. Tom and another police officer rushed over to him. Tom put his arm around Peter and half carried him back to the squad car. There, he grabbed the first aid kit and pressed bandages against the gunshot wound, trying to stem the flow of blood. He settled Peter in the back seat while two deputies got in the front, powered up the car, and took off, with lights flashing and sirens blaring. One officer called in the emergency, letting the hospital trauma center know it was the chief of police who had been shot. Immediately the word went out to all the police forces in the area. The route from Sullivan's house to the hospital was soon lined with police cars, making sure Peter got to the hospital as fast as possible. Tom held on to Peter closely, swapping out bandages as they became sodden with blood. Peter had his eyes closed, looking very pale. Tom shouted to the driver, "Step on it!" The driver mashed the gas pedal to the floor as they roared through the countryside. Tom murmured to Peter, "Hang in there. We're almost at the hospital."

Peter mumbled something. Tom asked him to repeat it, he mumbled it again.

Tom put his head close to Peter's lips. "Say it one more time."

"Call Cathy. Let her know where I am."

"Will do," Tom reassured him. Peter drifted off again. Tom said to the driver, "Can't you go any faster?"

They shot through town to the hospital, pulling up to the ER, tires squealing. A trauma team was ready and waiting for Peter.

Immediately they opened the back doors of the patrol car and gently lifted him out, moving him onto a gurney and into the hospital as fast as they could. They quickly attached monitors to check his vitals and got an IV ready to begin a transfusion. Peter lay very still on the gurney.

Tom stood outside for a few minutes, trying to gather his wits. He was intensely shaken up. So were the two cops who had been in the car with him. As they stood there, more police cars pulled up outside the hospital, with members of different forces rushing to see how Peter was. Tom elected to go inside and find out for himself. At first, the intake nurse would not let him near Peter but finally relented when he explained he was as close to being Peter's family as he had in the area.

Peter had a private hospital room. When Tom entered, he was sleeping peacefully, even with the IV in his arm. He was still very pale, almost bone white. The doctor came in while Tom was there. "How's he doing?" asked Tom.

"Peter lost a lot of blood," the doctor answered, "and is going to need additional transfusions."

"I have the same blood type. I want to donate blood if that would be okay."

"More than OK," said the doctor. "We're chronically short of blood, so any donations are welcome."

"I'll ask the officers outside to donate too," said Tom.

"Excellent. We will be keeping him for the next day or two for observation."

"Anything to worry about?" asked Tom.

"Just being careful," responded the doctor.

Tom walked outside and updated the crowd of well-wishers. He asked for blood donors, and a long line immediately formed.

One of Peter's team fought his way through the crowd to Tom. "I am going to run out to Peter's house and take care of his dogs."

"Great, thanks for thinking of that," Tom said. "I've got to call Ben out at the RV park and let him know what happened."

"What about Sullivan?" asked another cop. "He's at the station house now."

"Keep him under lock and key and double up on security," ordered Tom. "And get Smithy out of there. Give him some money to stay in a motel tonight. I don't want him anywhere near Sullivan."

"Got it," said the officer.

Tom walked a distance away from the crowd and called Ben.

Ben immediately picked up. "Are you coming to the party tonight?" he asked Tom cheerfully. Tom filled him in on what had just happened. Ben cursed quietly and asked, "Is Peter going to be all right?"

Tom answered, "Yes, the doctor seems to think so."

"I'll let the people here know," Ben reassured him.

"He especially asked to let Cathy know."

"I'll tell her personally."

Ben disconnected and went to find Luke. Together they went to look for Cathy. They found her with Linda and Betsy at the RV, getting ready for the farewell dinner.

Betsy was surprised to see them but invited them in. "What's up? We're just getting ready to come up to the ranch house."

Ben said, "We have something to tell you. Where are Linda and Cathy?"

"Linda is walking Charlie. She should be back any moment, and Cathy is in my bedroom changing. Can you tell me what's going on?"

"I'd rather tell all of you at once."

At that point Linda came back with Charlie, and Betsy called for Cathy to join them.

Once they were all present, Ben began telling them. "I wanted to let you know that something happened today. First of all, Peter is OK."

Cathy physically started when she heard Peter's name. "What do you mean he's OK?" she asked sharply.

Ben calmly continued, "He and his team went out to talk to Sullivan at his house. There was an altercation and Sullivan shot Peter."

There was a collective gasp among the three women.

Cathy said, "Oh my God."

Ben reassured them. "Peter is OK. Apparently, he did lose some blood, but it sounds like his whole department has donated blood for him. They will keep him there one or two nights, just to make sure everything is fine."

Cathy felt suddenly shaky and abruptly sat down. Linda put her hand on her shoulder.

Ben said, "Now a few of us are going over to visit him and see how he's doing. It will be a very short visit, as we don't want to tire him out. Alfreda has kindly agreed to drive us over in her van. Luke's coming. I think Izzy, too. Do you want to come with us?"

"Absolutely," said Betsy and Linda in unison. Cathy hesitated.

"Peter specifically asked me to let you know what happened," Ben told Cathy.

She took a deep breath and nodded firmly, "I'll come too."

"OK, we will leave in twenty minutes," Ben said. "Alfreda will pick you up."

Betsy asked, "Given the circumstances, I'm assuming our farewell dinner is on hold."

"Actually" said Ben, "a number of the staff and community members have been cooking for hours, so we're going to go ahead with the dinner. I don't want to waste people's efforts or food. It'll be a different feel of course. But at least Peter is doing well and recovering so that's a positive and something to keep in mind." He and Luke turned and started to leave.

"Wait a minute," asked Linda. "What about Sullivan? What happened to him?"

Luke said shortly, "He's been arrested and is probably going to be transferred to a maximum security prison."

"They won't allow him out on bail like before?" Linda asked.

Luke answered, "Not for shooting a police officer. They're going to throw the book at him now. I think it will be a long time before he sees the outside of a jail." Luke and Ben then left.

Betsy, Cathy, and Linda quickly got ready to go to the hospital. Before they departed, Linda looked at Cathy and asked, "Are you sure?"

"I'm not sure of anything right now," said Cathy, "but I'm going to the hospital even though this is exactly what I was afraid of."

They heard a horn and walked out to the van.

It was a quiet group that rode to the hospital. Each person was caught up in their own thoughts and emotions. Harry sat on the seat next to Luke, who had his arm around him.

As Alfreda pulled up to the hospital entrance, Betsy asked, "Shouldn't we have our own parking spot by now? We've been here enough times in the past week." It broke the tension and everyone laughed.

As they all got out of the van, Tom spotted them and made his way through the crowd. He informed them, "Peter is doing well. I'll take you to his room." As they walked inside, he continued, "Most of the time he's drifting in and out of sleep so don't be surprised if he nods off."

"That's quite a crowd out there," Betsy commented.

Tom replied, "Peter is well-liked and respected. Once word got out that he had been shot, every available police officer wanted to help. When they found out he needed blood, they immediately lined up to donate."

"Tom," Ben asked, "Have you contacted his daughters yet?"

"Thanks for reminding me. I called them initially when I didn't have a lot of information on Peter's condition. I need to call them again and give them an update."

At that moment, the doctor emerged from Peter's room.

Ben asked, "How's he doing, doctor?"

"Better than expected. He's lost quite a bit of blood, but we've given him transfusions and that's helped stabilize him." He looked at the group of people in front of him. Seeing Harry for the first time, he started to say something.

Luke pointed to Harry's service dog harness. "By law, he's allowed to go where I go." Luke's tone left no doubt that he was going to have Harry with him, no matter what.

The doctor nodded. "I'd like you to go in two at a time and keep it very short. He tires quickly."

"Will he be all right?" asked Betsy.

"Yes, he should be fine. But he needs to take it easy for a couple of days. We're going to keep him here at least one or two nights to make sure there's no complications. But he's generally in good health, so there shouldn't be any problems."

Tom quickly assumed the role of hospital visitor traffic cop. "Cathy, why don't you and Ben go in first. Then Linda and Alfreda, Luke and Izzy, Betsy and I will go in last."

Cathy and Ben entered Peter's room. The overhead

lights were low, but they were still able to see him lying under the sheets. He grunted in pain as he moved his legs restlessly. He suddenly became aware that there were people in the room with him.

He turned his head, "Hello, Ben."

"How are you feeling?" Ben asked,

"Like I've been run over by a truck. It's good to see you. Thanks for coming." He paused. "Is Cathy here?"

"I'm right here Peter." Cathy walked to his bedside and took his hand.

"I didn't see you at first. I'm glad you're here, Cathy."

"I am too," she said, leaning down to kiss his cheek. "You have a lot of friends who care about you."

"Friend?" he looked at her solemnly.

"Friend," She repeated.

He closed his eyes and sighed.

There was a knock, and Tom peered around the door. "Times up," he said.

Cathy squeezed his hand. "Feel better soon."

Linda and Alfreda were next. Linda sat quietly next to Peter, holding his hand while Alfreda bustled around straightening and rearranging things. Peter enjoyed watching her. Her chattiness and busyness soothed and comforted him. He soon dozed off. Tom peeked in as Linda and Alfreda were getting ready to leave.

"He's asleep," whispered Linda. Tom glanced over at Peter, who was beginning to snore softly.

"I think I'll suggest that Luke, Izzy and Betsy hold off on visiting him," Tom said.

Alfreda leaned over and kissed Peter on the cheek. They were about to leave the room when Elizabeth burst in.

"Oh my God," she said loudly. Peter started and opened his eyes. Elizabeth went over to Peter and took his hand. "I am so sorry. This was all my fault."

"How's that?" demanded Tom.

"I knew Sullivan had something on Benedict. I even knew what it was, but I hesitated to tell you and now Peter's been shot."

Peter asked, "What did he have on Benedict?"

"My brother had been having an affair with Sullivan's sister. Sullivan threatened to show Joan some nude pictures he had taken of the two of them. Joan and Benedict don't have a prenup, so he could potentially lose a huge portion of his assets." Elizabeth held onto his arm. "If I had told you at the restaurant yesterday, none of this would have happened. I made this stupid promise to Benedict, and it got me confused with where my loyalties lay. The reality is I should have told you. You got shot because of me."

Peter grabbed her hand and pulled her close to him. Fiercely he said, "This doesn't have anything to do with you. It's all on Sullivan. He made the choice. He picked up the gun, pointed it at me, and pulled the trigger. Nothing to do with you at all."

Elizabeth closed her eyes for a moment and shook her head. "I'll try to take in what you said and remember that. I still feel responsible. Maybe it's time for me to go back to New York."

Peter said, "Thank you for coming to see me and for sharing that information. Take care of yourself, Elizabeth. I hope you find what you are looking for in New York City."

"Goodbye, Peter." She leaned over and kissed his cheek.

Tom asked, "Elizabeth, do you have a ride home?"

Elizabeth no longer looked Fifth Avenue chic, she looked tired and pale, with dark circles under her eyes. "Yes, I do. Thank you, Tom." She turned and walked out.

Luke, Izzy, Betsy, Cathy, Ben, Linda, and Alfreda had all come into the room while Elizabeth had been talking to Peter. Now everyone stood quietly in an awkward, tense silence.

"Do I know how to throw a party or what?" asked Peter.

Tom grinned. "OK, I think it's time for us to hit the road. Let's give Peter a chance to relax and get some sleep."

"Tom, stay behind for a moment, will you?" asked Peter.

CHAPTER 23

The group got back in the van. Before she started the vehicle, Alfreda asked, "Are we ready to head home?"

"Yes, I think so," said Ben, looking around at everyone to see if anyone disagreed. "Are you all right to drive, or do you want somebody else to drive?"

"I'm fine. Thanks for asking, Ben."

He sat in the front passenger seat next to her. Alfreda carefully reversed the van since there were still crowds of people around the hospital entrance. She exited the parking lot and headed home.

Meantime, Tom let Peter know he had contacted his daughters and that they would be calling him. Peter thanked him for doing that.

Then, he asked Tom about Sullivan. Tom brought him up to date. "We've contacted the judge to get upgraded charges filed against Sullivan. He has rescinded the bail, but he's also talking about recusing himself because apparently Benedict called in a favor to get the bail lowered and have himself appointed as the bondsman. The judge agreed to it. So now he feels like his head is on the chopping block."

"It is," said Peter. "He should be removed from the bench. We'll deal with that later."

"Right now, Sullivan is currently in the station jailhouse, and I've temporarily moved Smithy out to a motel."

"Good call," said Peter.

Tom concluded, "I left a message for Benedict; I haven't heard from him yet."

"He may lose his license over this," said Peter, "which would not be a great loss to the legal profession."

"No," agreed Tom. "Time now for you to rest. I've placed an officer on guard outside your room."

Peter looked at him questioningly.

"Just in case," said Tom.

Peter sank back into his pillow and closed his eyes. Tom started to leave.

"Tom, thank you for everything," Peter murmured.

"No worries," Tom answered, his hand on the door handle.

"I'm thinking... I'm thinking maybe it's time for me to retire," said Peter.

Shocked, Tom turned back to him. "What are you talking about? You are at the top of your game."

"My heart's not in it anymore."

"You just got shot," pointed out Tom. "It takes time to come back from that."

"I just think I'd like to spend some time with my daughters in San Diego."

Tom asked, "And maybe take a trip to West Chester, PA?"

"That could be in the cards. I don't know. But I think that it's time for you to take over. You're certainly more than qualified and have proven yourself repeatedly with your professionalism, dedication, and compassion. I'd have total confidence in you being the new chief of police."

"B-but…" stuttered Tom.

Peter smiled and said, "It's just something to think about. Nothing is going to happen overnight. I'm not making any rash decisions here but talk to your wife, sleep on it, and see what you think. Now go home and get some rest."

At the RV park, Alfreda maneuvered the van up the driveway to the ranch house. Ben pointed out the throngs of people that were heading toward the building, many of them carrying casseroles and bottles of wine.

Ben said, "Looks like dinner is just about to get underway."

Linda leaned forward. "Alfreda, can you give us a ride down to our RV? We need to freshen up."

"Sure, I'll be glad to. I just need to first drop off those who want to get out here." Alfreda parked in front of the ranch house, and everybody, except for Betsy, Cathy, and Linda, piled out of the van. Then she carefully drove around the groups of people walking toward the party and eventually ended up at their campsite. Alfreda parked and turned to the three women. "I am certainly going to miss all of you. Frankie is going to miss you too."

"Thank you Alfreda," Betsy said. "It's going to be tough to leave. We've really gotten to know and care about the people here."

"I hope you can come and visit sometime," Alfreda said.

"I hope so too," Betsy replied. She leaned forward and hugged Alfreda. Then the three women got out of the van and went into the RV.

Once inside, Linda said, "Dibs on the shower."

"Fine," said Betsy, "I'm after you."

Cathy said, "I guess I'm last in line."

Thirty minutes later the women were ready to go to dinner.

Linda asked, "Betsy, are you okay walking up to the ranch house?"

"I am a little shaky right now. I will need my walker, and I'll need a ride home later."

"That shouldn't be a problem," said Linda.

As they walked up to the ranch house, they saw strings of white lights hanging from every surface dancing in the soft breeze.

"Oh, how beautiful," exclaimed Betsy.

"Is this all for us?" asked Cathy incredulously. Luke and Harry appeared around the corner of the ranch house, where he had been taking the big dog for a walk.

Luke had a smile on his face. "So, what do you think?"

"It's fantastic," said Cathy. Luke came over and helped Betsy maneuver her walker up the steps.

As she thanked him, he said, "We need to put a ramp

here for easier access."

"That would be helpful," admitted Betsy.

Luke said thoughtfully, "That could be a community service project for Smithy to work on with me."

"Oh my God," said Cathy who was the first one to walk through the doors into the ranch house proper. The others followed behind her oohing and aahing at the colorful decorations, crowds of people, and tables groaning with plates of delicious food. Servers moved smoothly around the room, dispensing drinks, juices, and water.

Ben came over to them, smiling broadly. "Welcome!"

"Well, I'm flabbergasted," said Betsy. "This is so much more than I expected."

Ben was curious, "What did you expect?"

"A couple of burgers on the grill. A six-pack of beer chilling in a Styrofoam cooler. That kind of thing."

Ben laughed. "We have a couple of professional chefs camping here, who I think are trying to beat out each other. There's definitely a sense of competition in the kitchen tonight."

Alfreda suddenly appeared in front of them. She put her arm around Ben and announced, "I have a party crasher with me."

They all looked at her in surprise.

Ben said, "Everyone in the park was invited. Who would crash this party?"

"This guy," she laughed and moved aside so that they could all see Charlie standing behind her, with his tail wagging furiously.

"Charlie! How did you get out?" Linda asked. He gave a happy sigh and lay down at her feet, tail still wagging.

Cathy said, "We secured all of the RV's doors and windows."

"Uh oh," said Betsy in a very small voice. They all looked at her.

Her face flushed red with embarrassment. "I left the window in my bedroom open. I mean, the screen was there... he must have gotten up on the bed and then pushed through the screen and jumped out."

"That is one determined little dog," said Ben.

"He found his way to my RV," explained Alfreda. "I was getting ready for the party, and Frankie started barking. Then I heard Charlie. They were definitely talking to each other." She smiled at Linda. "He was probably asking Frankie if you were inside. He clearly wants to be with you 24/7."

Linda said, "That worries me. I don't want him to get hurt trying to follow me somewhere."

Luke said, "I have something that might help." He disappeared into the crowd.

Ben led the women over to the head table. "Have a seat. We'll get started with dinner in just a few minutes. And then we'll have some dancing afterward."

Cathy asked a little nervously, "You're not going to ask us to make a speech, are you?"

Ben teased, "Possibly. I'll definitely be making a few remarks. But we'll see how the evening goes."

Luke reappeared and walked up to Linda. "This is an

LED light made especially for dogs. You can attach it to either his collar or harness, and it will stay put. He's so low to the ground that he really needs to be much more visible. This will do the trick." He handed it to Linda.

She was touched by his thoughtfulness and warmly thanked him. Linda immediately put the light on Charlie's collar and turned it on. Everyone agreed that it dramatically improved Charlie's visibility.

"OK," said Ben, "Let's get dinner started." Everyone followed him to the dinner tables, and he got them settled in their assigned seats. He talked on his phone briefly. Suddenly the sound of a gong rang out over the room. Then the lights blinked quickly on and off. The crowd quieted down.

Servers began bringing plates out to the main table where the women were sitting.

"Wow, this looks amazing," said Betsy.

"It's New Mexico barbecue," said Ben, "our house specialty."

"It smells fabulous," murmured Linda.

Cathy smiled at everyone but was unusually quiet. Linda and Betsy were sitting on either side of her, and they kept glancing at her to make sure she was all right.

"I'm fine," she said quietly to both. "Just tired."

Linda said, "I guess it really is time to go home."

Cathy said, "Yes, I think so."

"We still need to go to the Ghost Ranch," Betsy reminded them.

"Yes, I'm looking forward to that." Cathy gazed around

the room. "It will be good to focus on something other than my relationship with Peter. I just hope we'll find a good spot to spread Alice's ashes."

Betsy said, "I've read so much about the Ghost Ranch. I can't wait to see it in person."

Sitting next to Linda, Luke asked her, "Have you ever been there?"

"No."

"It is beautiful. Lots of canyons and scenic overlooks. The colors are amazing, especially at dawn and dusk. Do you have a good camera?"

"Just our phones," Linda answered.

Luke winced. "A phone camera won't do it justice. I have an extra camera I can lend you."

"Thank you, Luke, but we won't be coming back this way."

"Oh," he said, somewhat startled, "I thought you were coming back to say goodbye to Peter."

Betsy caught the tail end of this conversation, "We're leaving in the morning."

"That's too bad," said Luke. "I'm sure he'll miss not seeing you before you go."

At that point, Ben stood up and cleared his throat, tapping his wine glass. The room got very quiet. "Thank you all for coming to our farewell dinner for these three wonderful women." He swung his arm around to indicate them and nearly clocked Linda, who was sitting next to him.

Luke grinned and said to Betsy, "I think Dad has had a couple of glasses of wine over his limit." Betsy laughed.

Ben continued, "They've only been here a short while, but they've quickly become an important part of our community. We've all been through a lot together, and it's tough to see them leave. Their compassion, spirit, and willingness to get involved and help out has been invaluable to our community. I hope you'll join me in giving them a round of applause and see if they are willing to make a few remarks."

Everyone applauded enthusiastically. Linda and Cathy both nudged Betsy at the same time.

"Please stand up and say something," Linda whispered. "You're a wonderful communicator."

Hesitantly, Betsy stood up. She leaned forward heavily on the table to help with her balance. She took a few deep breaths and then began talking.

CHAPTER 24

"We never intended to stop here, you know," she said with a smile. "This is like the blind date you think is going to be awful and you are really dreading it, but it turns out to be the best thing that ever happened to you. That's how we feel about this place and all of you."

Ben said, "What, that we're the worst blind date you've ever had?" His words sparked laughter from the crowd.

Betsy laughed. "No, not at all. But this was so serendipitous, so unexpected. Who knew that stopping to help a small dog with an arrow in his side would lead us to Peter, who introduced us to Ben and Alfreda. Ben made us feel truly welcome, even when we arrived in the middle of the night with an injured dog. He found us a fantastic campsite that we love. Meeting Alfreda was a godsend. She took such good care of Frankie and saved his life. Even more than that she gave him a new future. He's part of her family now." Betsy looked down the table to Alfreda and smiled at her. "We're delighted that a little dog with such a big personality, and who battled so strongly to stay alive, ended up with someone so special.

"Then of course we met up with Charlie here who has clearly adopted Linda." Laughter rippled through the group as Charlie poked his head out from under the tablecloth at the sound of his name. He had been lying under the table, hoping somebody would drop some food. He looked around at everyone, wagged his tail, and went back under the table.

"Linda and I are now talking about setting up a sanctuary for senior dogs when we get back to Pennsylvania. Dogs, like Charlie, that have been dumped or dropped off at a shelter, just as they're getting ready to enjoy their golden years. Instead, they're abandoned to the care of strangers. They deserve better. At our sanctuary, they won't have to do anything but hang out on couches, enjoy treats, and watch dog and cat videos all day. Or they can lie in a dog bed in the sunshine and enjoy its warmth. They'll be pampered and loved for the rest of their lives." She paused. "None of this would have been possible without all of you. You welcomed us, even though we were strangers in a strange land. You lifted us up and supported us when we needed help. You celebrated with us when there was something to celebrate. You made us feel at home here. Thank you."

Everybody applauded and gave her a standing ovation. "Thank you so much," she said again and sat down rather shakily. Cathy hugged her, Linda grabbed her hand and held it, and Luke gave her a high five. Betsy took a deep breath, pleased that she had been able to do it at all.

Ben stood up again. "OK," he said, "Now it's time for dessert and then dancing." Everyone cheered. The servers brought in a massive five-tier cake and put it in the middle of the table, right in front of Ben. He looked at the three women, handed the cake knife to Linda, and said, "Would you do the honors?"

"With a little help from my friends," she said. All three women held on to the knife and carefully cut the cake. Everybody lined up for a piece.

"Absolutely fabulous," said Betsy. "Devil's Food with buttercream icing—yum!"

The women spent some time wandering around, talking to people they had met. Betsy was delighted to see Izzy and gave her a big hug. "Now we are staying in touch, right?" she asked.

Izzy said, "Of course." Sharon and George were standing next to Izzy, and they also greeted Betsy warmly.

As they were talking, the band started tuning up. Ben took over the mike and announced the first song would be a line dance. There were a few groans from the crowd, but most people eagerly got onto the dance floor and into position.

Linda and Cathy looked at each other questioningly. Betsy told them she was going to sit this one out.

"Are you OK?" asked Linda.

"Yes," she answered. "I am feeling very tired, so I just need to sit down for a bit."

"OK, let me know if you want to go back to the RV."

"Thanks," answered Betsy. "I think I'm OK for a while."

Cathy and Linda walked to where people were getting into one of several parallel lines. Sharon and George spotted them and called them over. Sharon asked, "Have you ever line danced before?" Both Linda and Cathy shook their heads. Sharon said, "Oh, it's a lot of fun. Just follow us and we'll show you what to do." As she said this, the music started in earnest, and immediately Linda and Cathy were lost.

Everyone around them seemed to know the steps intuitively. Linda and Cathy stumbled around, trying not to kick each other or anybody else for that matter as they tried to learn the steps on the fly. Within minutes they were both sweating heavily from the exertion. They suddenly realized they were standing in front of a large mirror. The sight of themselves as they tried to learn the steps cracked them up.

Linda called over to Cathy, "We look like we're being attacked by an army of ants."

Cathy said, "I think it's more like we're trying to stomp grapes into wine." But the music was infectious, and everybody was having fun so Linda and Cathy just let themselves go with the flow and stopped worrying about getting the steps right. Laughing, kicking, and stomping, they had a wonderful time. They danced a couple of numbers but then felt that they were winding down energy-wises.

Cathy leaned against Linda. "I think I'm done."

Linda said, "I think I'm done too. Let's collect Betsy

and Charlie and head for home." They worked their way through the crowd and saw Betsy and Izzy talking.

Linda waved to them. "Betsy, we've had it for the night; we're going to head home. Do you need a ride?"

Betsy hesitated and then said, "Yes, I do."

"OK, let me get that for you." Linda walked over to Ben. "Can we find a ride for Betsy?"

"Sure. Let me get somebody." He called over to Luke to see if he could drive Betsy home.

Luke said, "Of course." He asked Betsy, "Are you comfortable riding in a motorcycle sidecar?"

She looked at him and started laughing. "I've never been in one, but I rode on an ATV this week for the first time, so I think it'll be fine."

Luke got Betsy settled in the sidecar, with Harry sitting in front of her. Linda and Cathy came out to watch and take selfies.

"We'll be home shortly," said Linda. They watched as Luke, Betsy, and Harry slowly drove down the drive toward their RV.

"I just want to say good night to Ben," said Cathy.

The women retraced their steps into the ranch house, spotted Ben talking to Alfreda, and walked over to them.

"We just wanted to say good night and thank you for the best party ever," exclaimed Linda.

"Thank you so much," echoed Cathy, hugging both of them. She could feel herself beginning to tear up at the thought of leaving this remarkable group of people.

Cathy and Linda collected Charlie, tying a scarf around

his collar to use as a leash so that he wouldn't catch the scent of some animal and run after it into the night. They were about halfway home and just chatting when Linda happened to glance up.

"Oh my God," she said, stopping stock-still in the driveway.

Cathy asked, "What is it?"

Linda just pointed upward. Cathy looked up and gasped. There was little ambient light, so the sky was very dark. It arced like a giant bowl from horizon to horizon, as far as the eye could see. Overhead the night sky was filled with thousands of stars, so many it was dizzying to look at them. Cathy and Linda held on to each other as they stared up at the awesome sight. They drank it in until they heard Luke's motorcycle on his way back. It broke the spell. He waved as he went by. The two women giggled when they saw Harry sitting very tall and proud in the sidecar, with his goggles on.

At the RV they found Betsy already in bed with a cup of tea. They crowded into her bedroom, with Charlie eyeing the bed.

"No way," Linda looked sternly at him. He sighed and lay down next to her feet.

"Luke was really good," said Betsy. "He found the screen window outside that Charlie went through and replaced it back in its track. Thank goodness Charlie didn't get hurt when he made that jump."

Cathy sat down on Betsy's bed as Linda leaned against the doorway.

"You know, your speech was fantastic," said Linda.

Cathy added, "You really captured our whole experience here."

"Thank you." Betsy took a sip of her green tea. "Do you still want to leave tomorrow at the crack of dawn?"

Cathy and Linda looked at each other.

Cathy said, "I think we should just take it easy tomorrow morning. Not even set an alarm, but just wake up naturally, have a nice breakfast, pack up, and go. It is only a couple of hours drive. And we do have a reservation for tomorrow night at a campsite there, so we are all set." She stood up. "Does anybody want a cup of tea?"

"I have mine, thank you," replied Betsy.

Linda said, "I actually would like a cup of green tea with mint and maybe a cookie to go with it."

"That sounds good to me," said Cathy. "Coming right up."

A little later Cathy and Linda were sitting in the dining area. Charlie was lying on his back on Linda's bed, with his legs up in the air, snoring away. As Linda sipped her tea, she rubbed Charlie's belly. The two friends sat, sipping their tea, and munching cookies. They were quiet, caught up in their own thoughts.

At last, Linda turned to Cathy. "You know, I'm really glad we made this trip together, and I've gotten to know you better. I've never really had women friends before. You and Betsy have come to mean a lot to me. I consider you good friends."

Cathy said, "I feel the same way. It's heartening to

know that at our age, we can still make friends. Good lifelong friends."

They hugged, said goodnight, and went to bed. As Cathy reached over to turn out her light, she heard Linda talking quietly to Charlie.

"What are you saying to him?" she asked.

"Just telling him I love him."

CHAPTER 25

As the sun was coming up over the horizon, Tom arrived at the hospital with a newspaper, a Danish, and a large black coffee in hand. He peeked around the door to see if Peter was awake. He was and looking very frustrated. He spotted Tom and called for him to come in.

"At last, a normal person," said Peter.

Tom grinned. "A little grumpy this morning, are we?" He handed the coffee, newspaper, and Danish to Peter.

"You read my mind. This is so much better than what they tried to foist on me this morning."

"That would be the Dr. Seuss menu—green eggs and ham?"

Peter laughed. "Don't forget the green Jell-O."

"Yuck," said Tom. "By the way, you'll be glad to see you made the front page."

Peter said, "Seriously?" He unfolded the paper. "Oh shit."

Half of the front page was taken up by an image of

him covered in blood on a gurney being wheeled into the hospital. Surrounding him were worried looking doctors, nurses, and police officers. The headline read "Police Chief Gunned Down."

"Well," said Peter, "that will certainly sell papers."

"Yes," said Tom, "the station's communications system is already down for the count."

Peter winced. "I can only imagine."

There was a knock on the door. Tom checked who it was, then asked Peter if he was up to seeing Benedict. Peter shrugged resignedly.

When Benedict entered, it was a different Benedict than Peter had seen in recent years. A less confident, somewhat depressed, Benedict was facing him now.

Benedict asked Peter, "Can we talk? Alone?"

Peter added, "Anything you have to say to me, you can say to him."

Benedict nodded slowly, almost as if in defeat. "I just wanted you to know that I will not be representing Sullivan going forward." He stared out the window for a few minutes and then turned to Peter and said, "I'm relocating to New York City. Joan and I are divorcing. She will be staying here, running her nonprofit. I'd appreciate if you keep an eye on her. She's a good woman, and I treated her badly." He walked over to Peter's bed. Tom, who had been casually leaning against the wall, straightened up and moved a few steps toward him. Peter made a slight downward movement with his hand and Tom backed away and relaxed against the wall again.

Benedict continued, "I'm sorry for how I've treated you over the years, especially all those negative op-ed pieces." He started to walk toward the door.

Peter called to him. "Benedict, I think, at least I hope, there is a good guy deep inside you. I hope you find him. Good luck."

"Goodbye, Peter." Benedict walked out.

"Unexpected," said Tom. "How do you think he'll do in New York?"

"I don't know. He could go either way. Elizabeth is there, so she can be a good influence on him. Now, let's get to something really important. You've got to break me out of here."

Tom looked at him in disbelief. "No way."

"Come on Tom, I can't take it in here. Every couple of minutes someone comes in and takes my temperature or sticks me with a needle. I've got to get out of here."

Tom looked at him sympathetically. "I'm sorry, but the doctor said he wanted you here one more night. I am not going to be responsible for breaking you out of here and then having you drop dead walking into your office."

"I am not going to drop dead."

"I have no idea whether you will or not, but I'm not going to take that chance. The doctor says you stay here one more night, so you stay here one more night. And believe me, I know the nurses. They will take you down if you try to make it out of here. Actually, they will take both of us down for that matter."

Peter laughed. "We'll see. Hopefully, I can get out of

here this afternoon."

"OK, I'm heading back to the station now," said Tom.

"One last thing. Can you check and see if the doctor has any outstanding parking tickets?"

"Ha-ha. See you later." As Tom was leaving, he saw Peter's official cell phone on the table. He made sure he was blocking Peter's view as he casually slipped the phone into his pocket. He waved and left. Peter sighed, leaned back against the pillows, and closed his eyes.

A few miles away, at the RV park, Cathy, Betsy, Linda, and Charlie walked up to the ranch house and had a leisurely breakfast at a sun-drenched table on the veranda. Ben spotted them and, to their delight, joined them.

"So how long did the party go on for?" asked Betsy.

"Maybe another hour," Ben mused.

"Once you left, the party was over," commented Alfreda as she came up behind them.

"Though you did miss seeing Luke trying to teach Harry to line dance," added Izzy, sitting down next to Betsy.

"Another hour and he would have had it." Luke smiled as he joined them at the table.

Harry and Charlie touched noses and then lay down next to each other.

"Luke, when was the last time you fed this dog?" asked Alfreda.

Luke looked over. Harry had put his head in Alfreda's lap and was looking at her pathetically like he hadn't eaten in ages.

"Alfreda, he just had breakfast. Do not feed him anything. You know Labs. They have this down to an art form. They will make you think they haven't had anything to eat in three months, when they've just had three huge meals in a row."

Alfreda sighed. "I know, but he's just so darned cute."

Linda said, "Hopefully Charlie won't pick up that habit from him."

Betsy looked embarrassed, "Oops, too late. I'm so sorry. I just gave Charlie a little piece of bacon. I won't do it again."

"I'd appreciate that. I do not want to wind up having to put Charlie on a diet. He would not be happy with me," Linda replied.

"Any word on how Peter is doing?" Cathy asked with studied nonchalance.

Luke answered, "According to Tom, he is doing well and desperately trying to break out of his hospital room."

The group laughed sympathetically.

Ben asked, "Are you ready to go?"

"Almost," said Cathy. "Just a few more things to pack." At that, she stood up. Betsy and Linda reluctantly joined her, and they hugged everyone at the table, promising to stay in touch as they wiped away tears.

Slowly they made their way out of the ranch house and back to the RV. They packed away the table and chairs in the outside storage compartments.

"Betsy, where do you want your walker?" asked Linda.

"I'll keep it in my bedroom."

"Luke told me to be ready to take tons of photos on the drive over," said Linda. "Let's make sure our phones are completely charged up."

Everyone nodded and plugged their phones in wherever they could find an appropriate outlet.

"If we see a camera shop on the way, maybe we could stop and get an actual camera," suggested Linda.

"Good idea," said Betsy.

They disconnected the power, water, and septic hoses. Cathy climbed into the driver's seat. "This is so weird," she said, "it's been so long since I've driven this thing. I may be a little rusty."

"Just as long as you don't back us into the river," said Betsy.

Linda laughed but then said thoughtfully, "Cathy, if you are uncomfortable backing up, do you want me to get out and help?"

"No thanks. I'm okay driving this behemoth. I just felt a little anxious initially." Cathy started the RV.

Charlie let out an unearthly howl that made everybody jump.

"Jesus," said Linda, "I've never heard him make that noise before. It scared the hell out of me."

Betsy said, "Maybe he's saying goodbye."

Linda sat down on the floor next to him. "We're going home, Charlie. You're going to be living with me. You're my family now." She teared up as she leaned against Charlie and kissed the top of his head. He stopped howling and licked her face. She put her arms around him, lifted him onto the chair with her and put a seat belt on. "We are ready to go," she told Cathy.

"I'll back up carefully." Cathy swung the wheel around and began to move the RV out of its parking spot. The aged vehicle squeaked and groaned as it rolled across the rutted driveway and began to move toward the ranch house.

Betsy said, "Oh there's Alfreda's RV."

Cathy stopped for a moment in front of Alfreda's but no one seemed to be there.

Linda said, "Cathy just tap the horn very lightly."

Cathy did so, and soon Alfreda appeared on the porch, holding Frankie. She waved and blew kisses at them. They waved and blew kisses back to her, then continued on.

They got to the ranch house and, again, there was nobody on the front porch. The three women waved and blew kisses anyway.

Cathy said, "Thank you, Arden RV Park for being so good to us and giving us such a great time."

"Thank you, RV park," echoed Betsy and Linda.

They continued down the driveway until they got to the septic station where they emptied out the RV's tank. Once they were done, they took off down the driveway until they got to the main road.

"Which way?" asked Cathy.

"We go right," said Betsy, checking the GPS.

"Do we need any gas or oil?" asked Linda.

"No, we are fine," responded Cathy. "I checked already."

Twenty miles down the road, they drove through the town of Candor. On Main Street, they saw Luke, Harry, and

Smithy about to walk into A Safe Place, Joan's nonprofit. Betsy pointed them out. Cathy honked the horn and they all waved. Luke smiled and waved back. Harry barked.

"I hope that works out," said Betsy. "Izzy said Smithy is a talented artist, so fingers crossed his community service will do some good there."

Linda said, "I saw you talking to Izzy quite a bit at the party."

"Yes, unfortunately her husband was diagnosed with Parkinson's a few months ago, so she was asking about it."

"Doesn't her husband have Alzheimer's?"

"Yes, he's got a double whammy."

"Oh, that is awful," said Cathy. "That's going to be tough for her to deal with, emotionally and physically."

"She's got a lot of spirit," said Betsy, "and a lot of support in the community. She's taught the kids here for many years."

Linda informed them, "By the way, I picked up a couple of books on Georgia O'Keefe."

"Great," said Betsy. "I want to know more about her."

"She led a fascinating life," said Linda, "I have one of the books on Audible. Want to listen?"

"Yes, please," said Cathy and Betsy at the same time.

Linda turned it on and increased the volume on her iPhone. The women relaxed, listening to the story of Georgia O'Keeffe and the Ghost Ranch, and taking in the beautiful vistas as they drove through the New Mexico countryside.

CHAPTER 26

"Well," the doctor said to Peter. "I'm not thrilled about this, but there's no real reason for me to keep you another night. Your vitals are fine, your blood count is good, and you seem to be in good spirits. Frankly, I'm afraid if I keep you here one more night, you'll start a revolt among the other patients and take over the hospital. I'm signing you out. Just promise me you will try to take it easy for the next couple of days while your body heals."

"Deal," said Peter.

He waited until the doctor left the room, then he got out of bed and immediately started getting dressed. Peter had a moment or two of dizziness but felt his strength gradually creeping back the longer he stood up and walked around. Locating a pile of clean clothes on a chair, he started dressing but then couldn't find his phone. At that moment Tom walked into the room.

Peter asked him, "Where did these clothes come from?"

"From the lost-and-found closet," answered Tom.

"Why?"

Peter held up a brightly patterned polyester shirt that looked like it was from *Saturday Night Fever*. "Really?"

Tom cracked up. "You'll need some gold chains to go with that."

"Nice. Do you know where my phone is? I can't find it."

"Oops," Tom handed the phone over. "I must have picked it up by accident."

Peter gave him a dirty look. "Yeah right. OK, so tell me what's happening."

Tom brought him up to speed on the status of several cases, including Sullivan who had been moved down state to a maximum security prison.

"Good," said Peter, with a note of satisfaction. "OK, Tom, let's dust this joint." Peter grabbed his phone and keys.

"Wait," said Tom, "there's a protocol here for you being released. You need to be in a wheelchair." Without waiting for a response from Peter, Tom pushed the call button for the nurse. She arrived quickly, looking harassed. "Betty"—Tom smiled before continuing—"Peter is ready to check out of this lovely establishment."

Betty patted him on the cheek. "OK, Tommy. I'll get a wheelchair." She then turned to Peter, pointed sharply to a chair, and said, "You, sit. Do not move. I'll be right back."

Peter looked at Tom after she left. "Someone has a not-so-secret admirer."

"Actually," said Tom, "she's my mother's cousin. She worked an extra shift last night to make sure that you had good coverage."

"Really?"

"Yep. People were really worried about you."

"We'll have to do something special for Betty and the rest of the nursing staff. Any ideas?" Peter asked.

"Well, they do have a fundraiser for the hospital coming up, and they could use some visibility from the local police force to get people out for the event."

"Say no more," said Peter. "Done and done."

When Betty came back with the wheelchair, Peter said, "Thank you for taking such good care of me."

"I got it from here, Betty," said Tom, kissing her cheek and making her blush.

He pushed Peter down the hallway, as people applauded and called out well wishes.

"Yikes," said Peter under his breath. "Maybe this would be a good time to run for governor."

Tom chuckled. "You don't like chicken that much."

On the ride home, Peter asked Tom if he had talked to his wife about becoming police chief.

"Yes. As you can imagine, she has mixed emotions. On the one hand, she thinks that I would be a good police chief, but on the other hand, she worries about my safety, especially with what happened to you."

"What about you?" Peter asked. "How do you feel about it?"

"Well, I have mixed emotions, also. It's been wonderful working with you, and I have learned so much. More than that, I also feel like you've become a good friend. If you decide to retire, it would be difficult for me to not have you around to bounce ideas off of. On the other hand, I do think I'd be a good police chief. I get along with the staff and squad at the station. I care about the townspeople and want them to be safe and happy. I am interested in advancing my education to learn more about new technological advances. If you decide to leave, I want to be considered for the police chief position."

"Good for you, Tom. That's absolutely what I wanted to hear. You're not over the top with ambition. You are aware of the positives and the negatives, and you're willing to take the job, regardless, because you care about the community. That's good enough for me. It will take some time to put things into place. In the meantime, I want you to start going to the regional and state meetings that we have with legislators, criminal justice professionals, and different police forces. I want people to start getting used to seeing you operate at that level."

Tom asked, "Do you have a date in mind to make an announcement regarding your retirement?"

"Not yet. It kind of depends on what happens over the next couple of days."

Tom looked at him quizzically. "What do you mean?"

"I've been in touch with Ben, and he let me know where the women are, where their campsite is located up at the A&K RV Park. I'm going to go up there tomorrow morning and talk to Cathy. I'm planning on proposing to her."

Tom looked at him in shock and almost drove the squad car off the road. "What?! But you barely know her. You just met her, a week, a week and a half ago."

"I know, but I've had a lot of time to think in the hospital. Life is too short to not take a leap of faith when you meet someone truly special."

"That's one hell of a leap. It's more like taking a dive off Niagara Falls."

"Well, being shot changes one's perspective. I want to spend the time I have left with her. We can buy that RV that they've been renting and drive it around the country, visit my daughters, and visit Betsy and Linda in West Chester. Visit places I've always wanted to see, like Alaska, Wyoming, Florida, New York City. I've lived and grown up, gone to school, and worked in this town all my life. I joined the police department at eighteen and never left or moved on. It's time to spread my wings a bit."

Tom said, "Whatever I can do to help."

"You can find me a ride out to Ghost Ranch."

"I'll take you myself."

Peter called Luke, who picked up quickly. He could hear a lot of kids laughing and talking in the background. He asked Luke, "Where are you?"

"I'm with Smithy at A Safe Place. Peter, he's fantastic with the kids. He's a natural-born teacher. The kids are having a wonderful time and learning so much. He's going to be a real asset here."

"That's great. Luke, I have a question for you. Tom is driving me up to Ghost Ranch tomorrow morning early, probably leaving around nine. I wanted to know if you would like to come with us."

"Why, what's going on?"

"I'm going to see if I can track down Cathy and ask her to marry me." Peter laughed when he heard the phone drop on the floor, followed by Luke's voice exclaiming, "Holy shit!"

Once Luke came back on the line, he asked, "Are you serious?"

"Yes," answered Peter.

"Of course, I'll go with you. But only if you promise that Harry can be best dog at your wedding."

"Absolutely. I'll be at the RV park tomorrow morning at nine if you want to come."

"Sounds good," said Luke. "See you tomorrow."

Peter said to Tom, "Okay, we'll leave about nine o'clock tomorrow morning, get there around eleven or so, and track down their campsite."

Trying to be as tactful as possible, Tom carefully said, "Now there are a few things we need to do beforehand."

Peter looked at him. "Like what?"

"First of all, you need a haircut. Peter, I say this with great affection, but your hair is getting shaggy. Pretty soon you will be wearing a mullet. And no one looks good with a mullet."

"Point taken. I agree with getting a haircut."

Tom continued, "Then you need to get a better shirt and jacket. The jeans are fine, but you need to look a little bit more dressed up if you're going to propose. You want to stack the odds in your favor, after all." He paused, "Speaking of which, do you have a ring?"

"I didn't think of that. However, I do have my mother's

engagement ring which my father designed. It's beautiful, all natural gemstones."

"That sounds perfect."

OK," said Peter, laughing, "I'll go with your recommendations. Maybe I should go home, take care of some of this stuff and then come back tomorrow morning to the station."

Tom said, "I think that's a good idea. It's important for you to get rest. But we'll get the hair cut first. I know Elaine at A Cut Above has been dying to get her hands on your hair for ages."

"Isn't Elaine your cousin?"

Tom grinned at him.

"OK," Peter said, "you can take me home after that." He leaned back in the car seat and closed his eyes as a wave of tiredness swept over him.

Tom noticed how pale he looked and became concerned. He determined he would make sure that Peter was not bothered by all the minutiae of the station's goings-on that might wear him down.

CHAPTER 27

The women arrived at the A&K RV Park in early afternoon.

"Ben set this up for us," said Linda. "He highly recommended it. It's supposed to be by far the nicest campground in the area."

"It looks beautiful," said Betsy, peering out the window as they drove slowly into the campground. They registered at the office and then found their campsite, which was situated on a hillside with an incredible vista.

"Oh my God! This is spectacular," said Linda.

"Let's get settled in, so we can enjoy the sunset," said Cathy.

They quickly set up the RV, attaching the electric, sewage, and water hoses, then got out the table and chairs.

"Charlie is staying on leash while we are here," said Linda. "I do not want him picking up the scent of some animal, going after it and getting lost. There are also coyotes here, which scares the hell out of me, as far as Charlie is concerned."

Cathy gazed out over the landscape of dramatic sculptured canyons and towering hoodoo formations. Red rock and sandstone blazed with color. A brilliant blue sky arced overhead, with no clouds in sight.

"Wow," said Linda, coming up beside Cathy. Charlie was at her side, seemingly very comfortable on leash.

"Where is Betsy?" asked Cathy.

"She's resting."

Linda and Cathy both stood there for a long moment and looked out over the landscape.

"It kind of takes your breath away," Linda marveled.

Cathy took a few photos with her phone. "It really does."

"I can see why so many artists have been inspired by this place."

"Alice certainly was," said Cathy. "That big watercolor in her living room could have been this exact same view."

Betsy came out to join them. "Oh, it's so amazing here. Look at the colors."

Linda turned to Betsy. "I've been thinking a bit about Alice's memorial service. We should have music to begin with, each of us could say something about Alice and her impact on our lives, and then we can distribute the ashes."

"Sounds good to me."

Cathy said, "I think I'll walk over to the office right now and see if they can suggest an overlook where we could watch the sun come up."

Linda said, "I wouldn't tell them what we're planning on doing."

"No. I think we'll keep that part to ourselves. I'll be back in a few." Cathy walked up the driveway.

"I'm kind of glad we're doing this at the end of our visit," said Betsy.

"Why?" asked Linda.

"Well, it was so difficult leaving Arden RV Park. I think if we left there and had to go straight home, it would have been too depressing. This way we get to experience this beautiful spot, and it lifts our spirits, even given our reason for coming here."

About an hour later, Cathy came back carrying a few grocery bags. She sat down by the two women and put the bags on the ground. "I got dinner for us, plus a couple of suggestions for a good overlook to watch the dawn come up. We will have to check on the map to see which one is in the best location, in terms of accessibility."

Betsy said, "If it is a dirt walkway, I'll have to see how far it is. I could have some trouble walking on that kind of path. Also, my walker doesn't work very well with dust and dirt."

As she was talking, Charlie got a whiff of the rotisserie chicken Cathy had bought, and he opened his eyes. Cathy saw him looking around and reaching out his long nose toward the grocery bags. She laughed and pushed the bags away from him with her foot. "Sorry Charlie. These aren't for you." He sighed heavily and closed his eyes and went back to sleep.

Betsy suddenly said, "Could you both just wait here for a minute? I have something for you."

Cathy said, "Sure, we're not going anywhere."

Linda added, "It's much too beautiful watching this sunset."

Betsy went into the RV and then came out with three small, gift-wrapped packages. She handed one to each of the women and kept one for herself. "I bought these before we came out here. Before I got to know both of you very well. These gifts have more meaning now because I feel so much closer to both of you, and I think I have a better sense of who you are. Anyway, go ahead and open them."

Cathy, Linda, and Betsy opened their presents at the same time. Each box contained a beautifully fashioned silver eagle feather pendant, decorated with a gleaming turquoise stone on a delicate silver chain.

"Oh my God, this is gorgeous, Betsy," said Linda.

"Absolutely stunning," murmured Cathy as the women helped each other put the necklaces on.

"I love it," said Linda. "Thank you."

Cathy asked, "Does the feather have a special meaning?"

"Yes. For Native Americans, an eagle feather means bravery and courage. I initially got the necklaces when we were planning on driving out here in the RV. I thought that it was going to take courage and bravery on our part to do something we've never done before. Little did I know everything that was going to happen to us on this trip." She smiled at both of them and held out her hands. They put their hands in hers. "I think that we all have a lot more bravery and courage inside us than we ever thought possible. I am happy that I was able to find these and share them with you, given everything we've been through together. This trip will be a bond that we will always have, no matter where life leads us."

Both Linda and Cathy teared up at Betsy's words.

Wiping her eyes, Cathy said, "Thank you so much, Betsy, for this gift and especially for your friendship."

They turned their three chairs to face the sunset. The colors of the different rock formations grew even richer and deeper as the sun sank toward the horizon.

Once the sun dipped below the horizon, the temperature dropped like a rock and the women quickly got chilled.

"Time to take this party inside," said Betsy.

"I'll make dinner tonight," said Linda. "You two have been really good about cooking. Now it's time for me to step up to the plate."

"No argument from me," said Cathy. "Of course, we do have that rotisserie chicken."

"Chef salad it is then." Linda laughed.

"You lucked out," Betsy teased her.

"As you're making dinner," said Cathy, "we'll put the music together for the memorial."

Linda started puttering around the kitchen, getting dinner ready. Betsy and Cathy began listing songs that they thought would celebrate Alice's life and legacy.

"Definitely 'Here Comes the Sun' by The Beatles," said Cathy. "She also liked to listen to Caitlin Canty's 'Get Up' in the morning to help her get ready for work."

Betsy said, "I'm not familiar with her music."

"She's a singer/songwriter from Nashville. Alice loved

that song."

"We definitely need 'Imagine' by John Lennon.

Cathy agreed, "Yes, and 'Don't be Shy' by Cat Stevens. That's an excellent song. Then there's 'I Can See Clearly Now' by Johnny Nash. That's an uplifting song as well. How about ending with 'What a Wonderful World' by Louis Armstrong?"

Betsy mused, "I think it's a great playlist. It captures Alice's personality—hopeful, loving, and joyful. I'm sure she'll be with us tomorrow in spirit."

Dinner was ready, so they put aside the music and enjoyed the meal, laughing and talking into the night. Linda took Charlie for his last walk of the day but came back in a rush. She had heard coyotes howling nearby, and it had made her uneasy.

As the women prepared for bed, Cathy mentioned that she wanted to go on a trail ride the next day.

"Anyone want to come with me?"

"No thanks," said Betsy.

Linda shook her head ruefully. "I am not very comfortable riding horseback."

"Okay," said Cathy, "I am fine going alone."

They each set their alarm for 4:00 a.m., figuring that out of the three of them, the multiple alarms would at least wake up one of them in time.

CHAPTER 28

It was still dark out when the alarms began going off. The women all woke up slowly, gingerly stretching and yawning. They took their turns in the bathroom.

"Cups of tea all around?" asked Betsy.

"Sounds good," said Linda. "I'll put the water on."

"We should at least have a light breakfast, maybe scrambled eggs and toast," suggested Cathy. "I think we still have some of Alfreda's homemade blueberry jam left."

"Do we have time for breakfast?" asked Betsy.

"I think we're fine," answered Linda.

They had looked at the map the previous night, and the overlook was close enough that it wouldn't be an issue for Betsy. A paved path ran most of the way then it turned into a dirt path for about ten yards to the overlook itself.

Linda said, "I'm concerned about leaving Charlie here, especially given his Houdini trick the night of the party. But I think if we close everything up and make sure it's all locked, he'll be OK for the time that we're gone. Those coyotes last night scared the hell out of me."

"It's frightening to have a predator like that around," agreed Betsy.

"I need to get him chipped when we get home, so people will know where to call if he gets lost and they find him."

Betsy said, "You got him that nice leather collar. Why don't you write your phone number on that in permanent marker?"

"Brilliant idea, Betsy," said Cathy. She immediately grabbed a marker and handed it to Linda who started writing contact information on Charlie's collar.

"It's 40 degrees outside, so everybody needs coats, hats, and gloves. Maybe even a light blanket," advised Cathy. "I also have a surprise for you both. Look out the windshield."

There in front of the camper was a totally tricked-out golf cart. "It even has a heater," said Cathy. "I rented it from the campground office. They dropped it off overnight."

Betsy clapped her hands. "Oh, that's awesome. Now I don't have to worry about whether I can walk the distance." Betsy hugged Cathy. "Thank you. That's a load off my mind."

"You're very welcome." Cathy smiled at Betsy.

Linda said, "I've got a knapsack with blankets in it, two thermoses of hot tea, some water, and my iPhone with the playlist on it."

"Great," said Cathy. "I have the playlist on my iPhone too. We'll have our music in stereo."

The women started climbing into the golf cart when

Cathy said, "Oh my God. I forgot Alice. I'll be right back."

"Not to be paranoid, but make sure Charlie's secured in the RV when you close it up again," said Linda.

Cathy came back with the urn and handed it to Linda. "All secure." She turned on the golf cart.

With the headlights cutting through the darkness, they started down the path toward the overlook. Betsy nudged Cathy and pointed out the reflective eyes of animals in the undergrowth. Cathy slowed down even more to avoid hitting anything.

After about twenty minutes, Linda said, "It is a little hard to read the GPS in the dark, but I think we're approaching the turn-off for the overlook. Keep your eyes peeled."

Cathy pointed, "I think I see a turn-off coming up on the left."

"This may be it," said Linda. "Do you want to pull in a little bit, so we can walk in just to see if we are in the right place? Betsy, why don't you wait here until we're sure."

As they made the turn to the left, they saw that there were a couple of parking spots. They parked in one of them and walked through the foliage, with their flashlights picking out the footpath in front of them. Soon they came to the well-marked overlook and paused for a moment.

"I think this is a perfect spot," Cathy said. "You can see the horizon just getting very slightly pink."

"Let's go back and get Betsy," said Linda.

"Remind me when we get there that I have a couple of folding chairs in the back of the cart."

"Cathy, you think of everything."

"I try."

Linda helped Betsy out of the cart and got her walker out for her. Betsy turned her headlamp on and started moving slowly to the overlook. Cathy grabbed the folding chairs and Linda carried the urn down the path.

They quickly put a blanket on the ground, placed the chairs on it, and set up a small folding table. They put the urn on the table with the iPhones next to it and turned the music on.

The first strains of "Here Comes the Sun" by The Beatles paired perfectly with the world around them, as the sky grew lighter and a thin sliver of sun appeared on the horizon. Everything around them was soon bathed in glowing pinks and glittering golds. The music rotated through the playlist, the sound and meaning of each song deeply affecting the women. Betsy shivered. Linda reached in her knapsack for a light blanket and gently wrapped it around Betsy's shoulders.

"Thank you," Betsy whispered. They listened in silence as John Lennon's iconic 'Imagine' echoed out over the canyon.

They held hands as Louis Armstrong began his beautiful prayer to the world. As the song drew to a close, Cathy said, "I added one more last night."

Linda and Betsy looked at her in surprise and then smiled as the familiar strains of Beethoven's 'Ode to Joy' filled the air around them.

As the music ended there was a pause. Cathy cleared

her throat and took a sip of water and started to talk.

"I first met Alice," she started, "when we lived in the same neighborhood. We both had dogs—bichons. We began running into each other as we were walking the dogs up and down the street. As time went on, we just began talking more and more during those encounters. We talked about books, music, movies, and all kinds of things. After my husband died, she would invite me over for holiday meals. It was always a door wide open with her, figuratively and literally.

"One time I had a bad accident in the middle of a snowstorm. I had our wood stove going at high heat. I was distracted, thinking about something else. After I put the wood in, without thinking I put my hands down on the top of the stove to lever myself up. I immediately burned both my hands badly. I called Alice, knowing she was a nurse. Regardless of the severity of the storm, she came down to my house to help. She had a gentle soul and a kind heart."

"I met her," said Linda, "at the hospital. We both were nurses, and we began talking in the break room about how to handle different situations, plus coping with the emotional strain of being a nurse. I found her to be tremendously supportive, very honest, open, and willing to allow herself to be vulnerable. She showed me that what we traditionally think of as a weakness, the ability to show feelings, is actually a core strength. Showing feelings is what connects us as human beings. It's what enables us to truly empathize with one another.

"I still struggle with letting people in, but I carry the

memory of her with me as my role model. And it reminds me to break down the walls. I remember visiting her in the hospital shortly before she died. She was in the children's wing, playing games with them, telling stories, making them giggle. She did not have a lot of energy at that point. But what she did have, she wanted to share with others."

Betsy said, "I met Alice at an author's night at a local bookstore. We had similar tastes in books and the same sense of humor. When I shared my diagnosis of Parkinson's with her, she reached out to me to talk about what it meant, how was I going to deal with it, and what did I have in place to help. She was a great comfort to me. She knew my disease was getting worse, so she would call me, check on me and talk to me about it.

"I'll never forget when she told me she had pancreatic cancer. I was devastated. But she had an extraordinarily strong faith and wasn't afraid of dying. We often talked about death. I found that to be a great comfort. We didn't share the same faith, but she totally accepted me for who I was, even though our paths were different. Once Alice got the news there wasn't anything more to be done she was very calm about it.

"We have her ashes here today, but that's not who she was or how she would want to be remembered. That's merely the scant evidence of a life well lived. I believe she is here with us. Her love is all around us."

The sun was now fully up over the horizon, brilliant in a bright blue sky. The three women walked to the edge of the overlook, standing close by the safety railing. They put their hands on the urn at the same time and opened the top.

"Ready," said Cathy.

"Ready," said Betsy.

"Ready," said Linda.

They carefully tilted the urn and shook out the ashes, releasing them into the canyon below. A sudden updraft caught the ashes and swirled them upwards, the sun's rays illuminating them. With their arms around each other, the three women watched as the updraft carried the ashes soaring upwards to the sky and out of sight.

The women stood gazing out over the canyon, each caught up in their own thoughts. Finally, they looked at each other and spontaneously hugged. Then it was time to go. They packed everything up and walked to the golf cart. Cathy turned the vehicle on, and they rode back to the RV.

CHAPTER 29

Peter groaned as the alarm went off at 6:00 a.m. He tentatively stretched, stopping when he felt sharp pain around the bullet wound. Slowly he got out of bed, carefully maneuvering around his still-sleeping dogs.

After scrubbing his face and shaving, Peter ran wet hands through his newly cut hair, trying to shape it into some semblance of a style. He looked in the mirror again and grimaced. His blue eyes were bloodshot and his face was pale beneath the tan. He looked tired. Actually, he looked exhausted. His bandage had shifted during the night, and he had some blood oozing around the edges, turning it from pristine white to pink. Peter grabbed some bandages from a first aid kit and tried wrapping a few new layers around it. "That will have to do," he muttered.

He dressed in jeans, a white cotton shirt, and cowboy boots and then let the dogs out to do their business while he finished getting ready. Peter debated whether to take his gun or not but decided to err on the side of caution. He unlocked the gun safe, grabbed his service weapon, ammo, and holster, then strode out to his SUV.

Luke and Harry were sitting on the steps of the ranch house waiting for him when he arrived at the RV park.

As he parked, Ben spotted him. "How are you doing, Peter?"

"I'm feeling much better, thank you."

"Even though I am happy to see you up and about, what the heck are you doing here? You should be home in bed, resting."

"I have some errands I have to run. In fact, I'm going to grab some coffee right now." Peter yelled to Luke, "Do you want coffee?"

Luke responded, "That would be great. Thank you."

Once Peter was out of sight in the ranch house, Ben walked over to Luke. "OK, out with it. What's going on?"

Luke tried to look innocent. "Nothing."

Ben just stared at him, patiently waiting. Luke finally said, "All right, all right." He looked around, checking to see where Peter was, making sure he wasn't close by. "OK, this is what's going on. We're heading up to the Ghost Ranch because Peter wants to propose to Cathy today."

"What!" exclaimed Ben. "But he barely knows her."

"I understand that" said Luke, "but I think that getting shot has kind of changed Peter's perspective. All I know is he wants to go up to the Ghost Ranch and propose to Cathy today. We're picking Tom up at the station, on the way."

Ben said, "Maybe we should follow you up."

Luke said firmly, "No, that's not a good idea. We don't

want this to turn into a circus."

At this point, Alfreda showed up, walking toward the ranch house. She smiled and waved.

"Dad, please…" begged Luke. "Don't tell anybody else about this."

Ben said, "But Alfreda is family; she has to hear this. Now are you going to tell her or am I?"

Luke sighed.

Meanwhile Izzy had joined Alfreda. Ben went over and told them what was going on.

Alfreda immediately said, "We have to go. We have to follow them."

Izzy said, "I want to go too. I'll get Smithy to sit with my husband. They get along very well. They play checkers a lot." She said to Ben, "I am very happy with this community service arrangement."

Ben smiled. "I'm glad."

Alfreda said to Luke, "We'll take my van and follow you."

"We're going to the police station first," said Luke, "to pick up Tom. If you are determined to do this just be sure and keep the van out of sight."

Ben promised, "We will do our best to be inconspicuous."

Luke laughed. "Yeah right. You're going to be in a van that has a huge picture of a dog on it, with the word "veterinarian" in enormous font and Alfreda's name. That's inconspicuous?"

Alfreda laughed. She turned to Ben. "He does have a point."

Ben said, "We will just keep way back, out of sight."

Luke said, "OK, I think I see him coming back."

Peter came out of the ranch house, with two big containers of coffee. He nodded to Ben, Alfreda, and Izzy, and got in the driver's seat. He handed Luke his coffee, started the SUV, made a tight turn, and headed out the driveway.

"OK," said Ben. "If we are going to go, we need to go now."

"This is turning into a major expedition," said Alfreda, smiling.

Once in town, Peter parked his SUV in the station lot and called Tom. There was a delay of about fifteen minutes until Tom came out of the station, shrugging into his jacket. Peter moved into the back seat, Luke and Harry were in the front passenger seat, while Tom got into the driver's seat.

Peter said, "Thank you for coming, guys. It means a lot to me. Now if you don't mind, I'm going to lie down and just close my eyes for a bit. I'm still wiped out from being shot. Not that I'm using that as an excuse, but, you know, I will if I can."

Tom said, "Peter go ahead and sleep. It's a couple of hours, so relax and take it easy."

"OK."

Luke added, "Let me know if you need anything."

Tom drove off as a couple of police officers walking into the station waved. Alfreda pulled out from where she'd been parked down the street and followed them.

"Remember to keep back," said Ben.

"I will. No worries."

In addition to Ben, Alfreda, Frankie and Izzy, Sharon and George were sitting in the back of the van with their dogs, Hansel and Gretel. They had wanted to come along when they found out what was going on. Alfreda's van was packed pretty tight with three dogs and five adults.

After about forty minutes on the road, Luke noticed Tom glancing quite a bit into the rearview mirror. Tom and Luke hadn't been talking much as they wanted Peter to get some rest.

"What's up?" he asked quietly.

Tom answered, "I think the word is out about what's going on."

"What?!" said Luke. He turned around and looked out the back of the vehicle. "Oh my God. There are ten to fifteen cop cars back there. Do you think those cars are for us? What am I saying? Of course they are. That was a stupid question." He glanced at Peter sleeping peacefully in the back seat.

Tom looked over at him. "I think our administrative assistant used our phone tree to let people know what was going on."

"But how did she know?" asked Luke.

Tom looked guilty. "Actually, I told her. I said we were going to be off-site for the day, and she asked where we were going. I couldn't lie to her. She's my cousin."

Luke looked at him. "Just out of curiosity. Is there anyone in this town you are not related to?"

"I haven't run into anyone yet."

Luke looked behind them. "I think there are even more

cop cars now. Boy, this is going to turn into a circus with so many people. Peter is not going to like it."

Tom looked over at him and said worriedly, "I know, I know."

"Well, the one good thing is"—Luke chuckled—"he won't have to worry about finding a witness."

About ten police cars back, Alfreda was driving very carefully. "I don't want to get a speeding ticket."

"I think you'd have a hard time talking your way out of one with this many cops around." Ben laughed.

"It'd be like a feeding frenzy," said George. "Hey!" he exclaimed as Sharon elbowed him in the ribs.

Ben added, "You needn't worry about staying out of sight I think we're camouflaged right now by the ten to fifteen police cars in front of us."

"I thought this was supposed to be a secret," said Alfreda. "It looks like half the police force is on the road with us."

CHAPTER 30

In the meantime, Linda, Betsy, and Cathy had set up their table and chairs outside the RV and had breakfast out there with the pastries Cathy had brought back from the campground store. They weren't talking much; they were still absorbing the emotional impact of the memorial ceremony they had just had for Alice.

Finally, they got themselves together. Cathy stood up and started to stack the dishes and cups. She said, "Don't forget. I'm going on a trail ride this afternoon, so I will be gone for a couple of hours."

Linda said, "I'm going to go through the photos I took on my iPhone, do some editing, and transfer them to my iPad. It should take me about…forever."

Betsy said, "I can't help you with that, but I think I'll sit here and read one of the Georgia O'Keefe books that you got us."

"Speaking of which, we need to visit the museum here before we leave the area," added Linda.

"Definitely," Cathy and Betsy echoed at the same time.

A short while later, Cathy told Betsy and Linda, "I'm going to get ready for the trail ride." She put on a pair of jeans and a tee shirt and grabbed her sunglasses. "I should be back in about three hours."

"Have fun," Betsy told her.

Cathy walked up the pathway to the campground's main office and camp store. "Hi, I'm here for the trail ride."

"It's right outside our back door. Just walk out there and you can't miss it. They will choose the right horse with the right temperament for you, familiarize you with your horse, get you a good saddle, and get you all set up. You have about half an hour to go before the ride starts."

She thanked him and said, "I'm really looking forward to it."

"It's a beautiful day for a ride."

A woman standing at the register said, "Hi, I'm Anna and this is my husband Kevin. We own A&K RV Park." She asked Cathy, "Do you have a hat?"

"No."

"It's very sunny out there today. With your lovely porcelain skin, you have to be extra careful not to burn. Nothing ruins a vacation like a bad sunburn." She came around from behind the register. "You definitely need a hat. Let's go into the store and I'll help find you one."

"Thank you," Cathy said. "That's a good suggestion. I'd appreciate your help."

They walked into the camp store, and Cathy immediately gravitated toward a colorful display of cowboy hats.

"These are great."

Anna pointed out that some cowboy hats were just stylish, while others were both stylish and functional in terms of weather and sun resistance. "The ones that combine both are the ones you want to think about buying." She looked at the display for a moment, then snapped her fingers. "I have the perfect hat! This is the one I would choose for you." Anna handed Cathy a gorgeous black cowboy hat decorated with a colorful Navajo patterned hat band. Cathy tried it on. It fit perfectly.

She turned around and looked in the mirror. "Oh, I love this!"

"It looks great against your silver curls."

"I'll take it!"

Anna said, "I also have some sunblock here. It has a 50 SPF and is made by a local dermatologist. It's really good. I use it all the time."

"I'll take that," said Cathy, "plus this water bottle. Is there anything else you think I need?"

"Do you have a daypack to put all this stuff in? Oh, and you'll probably need a windbreaker. The forecast is for high winds this afternoon, so it might be a little chilly up there. We have nice windbreakers over here in the corner that are on sale."

Cathy was beginning to feel like she was running out of time and needed to get over to the stable, so she quickly grabbed a windbreaker, and a bandana.

Anna rang her up. "You're all set; have a great time."

Other than her hat, Cathy put everything into her daypack and swung it over her shoulders. "Thank you so much for your suggestions. I have a feeling I would have been miserable without a hat or sunblock." She walked out the back door to the stable.

The trail boss, Dan, introduced himself and led Cathy to her horse, Star, a small chestnut with dainty white feet and a white star on his forehead. He seemed friendly, reaching to sniff Cathy. She had googled the night before how to say hello to a horse. So, she walked slowly up to him, talking continuously with a low, calm voice.

"You're doing great," said Dan. "Now let's get a saddle on him, and we'll take the next step. But you're doing very well. Not only is he calm but so are you."

"Thank God for Google," said Cathy. Dan laughed.

There were three other people sitting on their horses waiting for her. Cathy got into line behind them. She felt less stressed when she saw a staff member from the stable getting on a horse and lining up behind her.

Dan told them what they could expect on the ride. The first break was going to be in about half an hour, when they would get a chance to get off the horses to stretch their legs, take pictures, and get some water. He introduced the stable rider bringing up the rear as Sam.

Dan said, "Okay, let's head out." He clicked to his horse and they started walking out through the paddock and onto the trail. Dan turned in his saddle to look back at the riders and check how they were doing. The three people in front of Cathy were laughing and talking to each other. Clearly they knew each other well and were comfortable together. Cathy hoped she wasn't going to feel like a third wheel on the ride. Or in this case, a fourth wheel.

CHAPTER 31

A short while later, Tom, Peter and Luke arrived at A&K RV Park. Luke looked out the window as they entered the campground. "Nice place."

Tom said, "I think we'll drive around for a bit and look for the women. If we can't find them that way we'll stop by the office and ask."

"Sounds perfect," said Luke. "It will give us a chance to reconnoiter."

Tom asked, "How's Peter doing? Is he still asleep?"

"Yeah, he's still out. Want me to wake him?"

"Not quite yet. Why don't we find the women first."

A few minutes after they drove into the RV park, a couple of police cars also entered. A security guard was heading into the main office for a meeting when he spotted the police cars. He stood by the side of the road and watched them drive onto the property. There were no sirens or lights. No sense of hurry or alarm.

As he watched them, he saw a few more police cars drive in. They waved at him and gave him a thumbs-up. This relieved his anxiety somewhat, but he still needed to talk to Kevin, his boss, to cover his bases.

Kevin met him at the front door. "What the hell is going on, Fred?" he asked the security guard.

"I don't know for sure, but a number of the police officers gave me a thumbs-up, like everything was OK."

Kevin stood looking over the campground. "Let's ensure everything is indeed okay. Take one of the golf carts and follow them and make sure there's no problem."

"Will do," said the security guard.

Tom drove slowly through the campground. At the farthest campsite from the entrance, he spotted Linda and Charlie taking a walk. He waved. Linda looked up and waved back once she saw him. He pulled up next to her and rolled the window down.

Linda leaned in. "What are you doing here?" she asked, with some confusion.

Tom and Luke both gestured toward the back seat. Linda glanced back and saw Peter stretched out, still asleep.

"He wants to talk to Cathy," said Tom.

"He has heard of a phone, right?" She looked up at the sound of a car and was shocked to see a line of cop cars coming toward them.

"Is that Alfreda's van?" she asked.

Luke winced. "They insisted on coming."

More cop cars and a couple of pickup trucks came down the drive. Linda felt she was standing in a sea of blue uniforms. Alfreda pulled up in her van, the door slid open, and Ben, Izzy, Sharon, and George piled out.

"What the hell is going on?" demanded a gruff voice from Tom's back seat. Peter was awake.

Everybody clapped when Peter emerged from the backseat. Rumpled and stiff, Peter took his time getting out of the car. A tall and distinguished police captain from a local police force came striding over.

Peter's face lit up. "Larry."

"Good to see you," said the captain. "We heard the happy news that you might be joining the ranks of the married soon."

"What?!" said Linda. "Peter is that true? Are you here to ask Cathy to marry you?"

Peter looked shocked. "How did you hear about that?" Everybody turned and looked at Tom, who was now beet red.

He explained, "I think our administrative assistant Abby used the phone tree to let people know what was happening."

Peter stared at him. "And how did she know what was happening?"

Tom was apologetic. "I might have mentioned it."

Linda decided to go get Betsy.

Betsy was humming to herself as she wiped down their outdoor dining table. Because of the angle of the RV, she had not seen any of the cop cars and she couldn't hear them because of the wind. Now Linda came barreling around the corner of the camper.

"Betsy," she called, "you're not going to believe this."

"What's going on?"

"Peter's here and Tom, Luke, Ben, and Alfreda, Izzy—they are all here."

Betsy was stunned.

"Apparently Peter has decided to ask Cathy to marry him."

"Oh no," said Betsy, "where did he get a crazy idea like that? I don't think this is a good time for that."

"Well apparently it's a good time for Peter," said Linda, "because he's here with about three thousand of his closest friends."

"Yikes," said Betsy. They walked around the corner of the RV and got a full overview of just how many cars and people were there. "Holy cow!"

Larry stepped up and clapped Peter on the shoulder. "It couldn't happen to a nicer guy. Where is she? This lucky woman."

"Peter," Betsy walked over to him, "Cathy is on a trail ride. She won't be back for several hours."

Linda asked him, "Are you really going to propose?"

"That's my plan."

Betsy started to say, "I'm not sure, Peter—"

Linda interrupted her, "We just don't know if this is the best time or place if you really want to propose. It's just, you never know how things are going to work out."

Peter looked at them. "Sounds like you don't think she's going to say yes. In fact, it sounds like you are pretty sure she's not going to say yes."

"Oh hell, Peter," said Betsy, "we have no clue what

she's going to say. Last time we talked to her about you, she was not in a great place. She felt like she didn't really know you. If you put her on the spot today, by proposing, who knows what her answer will be. It might be something you don't want to hear..."

Linda added, "There are a lot of people here right now, and that's a lot of pressure."

Peter said, "I can't just tell them all to leave. I mean they're here out of the kindness of their hearts."

Betsy said, "I know, but asking somebody to spend the rest of their life with you is a powerful moment. It's really between the two of you."

Ben, Alfreda, Izzy, Sharon, and George all made their way over to Peter.

After greeting Betsy and Linda, Ben pulled Peter aside and asked, "What's up?"

"I don't know, Ben. It seemed so clear cut, so definitive, at three in the morning. I would ask her to marry me and she would say yes, and we would go forward from there. But here in the bright light of day, I'm just not sure anymore how this is all going to work out."

Joining them, Alfreda chimed in, "Listen, Peter, nobody knows what's in somebody else's heart until they talk about it. Until they get it out there in the open. She may be totally surprised by her response. You may be totally surprised by her response. But if you really feel strongly about her, you have to give it a chance."

Peter hugged her and whispered in her ear, "Thank you."

She smiled. "Good luck."

Tom pulled out his phone and started to call the campground office, when the security guard walked up to him and introduced himself, "Hi, I'm Fred, can I help you?"

"We need to get this man together with a woman who is on one of your trail rides."

"I'll contact the owner of the campground and set up a rendezvous."

"That would be great," said Tom, relieved. Another couple of cop cars pulled in and parked.

Luke said to Tom, "With all these people, I think we should put together a big BBQ and have a party."

Larry overheard him. "I can get my team to bring over food and drink as long as we have grills to cook on."

"I think we can make that happen," said Tom.

"Peter is a good guy, personally and professionally," Larry added. "He has gone above and beyond to help people all over this part of New Mexico. Now let's see what we can do to make this a real celebration for him."

Fred said to Tom. "I just talked with my boss. They have a horse ready and a trail rider on tap to lead the way to find the group that went out this afternoon."

"Perfect," said Tom. He yelled, "Peter!"

Peter walked over to him.

"Fred, the security guard here, will give you a ride to the office, and they will put you on a horse so that you can catch up with Cathy."

"Sounds good. Let's go."

Fred took Peter up to the office in his golf cart. When

they got there, Kevin and Anna were waiting to greet him.

"Is it true you're going to ask her to marry you? This is wonderful." Anna clapped her hands in excitement.

Kevin said, "We have a horse waiting for you." He walked Peter out to the stable and introduced him to Bud, the trail rider. "Have you ridden before?" asked Kevin.

"Most of my life."

"Well, you are a big guy. We have a big horse for you. He has some spirit to him."

"I'm fine with that."

Bud introduced Peter to a huge black horse pacing in the paddock. "This is Midnight."

Peter approached very slowly, talking quietly and calmly to the horse. He could sense tension in the horse. He backed off for a little bit without touching the horse. Then he quietly approached again, calmly talking to the horse the whole time. He put his hands against its withers, feeling the warmth of the animal, the faint quivers of muscle under the sensitive skin. He could feel the tension slowly drain out of the horse. Curious, the horse looked at him and then reached over to sniff him.

The horse stood calmly as they put his saddle on. Finally, he was ready to hit the trail and Peter swung up into the saddle. Bud bought his own horse around, and they rode out of the paddock. They waved at Kevin and Anna, who were watching. They waved back.

Bud told Peter it would take about half an hour to catch up with the group. "Kevin is going to call ahead and make sure they wait," Bud reassured him.

Worried about Cathy's reaction, Peter hoped he wasn't making a big mistake.

CHAPTER 32

The trail riding group had stopped to water the horses and take a break. As they were stretching their legs, Cathy got to know her fellow riders. They introduced themselves as Mike O'Neal, a Catholic priest; Isaac Rubin, a rabbi; Emma Sterling, a Buddhist monk.

Isaac said, "I know it sounds like a joke—you know, three priests walk into a bar… yadda, yadda, yadda. But we met at a conference on spirituality and politics, about ten years ago. We ended up cutting out early to go spend time talking to each other and became fast friends."

Emma took up the thread, "So every year now, we've gone on vacation together for a week or two to try something new we haven't done before. Last year was surfing in Hawaii, which didn't go too well."

Mike said, "Show her the picture, Em."

Emma pulled out her phone and showed Cathy a picture of the three of them on a beautiful beach, with their priestly garb on, posing on surfboards and giving the traditional Hawaiian shaka sign for 'hang loose.'

"Oh, this is great," said Cathy, grinning.

"About a second after that picture was taken," said Mike, "we all fell over into the sand."

"It's hard to keep your balance on those things," said Isaac, laughing.

Cathy asked curiously, "Do you talk about spiritual things when you're on vacation?"

"Well," said Isaac, "we really try to keep our vacations separate from our work lives. But spirituality is a big part of everyday life, so it's not something you can really compartmentalize."

Emma asked, "Is something bothering you, Cathy? I'm getting the sense that there's something on your mind."

Cathy hesitated.

Isaac said gently, "You know, for whatever reason we have all ended up at this place, at this time. If there is something worrying you, I think that we are all open to hearing it."

"Really?" Cathy asked.

Mike said, "Yes, absolutely."

"I feel a little silly bringing this up, especially at my age. I mean, this sounds more like something a teenager would be concerned about."

Isaac said, "Oh, this is about sex then."

Cathy laughed. "No, not quite."

"That's a relief." Mike smiled.

"Go on, Cathy," said Emma. "Just ignore him."

"It's about a man I've met recently, only about a week

ago. Honestly, I'm crazy about him. I really like him. But I lost my husband some years back to cancer, and it devastated me when he died. I haven't let anybody into my life since then, and I'm afraid to let this man in because it might hurt even worse if something happened. I don't know if I can go through another loss like that."

"You know, the Dalai Lama talks about when you have a difficult choice to make, you should ask yourself if you are going toward happiness or away from happiness," said Emma.

Isaac added, "I was actually going to bring up Robert Frost's 'The Road Not Taken.' So often, fear stops us in our tracks, and from taking the path that we would like to take."

Emma said, "It sounds to me like you're making this decision very black and white."

Cathy asked, "What do you mean?"

Isaac agreed. "There's another option than strictly yes or no... there's maybe."

Mike nodded.

Cathy said, "What do you mean by maybe."

"Maybe you can get to know him better first before making such a big decision," Isaac explained. "After all, you don't really have all the data in order to make a reasoned decision."

Mike rolled his eyes. "That's my friend, the brilliant mathematician speaking."

"Spend some time with him," suggested Emma.

Cathy said, "That's a problem; we live across the country from each other."

"There may be an easy enough solution for that," offered Mike. "Stay here. Don't go back to your hometown yet."

Emma said, "If you can, spend some time here with him, share the minutiae of everyday life—the things that help you get to really know each other and enable you to build a solid relationship. Not the big grandiose things, but the everyday things that give you get a true sense of who a person is."

Cathy stared at the three of them. "You know, I never really thought about doing that, staying out here for a while, getting to know him. That's the maybe. I will vote for the maybe."

Isaac said, "I vote for the maybe."

Mike nodded, "Me too."

Emma joined in, "I vote for the maybe."

Dan, the trail boss, who had been sitting quietly and listening to all of this, startled everybody by suddenly speaking up, "I vote for the maybe too." Sam sitting next to him nodded in agreement. Suddenly Dan's phone rang. "I've got to take this. I'll be right back. In the meantime, you can start putting your stuff together. We need to move on to the next section of the trail ride. Everything you brought has to be carried out. Carry in, carry out."

Cathy said, "Emma, Mike, and Isaac, thank you so much. You have no idea how much you've helped me. One of you has to give me a contact number, so I can let you know what happens."

Emma said, "Thank you. I would appreciate that."

The trail boss came back with a message for everybody. "OK, we are going to stay here for a little bit longer. We have someone coming out to join us. Another person for the ride. So just relax for a few more minutes, they should be here shortly."

Suddenly he turned and looked up the trail. "I'm hearing horses coming in fast. Everybody off the trail. Watch out for snakes."

He and Sam quickly gathered the horses and made sure they were tied up securely out of the way, so they wouldn't spook. Everybody was a little tense, listening to the sound of the horses running down the narrow path. But then everything got quiet.

The trail boss relaxed. "It's OK. They brought them down to a walk."

Two men on horses came around the curve. Cathy was busy putting everything in her daypack to get ready to go when she heard her name. She looked up, and there was Peter sitting astride a handsome black horse, coming toward her.

"Peter," Cathy softly breathed out his name. She could feel her heart beating. "Peter," she repeated.

He looked down at her and smiled his beautiful smile. She looked up at him and smiled back, feeling her heart open up at that moment and fill with love.

"Cathy." Peter slid off his horse and came over to her.

"What are you doing here?" she asked.

"I came to talk to you. Can we talk someplace,

privately?"

Cathy looked around at everyone and said, "You can talk in front of them. They know everything already."

Peter said, "What... everything?" And laughed.

Emma nudged Mike and whispered, "Now that's a good reaction."

Everyone introduced themselves. Peter cleared his throat somewhat nervously and said to Cathy, "I had a lot of time to think when I was in the hospital about what I want to do with my life, with the years I have left. I want to take the time to explore the world, experience new things. And I want to do all of that with you. Cathy, I don't want you to leave. So, I'm going to ask you something, and I want you to think about it. Will you—"

"Maybe," interrupted Cathy, with a slight smile and tears in her eyes.

He looked down at her quizzically. "Maybe. What does that mean?"

She took a deep breath. "It means I'm not choosing yes or no. I'm choosing maybe. It means that I'm not going to go home right now. I am going to stay here for a while and spend time getting to know you better."

Peter's face lit up with the brightest of smiles. "That is exactly what I was hoping you would say." He gently put his hands on either side of her face. "I want to go to sleep every night and wake up every morning, looking at this beautiful face."

Cathy put her hands up to his face and tenderly caressed it as she kissed his lips and felt their warmth.

She felt her heart start beating faster. He softly kissed her face and traced her tears with his fingers as they ran down her cheeks.

There was a long sigh from Emma. "Oh, I do so love a happy ending."

Both Cathy and Peter laughed. Peter said to Emma, "Stay tuned." He then leaned over to Cathy. "By the way, I like your hat."

She grinned. "I like your hair."

Dan said, "OK, we have to head back now. Everybody, pack up. Make sure you've got everything."

Peter asked, "Can someone take Cathy's horse back to the stable, and she'll ride with me on Midnight."

"Sure," said Dan.

"Oh," added Peter, "by the way, there's a big celebration at the campground tonight, and you are all invited."

Emma gave Cathy a quick hug. One by one, everyone mounted up and started back. Peter and Cathy let everyone go ahead of them. He lifted her up onto Midnight. Then swung up after her, pulling her back against him so that they were settled in comfortably. Peter softly clicked to Midnight, starting him walking slowly.

Cathy leaned against Peter—feeling his arms around her, keeping her secure. She asked him, "So what are we going to tell everybody?" There was a pause, and she felt him suddenly start shaking with laughter.

He whispered in her ear, "Maybe."

Cathy turned her head up at him and smiled. "Definitely maybe."

Peter clicked to Midnight again, turning the big horse toward home.

CHAPTER 33

One year later…

"Betsy," called Linda, "our ride will be here any minute. Are you ready to go?" She stepped carefully around three elderly bichons who were sharing a large dog bed. Known collectively as the bichon sisters, Sadie, Zoe, and Sophie had separately come into Charlie's Place—Linda and Betsy's shelter for senior dogs—but had quickly formed a fast friendship. Inevitably where there was one, the other two were not far behind.

Linda reached down and stroked their heads. "Be good girls. We'll only be gone for a week."

Betsy appeared in the doorway, carrying her walker, and arranging her purse. "I'm ready. This is the first we've spent any time away from these guys, and I'm already missing them."

Linda agreed and gently moved Gracie, a seventeen-year-old mixed breed, out of the way so she could get her suitcase.

A car honked. The shelter manager came in to say their ride was there and asked if they needed help with their luggage.

"Thanks," said Betsy. "You have all our numbers if you need to get in contact with us?"

The manager smiled. "Everything will be fine. Relax, enjoy yourselves."

When they opened the front door, they saw a big stretch limo.

"We didn't order that," said Betsy as the driver came up to them.

All he said was, "I'll take your luggage. Is there anything else you need help with?"

Betsy said, "If you could take this walker and put it in the trunk, too, that'd be great."

Linda said to the manager, "But we didn't order a stretch limo. It's beyond our budget."

"This is on the house," said the driver. "My boss saw you on one of the local morning talk shows and was impressed by your work. She has a senior dog who goes everywhere with her, so she decided to upgrade your ride."

Betsy said "Well, tell her thank you very much."

Linda helped Charlie get into the car and up onto the back seat, where he stretched out and promptly fell asleep.

"Everyone ready?" asked the driver.

"As we will ever be," answered Betsy.

The limo driver got them to the airport in plenty of time. They checked in and picked up a wheelchair for Betsy so she wouldn't have to walk the long distance to the gate. Once they reached the gate, they put Charlie in his travel crate for the flight and got on the airplane.

About an hour into the trip, a flight attendant came up to them and asked if a young girl traveling by herself could come up and say hi to the dog. She was feeling anxious, and maybe seeing the dog would help calm her down.

Betsy said, "I'm a terrible flyer myself, but having Charlie around helps me."

Linda said to the flight attendant, "He's actually a certified therapy dog. We visit schools and libraries where children, as part of a special program, read to him. If the little girl has a book with her, have her bring it up here and she can read to Charlie."

The flight attendant said, "That would be great. I'll be right back with her." Within a few minutes, the flight attendant brought the little girl up to their seats. She was dressed in jeans and a sweater and had pigtails tied with bright ribbons. She looked nervous and had tear stains on her face from crying. But then she saw Charlie. Linda had taken him out of his crate and placed him on the middle seat. The girl uttered a little "oooh," and put her arms around his neck, hugging him tightly. He licked her face, making her giggle. The little girl happily settled in next to Charlie and started reading her book to him, carefully showing him all the pictures. The rest of the flight went by quickly. Before they knew it, the pilot announced over the intercom that they were descending into Phoenix. The flight attendant came to get the little girl and bring her back to her seat. Betsy and Linda made sure Charlie was secured in his travel crate under the seat.

A woman sitting across the aisle from them asked, "Are you from the Philadelphia area?" When they nodded, she said, "I want to find out more about the reading program you were talking about. I think it would be helpful for my granddaughter. She is shy about reading aloud in school."

Linda said, "Sure. Charlie was certified by PAWS Pet Therapy for People. It's headquartered in Delaware, but they have pet therapy teams in Pennsylvania, New Jersey, and Maryland too."

"Great," said the woman, "thank you."

As Linda, Betsy, and Charlie left the plane, the flight attendants thanked them profusely for helping to make it a comfortable quiet flight. The pilot and first officer came out to meet Charlie.

The first officer squatted down to pet him. "I grew up with a basset hound. They are great dogs." Charlie wagged his tail furiously and licked his face.

In the meantime, a few miles away, Cathy looked at her phone. "Oh yeah, they're here! They're here!"

Peter looked over and smiled. "It'll be good to see Betsy and Linda, and Charlie of course."

"OK, they're at baggage claim right now," said Cathy, "so if we pull up there, they should definitely spot us."

"In this RV," said Peter, "They should be able to spot us from outer space."

Cathy grinned and reached forward to pat the dashboard affectionately. "A lot of good memories have been made in this RV."

Peter looked at her and quirked an eyebrow. "How much time do we have?"

"Not enough," said Cathy.

They pulled up to the baggage claim, and Cathy got out. She heard her name being called and spun around. Betsy and Linda were wildly waving at her. The three women came together in a rush and hugged each other tightly. Charlie danced around them, barking. The women were all talking and laughing at the same time. Peter turned on the RV's blinkers and got out to help with the luggage. The women were still talking excitedly as he guided them into the vehicle and got them settled. He lifted Charlie up into the vehicle and introduced him to his dogs, Apollo and Pippin, who were in their dog beds. They all sniffed each other and then settled down again.

"They are getting along fine," Peter reassured Linda as he walked to the front. He hugged and kissed the two women and then settled into the driver's seat. "Is everybody strapped in?"

"Yes," chorused all three women.

"OK then, we're on our way."

"Yeah!" shouted the women.

Peter smiled broadly as he turned the blinkers off and pulled out into traffic.

Meanwhile, Ben and Alfreda were sipping their morning tea on the deck of the house they had leased from Peter once Ben had semi-retired from running the RV park. Luke now managed the day-to-day operations. Ben said, turning to Alfreda, "They just picked them up at the airport. They should be here in a couple of hours."

Alfreda said, "I can't wait to see them."

"According to Peter," Ben said, laughing, "the decibel level in the RV is off the charts."

Alfreda smiled. "They have a lot to talk about."

"So do we," said Ben.

"We'll have to remember to thank Peter and Cathy for the wedding present they gave us," said Alfreda.

Ben put his arms around his wife and kissed her cheek. "I have a lot to be thankful for." They leaned against each other. Ben looked down over the pasture where the retired trail horses, Midnight and Star, were grazing peacefully. "Who could have guessed those two would become best friends. Do you want to ride over to the park this afternoon, or take the car?"

"I'd rather take the car. I want to bring Frankie."

He nodded. "Frankie should be there to greet them. After all, he's responsible for bringing all of us together. Wait till Peter and the women see the changes at the park that Luke has instituted. The bed and breakfast, the small animal veterinary clinic, the rescue shelter, and the service dog training facility."

Alfreda took his mug from him, picked up their breakfast dishes, and started to walk inside. Abruptly she turned around. "Do you know if Cathy's three friends from the trail ride got here yet?"

"Luke said they checked in a little while ago. Apparently they rented one of the biggest RVs he's ever seen. He's not sure they know how to deal with it." Chuckling, Ben added, "He thinks that they may have taken out a couple of small trees when they parked."

"I can't wait to see everybody. Let's get ready to go over."

A short while later, they arrived at the RV park and checked in with Luke at the ranch house.

"How's it going?" Ben asked.

"Great, Dad," said Luke. "Everything is coming together nicely. Tom should be here shortly, and he's bringing Joan and Smithy. Izzy is here, of course. Sharon and George just pulled in a little while ago, and Cathy and Peter's friends are here with their humongous RV."

"What about the big surprise for tomorrow?" asked Alfreda.

"I'm not sure how much of a surprise it's going to be at this point," Luke answered wryly. "This group is not known for keeping secrets. But we got the main room decorated beautifully. It looks fantastic."

Suddenly they heard a wild honking.

"That has got to be them," said Luke, walking out the entrance as the aged RV pulled up to the front steps in a cloud of dust. The RV's door opened, and everybody piled out—people and dogs alike—talking and laughing. Peter grabbed Alfreda and gave her a big hug. Luke went down the line greeting Cathy, Betsy, and Linda. Ben gave them all a hug.

"It's so good to see you," Luke said to Peter.

Peter grinned at him. "It is good to be back."

Tom pulled up in his police cruiser, with a smiling

Smithy and Joan getting out of the vehicle. In the meantime, Izzy, Sharon, George, Emma, Mike, and Isaac were all walking up the driveway, toward the main building. They quickly got caught up in the hug-fest as they happily greeted each other.

Frankie and Charlie immediately began to play. Luke reached down and took off Harry's service dog vest so he knew he was off-duty and could join in the fun. Apollo and Pippin walked through the crowd like foreign dignitaries, sedately saying hello to everyone.

Cathy hugged Luke and then looked around. "The place looks great. What have you done to it? I see a number of new buildings."

"We'll give you a tour in just a little bit," said Luke, "but first I want to make sure nobody needs anything." He walked to the top of the steps and tried to get everybody's attention. It took a while, but he finally got everyone to quiet down. He put his hand up and asked, "Does anybody need to use the bathroom, number one?"

Somebody from the back of the crowd yelled, "What about number two?"

Luke winced and said, "Oh my God. OK, this is the level of humor we're going to have this weekend I can tell. Does anybody need any water or food?"

"No!" the crowd yelled back at him.

"Good," he said, laughing. "Now Peter wants to say a few words."

Peter made his way through the crowd and up to the top of the steps. He motioned for Cathy to join him.

He said, "I have some news. As you know, Cathy and I have been spending time together this past year, getting to know one another, and we've decided that…" He took a long pause.

"Out with it!" somebody yelled.

He and Cathy smiled at each other. Then at the same time, they turned and faced the crowd, shouting, "We're getting married tomorrow! And you're all invited!"

There was a lot of cheering. People were yelling and hugging each other. It was pandemonium.

"Anything for a free meal," said Peter to Cathy and Luke. They cracked up.

Luke quieted the crowd with an earsplitting NYC taxi whistle. "Now tonight," Luke said, "we have a big barbecue planned, with music and dancing. Then tomorrow at 8:00 a.m. we'll have a pre-wedding breakfast. At noon we'll have the actual wedding. We'll have dinner at about 3:00 and then another party. So, I hope you brought your dancing shoes."

Cathy took the microphone from Luke. "I want to thank everybody for being here and sharing this very special time with us."

A familiar voice called from the back of the crowd, "So no more maybe?"

Cathy shaded her eyes. "Is that Emma? I'm so glad you're here. Everyone, that is Emma, a Buddhist monk, who along with Isaac, a rabbi, and Mike, a Catholic priest, will be officiating at our wedding."

There was a round of applause.

Isaac shouted, "We're covering all the bases!"

Everyone laughed.

Cathy said, "To answer your question, Emma... no more maybe. It's yes, definitely yes." She looked at Peter, who leaned over and tenderly kissed her. The crowd applauded and yelled encouragement. Cathy blushed.

Luke said to Cathy and Peter, "I've got to check on the food."

"Anything I can do to help?" asked Cathy.

"No, you're the bride. You just get to sit around and have everybody wait on you."

Tom worked his way through the crowd to Peter, who grabbed him and gave him a big hug.

"It's so good to see you, Tom. I've been hearing such wonderful things about you and the job that you're doing. I have even heard talk that you might be asked to run for political office."

Tom looked embarrassed. "You trained me well, Obi-Wan."

Peter laughed and drew Tom over to where Cathy was excitedly talking to Alfreda.

"Cathy, look who it is," he said, turning her around to face Tom.

She squealed and threw her arms around him. "Hello, Chief Tom." She smiled broadly. "We are so proud of you. Peter keeps up with all your doings. He follows your social media postings religiously." She hugged him again. "Is your wife here? And your daughter?"

"Actually," said Tom, "we are expecting again."

"Congratulations! That's fantastic news," said Peter, clapping Tom on the back.

"Great!" Cathy hugged him again.

"Well unfortunately she's not feeling too great right now. That's why she's not here today. But she really hopes that you will stop by and see her while you're in the area."

"Oh, absolutely," said Cathy.

Smithy and Joan came up behind Tom. Smithy shook Peter's hand. "I can't thank you enough for everything you've done for me. It's turned my life around."

Peter smiled. "Well, you're putting in a lot of hard work. I hear you're doing very well at Joan's nonprofit."

"The kids love him," said Joan. "You should stop by and see how creative they have become. All thanks to Smithy."

"They're great kids," he said.

Cathy asked him, "How's your teaching degree coming along?"

Smithy said, "It's coming along really well. Between Joan and Izzy, they're keeping my nose to the grindstone and making sure I'm putting in the study hours."

"So far, 3.2 GPA," said Joan, beaming with pride.

At that moment Izzy walked up behind Smithy. "He's doing great!" She put her hand on his shoulder.

Cathy and Peter hugged her. "How are you doing, Izzy?" asked Cathy. "How's your husband?"

"He's in a memory care facility now," Izzy explained. "I think it's better for him; it's a more secure environment. He was beginning to wander and then get confused about where he was. It was very scary. Even with a GPS tracking device, it was tough to find him sometimes."

Peter said, "Sounds like he's in a safer place."

"Yes. But I miss him," said Izzy. Cathy saw the sadness in Izzy's eyes and put her arms around her.

Peter said to Cathy, "I need to move that RV out of the way." He looked around for Ben and spotted him talking to Linda and Betsy.

Walking up to them, he asked Ben, "I want to move the RV away from the entrance. Where did you put us in the campground?"

Ben said, "Oh you have the original campsite where the women first parked when they got here a year ago."

"Oh, perfect," said Betsy, "that's a beautiful spot."

"That's where it all began," said Linda, coming up beside them. Charlie was at her side. He plopped down, and Frankie immediately climbed on top of his best friend to join him in a snooze.

"They are worn out from all the excitement," Betsy smiled.

Alfreda said to the three women, "I can't tell you how much I love that little dog."

"I am so glad. Oh, I just had an idea," said Cathy. "I think Peter should stay in the ranch house, and Betsy and Linda can stay with me in the RV. It will give us time to really catch up."

"That would be great!" said Betsy.

Everyone else agreed to this new plan.

After dinner, the women walked back to their campsite. They gazed upwards trying to identify the different constellations. All three oohed and aahed at a brilliant shooting star streaking across the night sky.

Betsy nudged Cathy, "Well there's a good sign for tomorrow." Cathy smiled.

They settled at the dining table and opened a bottle of wine. Linda poured some for Cathy and herself, handing Betsy a glass of sparkling water.

"This feels like old times," said Betsy.

Linda agreed. "I'm so glad we're doing this. I really miss having you close by Cathy. Even though we stay in touch on Facetime, it's not the same. We can't just go out for a cup of tea or grab a bite to eat somewhere on the spur of the moment."

"I know," said Cathy. "It's hard not having you guys around. Now bring me up to speed on how Charlie's Place is doing."

"Well, first, just to update you on the book club," Betsy informed her, "we found a couple of women who wanted to take it over and run it, and they're doing a fabulous job. In fact, we've even had some club meetings at the shelter. That's been fun. It's also brought in some donations and volunteers."

Linda sipped her wine, "Charlie's Place has been going gangbusters. We have gotten some good coverage from our local media. Our donations have increased by 18% over the past six months, and we have new volunteers signing up every month."

"Wow," said Cathy. "Congratulations."

"One thing that never ceases to amaze me," said Betsy,

"is how much the dogs get along with each other. It doesn't matter what breed they are or how old they are. They all just get along really well. They snuggle up together on the couches and dog beds. When a new dog comes in, they all go and say hi and then just fold them right into the pack."

"We have about twenty-five dogs right now," added Linda.

Cathy said, "I'm hoping that we can get over to West Chester in a couple of weeks and stay for a while. We are looking to head east soon."

"Oh, that would be great," said Betsy.

"Now tell us about you," said Linda. "You and Peter seem very happy together."

"We are. He really is the man of my dreams. Funny, kind, playful, caring, communicative, and sexy as all get out.

Betsy questioned, "So you're fully ready to take that step tomorrow? To get married again?"

"Oh yes," said Cathy.

"That's fantastic," added Linda.

Betsy asked, "So here's the million dollar question. What are you going to wear?"

"I have a peach-colored satin dress. Very classic lines. I was just window shopping one day, and I spotted this dress. The color is fabulous, and I absolutely fell in love with it. It is ankle length. Long enough for formal but not so long that I am going to trip over it."

"A hat or veil?" wondered Linda.

Cathy made a face. "A veil is too archaic and a hat feels

too Kentucky Derby. I don't know."

"I have an idea; leave it to me."

"You got it."

"Shoes?" prompted Betsy.

"Peach-colored ballet slippers. Totally comfortable, and I can dance in them," Cathy answered with a smile.

"I noticed that beautiful ring on your finger," said Linda.

Cathy smiled and said, "Yes it was Peter's mom's engagement ring. I love that it's turquoise and jasper and coral."

There was a knock at the door. Cathy opened it to find Emma on the doorstep.

"Mike and Isaac are playing poker with the guys up at the ranch house. I thought I'd stop in and see what you are doing tonight."

"Excellent," said Betsy. "We'd love to have you join us. We are having a pajama party and talking about all things wedding."

Emma said, "That sounds perfect!" With a flourish, she handed over a bakery bag to Cathy. "Here's my price of admission. Homemade chocolate madeleines."

Cathy opened the bag and took a deep breath. "These smell fabulous." She looked at her in astonishment. "Emma, did you make them?"

"Actually, Mike made them, but I helped. I was the official taster."

Cathy passed them around and soon everyone was oohing and ahhing in delight as they sampled them.

"God, these are good!" said Linda.

"Okay, who wants what to drink?" asked Betsy. "We have wine, hot chocolate, juice, and, of course, tea."

There was another knock at the door.

"Come in," the women chorused.

Izzy and Sharon climbed into the RV.

"Poker game?" asked Cathy.

"You got it," said Sharon. "George is happy as a clam, playing cards up at the ranch house."

"We thought," said Izzy, "we would see what you were up to."

"Pajama party!" shouted Cathy, Betsy, Linda, and Emma.

"All right," said Sharon, "I haven't been to a pajama party since I was a kid."

"I've never been to one," said Izzy.

"Basically," said Cathy, "you eat everything that is supposedly bad for you…"

"And lots of it," finished Emma.

"What?" she said as everyone looked at her. "I wasn't born a monk."

Betsy started laughing. "I have this image in my head, of a maternity ward with all the little babies in white blankets, and there you are in a tiny saffron robe."

Emma giggled at the thought.

"Okay, we have all kinds of cookies," said Linda, "plus chips and dips."

Betsy said, "After the dinner we had tonight, I think I'm fine with just cookies and tea. These chocolate madeleines are just amazing. However, I would like to see Cathy try on her dress."

The women started chanting, "Try it on! Try it on!"

"OK, OK," said Cathy, laughing. "Just give me a few minutes."

She disappeared into the back bedroom and a little while later came out wearing a beautiful peach satin dress that clung to her like a second skin and then flowed softly to her ankles. The women were ecstatic.

Betsy said, "That color is a perfect match for your skin tone."

Linda said, "It fits like a dream."

Emma commented, "What a gorgeous bride you're going to make."

Izzy teared up, and Sharon snapped photos with her iPhone.

"What about the shoes?" asked Linda.

Cathy pulled up her dress slightly and showed off her ballet slippers that perfectly matched her dress.

"What about a bouquet?" asked Emma.

"Sunflowers," answered Cathy. "It's the flower I love most, and that's what I will be carrying down the aisle."

"You do have a photographer right?" asked Linda.

"It turns out Luke is a very good photographer, and he has agreed to take the photos for tomorrow."

"Have you written your vows yet?" asked Emma.

"No," Cathy said. "I'm still thinking about that and also thinking about the music too. We don't want to use the traditional wedding march music down the aisle. But we're not sure what music we do want to use."

Izzy suggested, "I think you should use John Legend's 'All of Me.' It's a beautiful song. Great message. Very current."

Betsy looked at her. "Izzy, you constantly surprise me. I would never think you knew John Legend."

"Well, I don't know all of his songs," responded Izzy. "But this one I do know, and I happen to like it a lot, especially for two people who have a lot of life experience under their belts."

Cathy laughed. "I don't know how I should take that. I'll look at it in a positive light."

"Of course," said Izzy, "that's what I meant."

The women talked, laughed, and noshed on goodies, far into the night. Eventually Emma, Izzy, and Sharon left to walk back to their own RVs.

The next morning dawned bright and beautiful. All three women were moving a bit slow, following their late night. Still dressed in her pajamas and bathrobe, Betsy poured herself a cup of tea, let it steep for five minutes, and then took a grateful sip to get going. Linda debated whether she wanted a cup of tea or a cup of coffee. She went with the tea. She poured a cup of hot water over loose tea leaves and set the timer.

"You've really got me got hooked on tea, especially English Breakfast," she said to Betsy.

Cathy said, "I'm heading up to the ranch house now for breakfast. Are you up for that?"

Betsy and Linda exchanged glances. Linda explained, "I think we'll have breakfast here. Then we have a couple of errands to run."

"Really?" asked Cathy.

"Yes," answered Betsy innocently. "I want to buy some postcards." Linda stifled a laugh.

Cathy gave Betsy a disbelieving look, "Uh huh." She grabbed a jacket. "Don't forget to be back here by about 10:30 to help me get ready." Cathy looked at both of them. "I'm pretty anxious, I have to say."

"Well, if you weren't, you wouldn't be human," said Betsy.

Later that morning, Cathy was back from breakfast, and Linda and Betsy were back from their errands. They started helping Cathy get ready for the wedding. They did her hair and got her dressed and made up. Then together they handed her two special gift bags.

Linda said, "These are from both of us."

Betsy handed Cathy the larger of the two bags. She opened it up and gasped. "Oh my God! This is beautiful!" She pulled out a soft yellow silk wrap that went perfectly with her wedding dress.

"In case you get chilled," Betsy said.

Linda handed Cathy the second bag. She opened it and burst into tears. Betsy sprang into action with tissues.

"Don't cry; your makeup will run." Betsy gently blotted away her tears.

"I can't help it," said Cathy. She held up a headpiece that Betsy and Linda had made by braiding together long peach-colored satin ribbons. "This is perfect!"

The two women carefully arranged it on her head amid her curls. Cascades of ribbon flowed down her back.

"How wonderful," Cathy said. "Thank you for helping make this day so special and for being here to share it with me. That means so much."

Betsy smiled. "I am so happy for you."

Linda checked her watch. "Okay, Alfreda is going to pick us up in a few minutes in her van to go up to the ranch house." As she said it, they heard a honk. Then a knock.

"Come in!" they yelled together, and then they started giggling.

"Nerves. It's all nerves," said Cathy, shaking her hands to try to relax.

Alfreda opened the door to the RV. When she saw Cathy, she put her hands up to her face. "You look so beautiful!"

"We have to go," said Linda. Charlie eagerly joined them at the door. "Sorry, Charlie, you stay here. But I promise you will get a special treat tonight."

They all climbed into Alfreda's van.

"Don't worry," Alfreda reassured Cathy, "I had the van detailed, and coverings put down on the seats and floors."

The ranch house looked deserted.

"There's nobody around," said Cathy, feeling surprised. "Where is everybody?"

Alfreda parked in front of the steps. As she pulled up, Tom came to the top of the stairs and rolled a red carpet down. He formally offered Cathy his arm as Luke, Smithy, and Ben came around the side of the ranch house and offered their arms to Betsy, Linda, and Alfreda.

Once they were at the top of the steps, Tom said to Cathy, "Now you need to turn away from the building and look out over the RV park while we all go inside."

Cathy did as he asked and then thought, "How will I know when it is time to go inside?" Then she realized she had totally forgotten to put a bouquet together. "Oh no," she thought, "do I have time to go pick some wildflowers?" She started feeling anxious. She heard the door open behind her. Over her shoulder, she said, "I should have asked when I'm supposed to go in."

A voice behind her said, "We'll go in together."

She turned around, and there was Peter looking drop-dead gorgeous in a black tuxedo, his blue eyes intently fixed on her as a warm smile spread across his face. She looked into his eyes and felt her heart overflow with love.

Peter handed her a bouquet of sunflowers tied with a white satin ribbon. "Betsy told me you didn't have a bouquet. I put this together for you." He looked at his watch and said, "It's time."

Cathy stood beside him as he pushed open the big double doors. She stared in amazement. The main room of the ranch house had been transformed. White-and-gold fabric softly cascaded from the ceiling and windows. Tiny white lights were everywhere, on every surface. The whole room glowed.

There were ten rows of chairs on either side of the main aisle. Each chair was draped in white satin. At the end of each row, a placard hung, featuring a word traditionally associated with sunflowers. Words like 'hope,' 'joy,' 'love' and 'optimism.'

As she looked down the main aisle, she saw the people she now considered family: Betsy and Linda, Ben and Alfreda, and Tom and Luke. In the front row, Peter's daughters, Jeanne and Ellen stood beaming with pride and love.

Emma, Isaac, and Mike were at the lectern, with bright welcoming smiles and open arms. On the lectern itself, there was a beautiful image of a sunflower in full bloom, with the word 'happiness' underneath it.

Her eyes brimming with tears, Cathy turned to Peter, who said, "Oh no, don't get me going. I've managed to avoid crying all morning, and I'm very close to it right now." She looked up into his face, loving every inch of it.

He looked back down at her, with great tenderness, held out his hand to her and asked, "Are you ready to begin?"

She put her hand in his and said, "Yes, absolutely," and they took the first steps on their journey together.

THE END

ADDITIONAL INFORMATION

Parkinson's Disease

Parkinson's Foundation

The Parkinson's Foundation makes life better for people with Parkinson's Disease (PD) by improving care and advancing research toward a cure. In everything they do, they build on the energy, experience and passion of their global Parkinson's community.

Website: parkinson.org
Email: contact@parkinson.org
Phone: helpline: 1-800-4PD info (473-4636)
FL: 200 SE 1st Street, Ste 800, Miami, FL 33131, USA
NY: 1359 Broadway, Ste 1509, New York, NY 10018, USA

Michael J. Fox Foundation

The Michael J. Fox Foundation (MJFF) exists for one reason: to accelerate the next generation of Parkinson's disease (PD) treatments. In practice, that means identifying and funding projects most vital to patients; spearheading solutions around seemingly intractable field-wide challenges; coordinating and streamlining the efforts of multiple, often disparate, teams; and doing whatever it takes to drive faster knowledge turns for the benefit of every life touched by PD. In principle, it means leveraging the core values of optimism, urgency, resourcefulness, collaboration, accountability, and persistence in problem-solving to work on behalf of the 6 million people worldwide living with Parkinson's.

Website: www.michaeljfoxfoundation.org
Email: info@michaeljfox.org
Phone: 1-212-509-0995,
Address: The Michael J. Fox Foundation
for Parkinson's Research
Grand Central Station, P.O. Box 4777
New York, NY 10163-4777

Service Dogs

Adele and Everything After

This powerful documentary captures the remarkable relationship between a woman with an untreatable heart condition and the service dog that transforms her life.

Website: https://www.adeleandeverythingafter.com/

ADI (Assistance Dogs International)

Assistance Dogs International, Inc. (ADI) is a worldwide coalition of not-for-profit programs that train and place

Assistance Dogs. Founded in 1986 from a group of seven small programs, ADI has become the leading authority in the Assistance Dog industry.

Members of ADI meet regularly to share ideas and conduct business regarding educating the public about assistance dogs, advocating for the legal rights of people with disabilities partnered with assistance dogs, and the setting of standards and establishing guidelines and ethics for the training of these dogs.

Note: ADI does not actually train or place service dogs itself. It can help in finding the location of organizations that do train and provide service dogs.

Website: assistancedogsinternational.org

Canine Companions for Independence

Canine Companions is leading the service dog industry so their clients and their dogs can live with greater independence. They provide service dogs to adults, children and veterans with disabilities and facility dogs to professionals working in healthcare, criminal justice, and educational settings. Since their founding in 1975, their dogs and all follow-up services are provided at no cost to their clients.

Website: canine.org

Pet Therapy

PAWS for People Pet Therapy

PAWS for People™ (Pet-Assisted Visitation Volunteer

Services, or PAWS) is a nonprofit organization committed to providing therapeutic visits to any person in the community who would benefit from interaction with a well-trained, loving pet. What makes PAWS for People stand above other pet therapy services is the emphasis they place on providing individualized therapeutic experiences for every person they visit. Their strict standards in training and testing dogs, cats and bunnies ensure every therapy team is capable of meeting the various needs of their diverse clientele.

PAWS is most active throughout Delaware, but also serves areas in southern Pennsylvania, northeast Maryland, and southern New Jersey. PAWS visits people of all ages, ethnicities, and levels.

Website: pawsforpeople.org
Email: info@pawsforpeople.org
Phone: (302) 351-5622
Address: 703 Dawson Dr, Newark, DE 19713

Rescue Organizations

Finding Shelter

Finding Shelter provides loving care for animals who need their help finding a permanent home. They are an organization based on love and respect for animals, supported by an incredible group of volunteers who work together to give these animals a quality life and the best chance for adoption.

Website: findingshelter.org
Email: Info@findingshelter.org
Address: P.O. Box 723, Southeastern, PA 19399

Animal Friends

For more than 75 years, Animal Friends has been saving, impacting, engaging, enriching and affecting the lives of pets and people. Since their humble beginnings in 1943, they have grown into a full-service companion animal welfare organization serving the pets and people of Pittsburgh and the surrounding area. With their progressive programs, Animal Friends is leading the way toward making their community a safer and more humane place.

Simply put, they are thinking outside the cage! Their Vision Statement: A humane and compassionate future for every animal friend. Their Mission Statement: To rescue, rehabilitate and rehome animals in crisis, ensure healthy pets through education, advocacy and affordable services, and inspire a community where the animal-human bond is celebrated and nurtured.

Website: www.ThinkingOutsideTheCage.org
Email: Speak@ThinkingOutsideTheCage.org
Phone: 412.847.700
Address: 562 Camp Horne Road, Pittsburgh, PA 15237

Made in the USA
Las Vegas, NV
26 November 2024